Crying Blood

Books by Donis Casey

The Old Buzzard Had It Coming
Hornswoggled
The Drop Edge of Yonder
The Sky Took Him
Crying Blood

Crying Blood

An Alafair Tucker Mystery

Donis Casey

Poisoned Pen Press

First Edition 2011

10 9 8 7 6 5 4 3 2 1

Library of Congress Catalog Card Number: 2010932085

ISBN: 9781590588314   Hardcover
       9781590588338   Trade Paperback

Poisoned Pen Press
6962 E. First Ave., Ste. 103
Scottsdale, AZ 85251
www.poisonedpenpress.com
info@poisonedpenpress.com

Printed in the United States of America

This is a book dedicated to all the men I love:
my husband, my brother,
my brothers-in-law and nephews, uncles and cousins.
But especially for my father.
For good or ill, our fathers are the first
to teach us what it is to be a man.

Acknowledgments

I owe a debt of gratitude to my editor, Barbara Peters, who held my hand through this book and basically showed me that I can still tell a story. Many thanks also to Jere Harris and Nancy Calhoun of the Local History and Genealogoy Department at the Muskogee Public Library for helping me to find Sheriff John Barger.

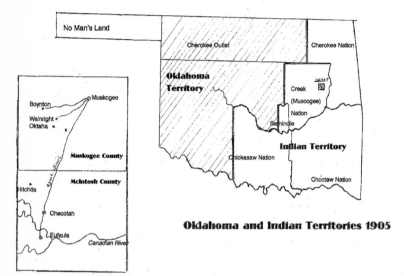

No Man's Land

Cherokee Outlet

Cherokee Nation

Oklahoma Territory

Creek
(Muscogee)
Nation

Seminole

Indian Territory

Chickasaw Nation

Choctaw Nation

Boynton

Muskogee

Walnright
Oktaha

Muskogee County

McIntosh County

Hitchita

Checotah

Eufaula

Canadian River

Oklahoma and Indian Territories 1905

Map Inset - State of Oklahoma 1915

ˣ The old Goingback place

The Main Characters

The Family

    Shaw Tucker, *farmer and breeder of horses and mules*

    Alafair Tucker, *his wife*

    Their children:

    Martha, *age 24, engaged to* Streeter McCoy

    Mary, *age 22, engaged to* Kurt Lukenbach

    Alice Kelley, *age 21, married to* Walter Kelley

    Phoebe Day, *age 21 (Alice's twin), married to* John Lee Day

        Zeltha Day, *age 1, their daughter*

    G.W. (Gee Dub), *age 19*

    Ruth, *age 16*

    Charlie, *age 14*

    Blanche, *age 10*

    Sophronia (Fronie), *age 9*

    Grace, *age 3*

    Sally Tucker McBride, *Shaw's mother*

    Jim Tucker (d.), *Sally's first husband*

    Six children, including

    Josie *(m. Jack Cecil)*

    Shaw *(m. Alafair)*

    James

        Jerry & Jimmy, *James' sons*

        Leroy—*one of Sally's bunch of grandkids*

◇◇◇

The Creeks
Crying Blood, *an enigma*
Odell Skimmingmoon, *tracker of fugitives*
Lucretia Goingback Hawkins, *who owns land*
and is the mother of two Goingback children
and two Hawkins children
Goingback, *Lucretia's first husband*

The Old Pony Soldiers
Peter McBride, *Sally's second husband*
Roane Hawkins, *Lucretia's second husband*
Doolan, *who won't take no for an answer*

The Law
Scott Tucker, *Town Sheriff of Boynton, Oklahoma. Shaw's cousin*
John Barger, *Sheriff of Muskogee County, Oklahoma*
Trent Calder, *Scott's Deputy*

The Clergy
The Reverend Edmond, *Methodist minister in Eufaula,*
Oklahoma

The Critters
Charlie Dog, *The Tuckers' family dog*
Buttercup and Crook, *Shaw's hunting dogs*
Happy, *James Tucker's bird dog*
Penny, *Gee Dub's horse*
Hannah, *Shaw's horse*
Red Allen, *Peter's amorous Tennessee Walker stallion*
An alluring mare
Two apologetic bloodhounds
Several mysterious snakes
Two unfortunate hogs

Indian Territory

1905

There was no place left to hide. It was sheer luck that he had managed to elude his pursuer for most of the day, anyway. He didn't know the country as well as his hunter did. Even if he had, there was no one within a hundred miles who would be inclined to help him.

He thought he had been going in circles, through woods, up and down hills and through gullies, across open spaces, crawling through brush and grass that moved like silk but cut like razors, behind rocks, following weedy creek banks, slogging through mud. Now he was trapped, boxed in at the end of a dry wash. The walls of the gully were severely undercut, forming a ledge that loomed out about fifteen feet over his head. The bare dirt was full of roots and for an instant the man held a dim hope that he could use them to climb the awkward angle. But every root he grabbed pulled free and every toehold crumbled under his weight. He only made it up three or four feet before the sandy clay gave completely away and he landed on his back with a thud, knocking the wind out of himself. From his new perspective, his eye fell on a small cave-like indent in the bank under the overhang that was partially hidden by a small stand of young chokecherry bushes.

He scrambled onto his knees and crawled behind the bushes that pushed up from the dry creek bed. The opening was maybe three feet high and a little less wide, barely deep enough that he could be able wedge himself into it. Perhaps it had been washed out by an eddy the last time water ran in the wash, but he thought it more likely that some critter had dug it for a night's shelter.

It was a desperate last effort, but he was grateful for the chance. He could already hear his pursuer moving toward him through the brush. He struggled to catch his breath, to regain some semblance of control over himself. He had never been so terrified in his life, even when he was fighting the Apaches in Arizona. At least he hadn't been alone, then. He was drenched in flop sweat. His eyes stung with it. Even if his pursuer hadn't been such a competent tracker, he could probably smell the reek of fear. The man's jacket and pants legs were covered with stickers, mud, stained with who knew what. The gnats and nosee'ums were eating him alive.

He sighed at the rueful realization that it was his own fault that he had come to this pass. He never could leave well enough alone. If he had never come to the Indian Territory he wouldn't be in this mess. If he'd never left the Army. If he'd never left Ireland…

Hindsight wasn't going to help him now. He drew his revolver and waited.

His pursuer broke through the brush and stopped dead. He was holding an axe in his right hand.

The hunter's eyes were aflame with hatred as he looked directly at his enemy hunkered down behind the shrub. The man in the hold twitched. A movement in the brush drew his eye. He realized with shock that the boy had followed them. Cruel.

The man leaped to his feet and his pursuer sent the axe flying through the air, end over end. "Jaysus!" he shrieked, just as the axe took off his ear and embedded itself in the cliff wall. His pursuer let out a whoop of triumph and drew the six-gun from the holster strapped to his hip.

Trapped like a rat. But he'd be damned if he was going to die cowering in a hole. The man was shaking so much that it was a miracle he was able to stand. He closed his eyes, leveled the pistol and pulled the trigger.

Oklahoma

1915

Chapter One

Six men spread in a line across the field, wary and still, shotguns at the ready. The sun had barely sunk below the tree line, but the few moments of the peach and pink of evening had faded, leaving the sky clear, cloudless, and the color of new cream. In the woods behind him, Shaw Tucker could hear the discordant gabble of birds gathering in the trees, settling down for night and making their plans for the following day. Grackles, sounded like. It was late in the season and any birds who were going to fly south for the winter were gone.

Shaw flexed the fingers of his free hand, trying to ease the stiffness out of them. It was getting cold. He had to resist the temptation to stamp his feet. A sigh of a breeze briefly ruffled the tall grass, making a shushing sound that faded quickly back into stillness. Nothing moved.

They were in there, he knew it. It was a test of nerves, now.

To his left, Shaw could just see his brother James and James' two teenaged sons out of the corner of his eye, arrayed across the clearing at twenty yard intervals. He turned his head to the right to look at his own two sons. Gee Dub and Charlie were standing tensely, watching the brushy field, unmoving as stone, only the fog of their breath in the sharp November air betraying the fact that they were alive.

It had taken the six of them a quarter of an hour to ease themselves out of the woods and into the clearing far enough to be able to get a clean shot, but Shaw figured that any further would be pushing their luck. Two black, tan, and white hounds were sitting close to his feet, one on either side, obedient but quivering with excitement. He could tell by their riveted attention that they had marked their quarry.

A speckled bird dog was working the field, back and forth in a zig-zag pattern, his nose to the ground. As the dog moved further into the field, only his back and feathery tail protruded above the tall, dried grasses.

The dog slowed and took a tentative step or two before his head popped into sight and his tail dropped, creating a straight line from nose to tail-tip as he froze on point.

Shaw emitted a tiny whistle between his teeth and his dogs shot forward into the grass like a couple of bullets, one to the left and one to the right, approaching the pointer in a wide circle. As they neared, James signaled the pointer with a piercing whistle of his own and the dog leaped forward. Faced with a three-sided assault and no escape route, the entire covey of quail flushed.

Shaw was peripherally aware that his companions raised their shotguns at the same time he did, aiming into the air above the dogs' trajectory. He barely had time to seat the stock on his shoulder before the half-dozen quail took to the air in a panic. He chose his prey and sighted it along the barrel of his gun as it rose above the treetops. A shot rang out to his right and one of the birds nosedived, but Shaw didn't allow himself to be distracted. He pulled the trigger and his target spun in the air, flapped a couple of times, then managed a crazy, zig-zag landing at the far edge of the field.

Shaw barely heard the blasts of the guns on either side of him. He had more than likely only winged his quarry. He huffed, torn between feeling disappointed that he hadn't killed the creature outright and pleased that he had hit it at all.

The dogs were still crashing around through the tall grass, each heading for dead or wounded birds to retrieve. Shaw had never seen his brother's bird dog hunt before. He was impressed. He had only had the opportunity to see Happy at family gatherings and hadn't thought much of the pup's brainpower. He was aptly named, though, as goofy and good-natured as a creature could be.

Shaw had owned his two hounds for years. He had trained them himself and he had to admit that Crook and Buttercup were two of the best hunters he had ever run. They were 'coon hounds, natural stalkers, and unusually smart. They seemed to know automatically what kind of game their master was after and exactly which skills were required of them on each hunt. They could tree raccoons, trail foxes, keep a bear at bay, flush birds, and were good retrievers on land or water. Their only defect was that they were both terrible watchdogs since they were friends with everyone they met. But Shaw couldn't fault them for it. They loved children, and for a man with ten of his own, that was a good trait for a dog to have.

James and the boys all descended on him, laughing and excited and talking at once.

"I didn't hit nothing, Uncle Shaw, but I think Daddy did."

"I don't know, Jerry, I think mine got away, too."

"Gee Dub sure got his, Daddy. Blowed his head clean off!"

"I saw two more go down, Dad. One looked to be still alive."

Shaw put his arm around his oldest son's shoulders. "That was mine, Gee Dub. I just nicked him, looked like. When the dog fetches him back, I'll have to wring his neck, I reckon."

As he said the words, Crook emerged from the grass with a headless quail in his mouth. Shaw praised the dog before he took the bird by the feet and held it up with a laugh. "Well, I'll be switched! I guess Gee did blow his head clean off! Go on, Crook, bring me another one."

Crook disappeared and Shaw handed the bird to Gee Dub, who put it in the satchel slung over his shoulder.

James nodded toward a wave of moving grass. "Here comes Buttercup yonder with another bird."

The hound trotted out of the field with something in her mouth, her head high and her tail awag, obviously pleased with herself, and sat down at Shaw's feet.

Charlie leaned over to inspect her treasure. "What do you got, girl? This ain't no bird. Why, it's an old boot!"

"Thanks, Buttercup." Shaw sounded more amused than unhappy about it. "I believe I've got plenty of footwear."

Shaw's nephew Jimmy moved up to take a better look. "That old thing has sure seen better days! Looks like it's been lying out in the woods for a spell. There's something inside it."

"Probably a dead critter or some such," Gee Dub said. "I bet that's what interested her."

Amid the sounds of disgust at this suggestion, Charlie turned the boot upside down and gave it a shake. Dirt and leaf litter fell out onto the ground with a plop. The boy stirred it around with his toe before peering back down the boot top. "There's something still in here. Looks like a couple of sticks." He shook it again, but his only reward was a rattling noise.

Shaw was suddenly struck by foreboding. He extended his hand. "Let me have that, son."

A glimpse of two jagged, grey protrusions confirmed his fear.

"What is it, Uncle Shaw?"

"Nothing, Jerry. Some furry little thing built a nest in an old boot, is all. You children check the field for more downed birds. Charlie, you find Crook."

The boys scattered but James didn't move. "Shaw?"

"It's bones, James. Seems we got us a boot complete with its own leg and foot."

An expression of dread passed over James' face. "Old?"

"Yes, right old, no worry about that. Stick with the boys a spell and I'll see what Buttercup has dug up." Shaw knelt down in front of the dog and held the boot under her nose. "Where'd you get this, gal? Show me!"

He gave a short warbling whistle and Buttercup took off through the grass, heading toward the curve of woods bordering the clearing to the north with Shaw hot on her heels.

◇◇◇

The dog put her head down and sniffed around in a little circle right at the edge of the woods. Because of the grass, Shaw was practically on top of her before he could see what had momentarily distracted her. Another small piece of grey bone with a finger-thick vine wrapped around it was lying on top of a flat rock that was half embedded in the dirt.

Shaw's first thought was that this shard of bone had fallen out of the boot when Buttercup was carrying it. He reached for it, but jerked his hand back when the vine moved.

A small, greenish brown snake lifted its head and regarded him. Shaw backed up a step. What on earth was a snake doing out at this time of year? The earlier part of the day had been mild and obviously the snake was soaking up whatever warmth remained in the rock. But still…

It was November and the evening was frosty! That critter should have been curled up in a hole with his kinfolks for the past month.

Yet there it was. A snake wrapped around a bone, giving him the eye. Shaw fought off a flood of superstitious dread.

Buttercup reappeared from the woods and emitted a *wuff*. *Are you coming?* Shaw looked at her, then back at the rock. The bone was still there but the snake had gone.

Shaw blinked. Had he actually seen what he thought he saw, or had it been a trick of the shadows? He shook himself.

"Come on, Buttercup. Let's see what you've found."

Chapter Two

Shaw stood next to his brother James and pondered the grinning visage that looked back at them from the ground. It was getting colder and a damp mist was forming close to the ground. There would be a frost before morning. Shaw's mustache felt stiff. He wondered if his breath was freezing into icicles above his lip.

Buttercup had led him several yards into the woods to a small, open area where a large tree had probably stood once, but was now overgrown with tall chokecherry bushes interspersed with fiery red sumac. After he had seen the leg bones protruding from the small mound under the bushes, he had walked back to the clearing and waved at James to join him. After a brief consultation the men sent the boys back to their campsite with the dogs and the day's kill, leaving the two of them to excavate the body. It had taken them nearly an hour to remove the rocks, dirt, and weeds from the makeshift grave, by which time dusk was pressing in on them and the woods were so gloomy that they were no longer able to make out much detail.

"Looks like he's been here a good long time," Shaw observed. "Five, ten years, at least, maybe longer."

James cocked an eyebrow. "Being as he's good and well reduced to bones I would reckon so." He glanced toward the clearing, barely visible through the thicket of scrub oak and sassafras trees.

Shaw bit his lip. "This looks like an old Indian burial. See how it was once piled over with rocks? Not deep, though. I'm guessing that the flooding we had back in January and February washed it out enough to finally expose that foot. He was more'n likely buried good enough to thwart any critters who might have been interested in him, until lately. These bones would have been dug up and scattered all over creation before long." He squatted down to get a better look. The body was stretched out on its back. The left foot, shod in a tall leather boot, protruded below. The similarly booted right foot was now standing sentinel at the side of its previous owner.

Dirt clogged the empty eye sockets and the lower jaw had been crushed and fallen over at an odd angle. Shaw dug his hands deeper into the pockets of his coat. "He was probably a Creek."

His brother's eyebrows peaked. "You expect so?"

"Well, look, James. He's been here a long time and this is Muscogee Creek country."

"Those look like army boots to me," James pointed out.

Shaw stood up. "That don't mean anything. Plenty of Creeks fought in the War between the States, on both sides. Can't tell by looking, though. He might just as well have been *yu-ne-ga*." He used their Cherokee mother's word for "White man."

"What do you figure happened to him, Shaw?"

"Who knows? Not a well-done burial. Maybe it was done in haste." Shaw removed his bandanna from his back pocket and knelt back down. He leaned over the body and carefully began to brush dirt away from the skull. A long crack across the forehead began to reveal itself, growing wider as Shaw worked his way across the brow. A dark clot of dirt fell away from a perfectly round hole at the point above the nose cavity.

Shaw's mouth quirked up on one side and he looked up at James, who was leaning over his shoulder. "Right between the eyes."

"I'll be switched!" James exclaimed. "Done to death! Now what do we do?"

Shaw stood, shook his head. "It's too late to make it into town before dark. Let's cover him up with one of them old blankets we have back at the camp and put some of these rocks back on top of him for the night. In the morning I can ride into Oktaha and see if I can rustle up a telephone, call the sheriff in Muskogee. Somebody around here may know all about this poor fellow. Let's see what the sheriff wants us to do. You and the boys stay and keep an eye on Slim, here, until I get back. Y'all can pack up the campsite."

James gave him a dry smile. "You expect our hunting trip is over?"

"I fear so, James."

James walked back to the clearing to send one of the boys for a blanket, leaving Shaw squatted down beside the grave.

Who were you, he wondered, without hope of an answer. His gaze wandered over the open hole, looking for a clue as to the identity of its occupant. There wasn't much to see; brownish-grey bones with shreds of degraded clothing still clinging here and there. A boot. The shallowness of the grave had at first led Shaw to think this was a hasty burial, but the bony hands had been arranged over the place the heart had once been. Perhaps the dead man had simply been interred by someone who didn't know how deep to make a grave.

He spotted something at the skeleton's side, something of a slightly different color than the surrounding soil. He leaned forward to dig it out with his fingers, then held it up to the fast-fading light. It looked like a small leather saddlebag with a short fringe on the flap. Years in the ground had done it no good, but it had held together better than its owner had.

The flap was stiff and cracked when he lifted it, but he was curious enough not to care. Water had seeped in over time, and frost, and all manner of things that live under the ground. Whatever the bag's contents had been they appeared to have melted together into a single mottled beige entity. Except for something white on top.

He drew it out. A necklace, it looked like, made of the vertebrae of a snake strung together on a stiff and degraded leather thong. He stared at it in the palm of his hand, mesmerized, until he heard James coming back toward him, crunching through the leaves on the ground.

Shaw often wondered in later years what possessed him at that moment. It seemed urgently important to him that this artifact not be seen by anyone. Not yet. He stuffed the necklace in his coat pocket and dropped the bag back into the hole as James came up behind him.

"Look at that!" James said. "Is that his medicine bag?"

Shaw's heart was thumping, but when he spoke he sounded nonchalant. "Could be. Kind of big. Maybe it's a saddle bag."

"Did you look inside?"

"I did. It's been in the ground too long. There's nothing in there but a waterlogged mess." A guilty thought arose. *True, now that I've taken out the one thing I could identify.*

Chapter Three

Their camp was set up at an old homesite. No one had lived on the property for many years, so even though the split log cabin had been fairly large and comfortable in its day, it had long since fallen into such disrepair that it was in danger of collapse. The boys had been eager to explore the house but were forbidden to go inside. So the Tuckers were camping rough, with three canvas pup-tents and blanket bedrolls around a fire in the forest clearing that once was a farm yard.

It had been a poor farm. A few sticks remained of a pig sty and a chicken coop. There had never been a barn, but there was a debris-filled well that if dug out and cleaned would probably be serviceable. The homesite was no more than a cleared circle in the middle of the woods. There had once been a path out through the woods to the main road that was now overgrown.

By the time Shaw and James had left the forlorn grave, it was so dark that they had some trouble navigating through the woods to find their way back. Shaw was in the midst of cursing himself for not keeping at least one of the dogs with them when James spotted the light of the boys' campfire through the trees. The mouth-watering smell of roasting rabbit hastened them along.

Fifteen-year-old Jerry stood up when the men crashed through the brush into the open. "There they are! What did y'all find? Was it a man buried up in the woods?"

They stacked their shotguns and made themselves comfortable next to the fire before James sated the boys' curiosity. "Some poor old devil passed into eternity back there in the woods, all right. Whatever happened to him happened a long time ago, but it looks like somebody helped him leave this life before God could call him."

Shaw took up the story so that James could stuff his mouth with rabbit. "We figured we'd better let the sheriff know what we dug up in case Slim's kin have been wondering about him all this time, so I'll ride into Oktaha in the morning. I don't know whether the sheriff will send somebody right out or not, or whether he'll want us to stay and answer questions or clear out. But I'm betting our hunting trip is done, boys."

A collective groan greeted this announcement and Shaw laughed. "I reckon the sheriff will want us out of the way eventually. Course, if y'all want to bag a few more birds before I return with with law in tow, help yourself."

They feasted on wild rabbit, saving the quail for the superior cooking skills of the womenfolk at home, then crawled into their pup tents, two by two, bunking together by age—the two youngest, Charlie and Jerry, the two eldest sons, Gee Dub and Jimmy, and the two patriarchs, Shaw and James. As he slid into his bedroll, Shaw could hear the boys' excited whispering about the intriguing twist their hunting trip had taken.

In good time, silence fell. Shaw was drifting between wake and sleep when James spoke.

"I'm sorry we have to cut this trip short, Shaw. I look forward to it every year. This a real good hunting spot. I'm glad you thought of it."

"I spent some time out here years ago, before Papa even bought it. The fellow who owned it before gave me a job helping him clear land."

"Well, we'll have to come back for sure. All these trees around here, this country reminds me of back home."

"Not so hilly as Arkansas," Shaw noted.

"Still. Makes me think of how our pa used to take us boys out hunting every fall. Sometimes we'd be out for days. Now, them woods back around Mountain Home are deep. Full of deer and bear."

Shaw smiled at the memory. "Never used any tents, either. Pa could whip up a shelter out of a couple of saplings and a bunch of branches quicker'n you could spit. All four of us would hunker down together in that lean-to, all wrapped in Ma's quilts, and Pa would scare the wadding out of us with tales about panthers dragging off little children and haints walking the hills."

James chuckled in the dark. "You and Charles told me that if a panther came he'd always go after the youngest 'cause they was the best eatin'. I bawled, so Pa gave me an unloaded pistol and said I was to shoot any panthers I caught sight of. I'd sit there pointing that pistol out the door until I couldn't keep my eyes open and fell over asleep!"

"You remember that? You were just a little feller when that happened."

"Well, shoot, y'all about scared me to death. I like to never got over it."

"Sorry!" Shaw's apology lacked conviction. "I reckon that's what you get when you have two older brothers."

James laughed. "I ought to thank you, I expect. It's one of the only things I remember very clear about Pa."

"I'm glad of that, then. We always came home with about as much game as we could carry. 'Coons and possums, rabbits and squirrels, all kinds of birds. One year we brought home a big old snapping turtle and Ma made the best soup out of it. Pa always took one deer every autumn."

"Oh, I had forgot how he'd dress that deer and smoke it in a hollow log!"

"You remember the razorback?"

James barked a laugh. "Ugh! Charles still has the scar on his leg to bear witness to that little scrape! Tasted like boiled shoes, too."

"Well, Mama made a passel of brushes out of its bristles and got a bunch of shoe soles and straps and hinges out of its hide."

"I'd rather eat one of my own pigs any day." James murmured. His voice was muffled by his arm.

"You know, there's a rime on the grass tonight. I figure it'll be butchering time pretty soon after we get home." Shaw waited a long moment for a reply that didn't come. James had fallen asleep.

Chapter Four

Shaw sighed and turned over. It always made him a bit sad to think about his father. He wasn't sure why. He had only been eight years old when Jim Tucker died. Over thirty-five years ago.

It had happened so fast. Jim fell ill one day and three days later he was dead. That sort of thing happened a lot in the Arkansas backwoods in those days. That didn't make it any easier, though. Shaw had felt like the bottom had fallen out of the world.

Shaw's mother had reacted with her usual Cherokee stoicism. She hadn't indulged in any hysterics, or even cried much that Shaw had seen. She hadn't done much of anything, in fact. It was as though she had turned to stone.

At the time Shaw had been too young and concerned with his own loss to have much compassion for his mother's feelings. He remembered long periods of time after that when she wasn't at home. To this day, he occasionally wondered how she could have left her six young children alone to cope with the loss. He had never asked her why she disappeared for days on end, or where she had gone. No one in the family ever talked about it.

His oldest sister Josie had mothered her younger siblings through that first dark year, feeding them and keeping them clean. Shaw smiled to himself. Her three little brothers hadn't helped her much in that department. The two littlest girls had been not much more than toddlers. Of course Josie had been not quite twelve years old herself. That realization filled him with awe.

His mother had slowly returned to this earth and resumed her life, even though there were still periods of absence. But she never smiled, never laughed, never played and teased like she had before Jim died.

Not until a carrot-topped, blue eyed, elfin Irishman by the name of Peter McBride showed up and brought light into the world again.

Shaw had never for one minute resented his stepfather. Peter had brought his mother back to life and had filled a void in the lives of her children. He had even added two more boys to the family. Even so, to this day Shaw felt a peculiar ache when he thought about his father. He pillowed his head on his arm, drifting again, and made an effort to remember the details of his father's face. He had had shaggy dark hair and green eyes. A ready smile that quirked up at one corner. He hugged his children a lot and his ill-shaven face was always scratchy. He had been twenty-nine years old when he died.

Come on, boys, y'all think you can rassle me? I'll take you all on at onest! Oh, no! Oh, no! He'p me, Ma! All these boys is got me pinned!

Chapter Five

Shaw blinked at the blackness over his head and wondered briefly where he was. Wherever it was, it was cold and dark. The inside of a tent, and his sleeping companion was his brother James instead of his wife, Alafair. It only took a moment for him to realize that a noise had awakened him. Something that didn't belong with the normal sounds of an autumn night in the woods.

He listened to his brother's even breathing. Whatever it was hadn't disturbed James. Shaw wondered if he had been dreaming. He had just turned over on his side when he heard it again. His eyes popped open. A rustling noise. He raised up on his elbow, not alarmed, yet wanting to place the unfamiliar sound before dismissing it.

He could see the glow of the banked fire pit through the slit in the tent flap. Nothing was stirring. He could see the tops of the heads of two black haired boys, Gee Dub's curly and Jerry's straight, in the tent directly across the clearing. Both were sound asleep.

He could hear the dogs snuffling and muttering to each other, and a soft *woof.* That's it, he told himself. Just the dogs moving around. But as logical as this explanation was he didn't lie down. *If I can hear it one more time I'll know for sure what it is.*

Something dark and noiseless passed between the tent flap and the light of the fire. Shaw froze. Had he imagined it? He reached out to shake James when a speckled dog brushed by the entrance, panting loudly. Shaw let out a breath he hadn't realized he had been holding. His relief was short lived. Following close behind the four trotting dog legs were two creeping human legs, shod in tall muleskin moccasins. Shaw yelped and sat up so quickly that his head scraped against the canvas.

James started awake as Shaw sat up. "What...?"

Shaw hushed him with a gesture and was outside in a fraction of a second, standing in front of his tent glancing wildly around the clearing and poised to bolt for the tripod of shotguns stacked nearby. Crook and Buttercup were lying next to one another by the fire, nibbling and worrying something on the ground between them. They lifted their heads and gave him a quizzical look. Happy was sitting on his haunches beside the younger boys' tent with his usual brainless grin on his face and what appeared to be a stick in his mouth. No human legs, attached or otherwise, were to be seen. James crawled out next to him and got to his feet.

"What'd you hear?" he whispered, still bleary with sleep.

"I thought I heard somebody moving around."

James yawned. "Look at Happy. He's got a squirrel or a rabbit haunch in his mouth. And your two hounds over there have the rest of it. You heard the dogs after a critter."

Shaw gave a tight shake of his head. "That's what I thought, 'til I saw a set of legs go strolling by the tent."

That woke James up. "Legs? Not one of the young'uns?"

"Not unless they took to wearing moccasins in the last few hours." Shaw kept his voice low so as not to disturb the boys.

"I don't see anybody. The dogs don't seem fretted."

Shaw was stalking around the clearing with James in his wake, taking inventory, listening and looking for anything amiss. "I don't see anybody either. He couldn't have got into the woods so fast without being seen."

"You more than likely just dreamed it."

Shaw looked up at the sky. The positions of the crisp, bright, points of light in the blackness on either side of the blanket of the Milky Way told him it was around two o'clock in the morning. "Must be," he mumbled. What else? Either that or their stealthy visitor had disappeared into thin air.

"It's hours to dawn," James observed. "Let's get some sleep."

That was the practical thing to do, Shaw realized. But the strange incident had shaken him. "You go on. I think I'll sit up a spell."

"Suit yourself." James gave him a crooked smile and clapped him on the back before crawling back into the tent.

After retrieving his boots, coat, and hat, Shaw sat down on a log they had dragged near the fire to serve as a bench. It was freezing, and unnaturally quiet. Every breath fogged the air in front of his face. He poked up the fire and fed it until it was a jolly blaze, big enough at least to hold off the worst of the chill. At the dim limits of the firelight he could barely see a low mist clinging to the base of the trees in the woods. He heard Charlie sigh and shift positions.

As he settled back, Buttercup sidled up and put her head in his lap, her soulful brown eyes gazing up at him. He sat by the fire with the dog until he lost track of time and had to check the positions of the stars to determine how long he had been there. He was shocked. He was sure he hadn't fallen asleep, but what seemed like a few minutes had apparently been a couple of hours. No hint of dawn yet. One of the older boys was snoring softly in his tent. There was no wind at all, just dead quiet and a bone-numbing chill in the air. Buttercup's head was still on his knee, her eyes open, staring up at him. He couldn't see the other two dogs.

She lifted her head and looked toward the woods, her floppy ears shifting forward. Shaw followed her gaze. The fire had died down and he could barely make out the edge of the woods beyond the perimeter of light. The low-lying mist had thickened and long tongues of fog licked out from the tree line into the clearing, illuminated by the sliver of new moon.

One of the slender blackjacks seemed to move. Shaw's breath stopped. Not a tree, but something upright. A bear? He glanced at the dog, whose attention was riveted upon the moving shadow. Her hackles raised and her lip curled, but she didn't bark or charge off, which made Shaw feel marginally better. She'd be going crazy if she had spotted a bear. He opened his mouth to speak to her, but reconsidered. He wasn't sure he wanted to alert whatever was watching that he was aware of it.

Buttercup stood and trotted toward the woods in a business-like manner and the shadow in the woods faded back into the darkness. Shaw gasped, leaped to his feet and made a lunge for one of the shotguns stacked in a tripod by the fire. He was into the woods in a trice. The thick carpet of leaves were damp with fog and his footfall was muffled, but the pop and crackle of dried twigs on the trees snapping as he plunged further into the forest stopped him in his tracks. The brush at the edge of the tree line was too thick and brittle for him to walk through without being heard.

But not for whatever creature he had glimpsed. Strain his ears as he may, the only sound Shaw could hear was Buttercup snuffling around. She was obscured by the mist and he couldn't see her. In fact, once he was ten feet into the woods he couldn't see his hand in front of his face.

He squatted down and breathed a tiny whistle. Buttercup materialized at his elbow. "What did you see, gal?" he whispered. He gave a low quavering whistle, a signal for the dog to track.

She disappeared again, nose to ground. Shaw remained hunkered down in the fog with the shotgun across his knee and listened to the dog range back and forth through the brush, left and right, further and further, then nearer again.

She suddenly reappeared, sat down in front of him and regarded him with a quizzical cock of the head.

She had been unable to pick up a trail. Shaw sighed. What had he seen? Something had been there. Buttercup had seen it too, so he wasn't hallucinating. An animal surely, considering how silently it had melted into the forest.

He stood up. He knew it wasn't an animal.

A single, icy, sigh of wind passed, causing him to clutch the collar of his coat, ruffling the remaining dry leaves on the trees.

The sound was like a voice. *Shaw,* it said.

The hair on the back of his neck rose. The dog was gone, probably back to the warmth of the fire like the sensible creature she was. Shaw turned around and took a few steps toward camp before another breath of wind passed by.

Shaw...

He stopped dead, rooted in his tracks. He knew that voice.

He managed to open his mouth enough to speak. "Pa?"

Chapter Six

The most irritating thing about a cold Saturday morning in November, as far as Alafair Tucker was concerned, was that school wasn't in session. She huddled over her rag basket, trying without much success to sort material for a quilt top and ignore her squabbling offspring in the kitchen. Their morning chores were done, so in an attempt to keep a screaming fight from breaking out she had sent the girls to wash vegetables and peel potatoes for dinner.

"Ma!" Grace's piping voice rose. "What's a garment? Blanche keeps saying that I have a garment on my back but I can't reach it and she won't brush it off of me!"

Alafair didn't look up from her task. "Blanche, quit saying that Grace has a garment on her back."

"Grace keeps bothering us, Ma," Blanche responded. "She's pulling potato peels out of the bucket and putting them on her head…"

"They're curls!"

"Grace, quit playing with the pigs' dinner and let your sisters do their work."

"Grace, stop it," Sophronia yelled. "Give me that carrot!"

Grace squealed. "Mama!"

Alafair bit her lip and forced a breath out her nose. No use. She placed a scrap of calico on the side table. "Grace, come here."

Grace ran into the parlor, her bare feet beating on the wooden floor. "Ma, I didn't do nothing!"

Alafair didn't argue with her. "Where's your socks? You'll catch your death! Go put on some shoes. But first go over there in the corner and bring me my quilting hamper."

The child rushed to the sideboard to retrieve a homemade honeysuckle vine basket nearly as big as she and brought it to her mother. "Are we going to quilt?" Grace was excited. At barely three years she wasn't yet old enough to ply a quilting needle, but she loved to watch Alafair lower the quilt frame from the ceiling. Once the wooden frame was down at lap-height Grace could spend hours playing house under the stretched material while the family females sat in a circle around it, sewing and swapping stories.

Alafair stood, walked over to the corner of the room and unlashed four cords wound around a knob high on the wall, far out of the reach of little children. The cords were attached to the four corners of the nine-by-seven foot board rectangle which served as her quilt frame. When not in use the frame was raised up to the ceiling by means of an ingenious system of bent-nail eye bolts, pegs, and pulleys which Shaw had fashioned for her years earlier, shortly after he and his brothers had built the house. All she had to do to lower the frame was loosen the ropes and let it down. When she finished a quilting session, a couple of tugs raised it back up to the ceiling, out of the way and out of sight.

Ten-year-old Blanche and nine-year-old Sophronia both appeared in the kitchen door. "Are we going to quilt?" Blanche echoed. Both the older girls were just beginning to learn the skill and were eager to practice.

"I'm going to stitch for a while before dinner. Y'all, on the other hand, are going to be busy getting things ready for me to cook. Blanche, you finish peeling the potatoes and skin an onion for me. Then mix up a pan of cornbread. Fronie, you run out to the cellar and bring back a couple of them acorn squashes and clean them out."

Sophronia loved to clean and carve winter squashes and pumpkins, so she was gone out the back door in a flash. Blanche loved the close and delicate art of quilting. She gave her mother a look full of longing and maybe a touch of resentment. But after a quarter-century of child-rearing, Alafair was immune to wheedling. Blanche knew it, so she did no more than frown before turning to her task.

Alafair had just stretched this particular quilt onto the frame a couple of days earlier, so most of it was wound around the side boards which had been attached with pegs through holes near the middle of the end boards, creating a long, narrow, strip of quilt to work with. Alafair stuck the ends of the frame through a couple of slat-back chairs to steady it, pulled up a chair for herself and sat down. She spent a couple of minutes rummaging through her sewing hamper, threading a needle, finding her favorite thimble.

She figured she had maybe half an hour until the girls had done as much prep work on dinner as they were able and she would be called to do the actual cooking. But she had planned a simple dinner just for herself and her three youngest. The two eldest girls, Martha and Mary, along with their middle sister, Ruth, had gone to town early that morning. Shaw and the boys were on a hunting trip with James and his sons and wouldn't be back until Sunday morning, so Alafair would be able to leave the frame down all day if she wanted.

Grace, now shod in mismatched socks, skipped back into the parlor from the bedroom and immediately crept under the stretched quilt. She would stay there, lost in a pretend world, as long as Alafair would allow it. Alafair briefly wondered if she had ever sat down to quilt without a child or two playing beneath the frame.

The quilt she was working on now was a crazy quilt that she and her daughters had pieced over the fall. Since most of the quilting would be done by her and the younger girls, Alafair wasn't taking quite as much trouble with the stitching as she would for a fancy quilt, like the double wedding ring she and several Tucker clan mothers were making for Mary's wedding in

May. No elaborate pattern of stitches for this quilt. She sewed simple outlines around the patches.

She had just gotten into the rhythm and was beginning to feel the sweet calm that came on her when she was absorbed in her art, when the back door banged and Sophronia ran into the parlor, her cheeks and nose rosy with cold, clutching an acorn squash under each arm.

"Ma, Daddy and Uncle James are back!"

Grace shot out from under the quilt and through the kitchen, crying, "Daddy!" But Alafair's eyebrows knit. "Already?" Even if they had bagged all the birds they wanted, her men wouldn't have come home a day early without another reason. The greatest pleasure of these hunting trips for them was camping out in the woods together.

"The boys, too. They just come in and rode up to the barn!"

Alafair anchored her needle through the material and stood up, a little worried at the unexpected turn of events.

Chapter Seven

"He was buried in a shallow grave way up in the woods." Charlie spoke between mouthfuls of fried potatoes and gravy. "Looks like he'd been there for years."

Six hungry males showing up unexpectedly for dinner had forced Alafair to abandon her plans for a leisurely meal for herself and the girls. She and her helpers had thrown together a pan of biscuits, opened several jars of canned vegetables, carved slabs of ham off the joint in her cupboard, sliced up Blanche's carefully peeled potatoes and fried them up in bacon grease, used the drippings with milk and flour for gravy, and had dinner on the table within twenty minutes.

Blanche and Sophronia did waitress duty. Alafair was sitting at the table with a mug of coffee in her hand and Grace in her lap, listening to her menfolk relate the tale of the discovery that had cut short their hunting expedition.

James took up the story. "We were on that piece of land that Papa bought back some years ago, the old Goingback place just southwest of Oktaha. Papa's never had a tenant out there, never goes out there at all to my knowledge, so the property has run wild. Shaw suggested it'd be a good place to hunt some birds. I'd never even been out there before."

"Mama, there wasn't nothing left of him but a skeleton and a couple scraps of clothes and his boots." Charlie made this contribution while ladling gravy over his second helping of everything. "Between the rain and the critters his rocky grave finally shifted and sank enough that his right foot was sticking out from under the bank and Buttercup sniffed it out."

"Then she took a notion to wrench it off and fetch it back to us," Jerry added.

At the mention of a booted skeleton Alafair had felt Grace shift in her lap. The child was now leaning forward with her elbows on the table and both hands over her ears. Alafair sighed. She didn't relish the idea of having to deal with a scared little girl in Mama and Daddy's bed all night. She crooked a finger and Sophronia came to her side. Alafair drew her down and murmured into her ear. "You and Grace bundle up real good and go on over to Phoebe's for a spell, puddin'." One of Alafair's two married daughters lived across the creek on the adjoining farm. "I'll come get y'all in an hour or two and you can have some pie and do some quilting if you've a mind."

Grace may have stopped her ears but she wasn't deaf to her mother's suggestion. She leaped down and seized Sophronia's hand, excited. Her year-old niece Zeltha was her favorite play-mate and most ardent admirer.

The girls disappeared and Alafair turned back to the conversation. "I always wondered why your Papa bought that piece of land, James. It's way out there on the edge of nowhere. It ain't close to his farm or not much close to any town either, and as far as I know he's never put it to any use."

James shrugged. "Tell you the truth, Alafair, I had kind of forgotten that Papa even owned it. Jerry asked if we could go to some different place to hunt. If Shaw hadn't suggested we try the woods out there I doubt if I would have ever thought of it again."

Shaw finally spoke up. "It's mostly heavy woods, James. Papa may have plans for that timber eventually. I don't know. But for some reason when Jerry mentioned finding a place that hadn't been hunted on for a spell that property of his came to mind."

Alafair gave him a sharp look. These were practically the first words Shaw had uttered since they returned. She had known from the moment she saw him that morning that something was eating at him and it wasn't just the discovery of an old burial in the woods.

He looked tired. His fine, black-lashed, hazel eyes were sunken and he seemed distracted. Almost haunted, Alafair thought. She shifted in her chair, itching to get shed of the company so she could ask him what was on his mind.

Shaw glanced at her, aware of her scrutiny, before he continued. "Funny thing is that parcel of land hadn't crossed my mind in years. Not until last month when Papa's feud with Mr. Doolan heated up again."

James snorted. "Not again? What is it this time?"

"Doolan wants to breed one of his mares to Papa's prize Tennessee Walker stud and Papa says he'd sooner kick Doolan all the way to Texas." Shaw shook his head. "Who knows what it is between those two old reprobates? The point is that I got to thinking what good friends Papa and Doolan used to be, along with the man that used to own that property, Roane Hawkins. They were in the Army together out in Arizona. Three Irishmen. Papa said they were like three brothers. Do you remember Hawkins, James? He married Goingback's widow."

James scratched his cheek thoughtfully. "I recall somebody called Mr. Hawkins used to work with Papa and Mr. Doolan back in Arkansas. That was when I was still at home."

"Same fellow. Hawkins came out here to Oklahoma when it was still the Indian Territory and ended up staying. That was even before we moved out here. A year or so after we came to the Territory I went out there over a summer to help Hawkins clear land for a sawmill. He was married to the widow by then. I was trying to earn money to build this house."

Alafair nodded. "I remember. You were gone out there for several weeks."

"I didn't enjoy it much, either. Hawkins was a sharp dealer and it took some persistence on my part to get my money out of him. Unless I'm mistook, Papa bought that land off him and his wife several years later. Seems I heard that Hawkins wanted to move on and Papa bought the section just to help out an old Army pal."

"Where'd they go?" Gee Dub asked.

"I don't know, son. Papa'd know, more than likely."

This information intrigued Alafair. "Could it be that this body has something to do with why those folks wanted to move away?"

Shaw's expression lightened. "Trust you to make that connection, honey. I think that Slim was some drifter who ran afoul of someone on the road. Or a Creek who got shot in a skirmish. I'd bet that whoever put him there wanted to find a likely looking ill-cleared or abandoned farm where he could get rid of a body and nobody would find it for a long time. And nobody did."

"But what about that poor dead man? Y'all didn't just leave him there! " Blanche was appalled at the very thought.

Shaw put his arm around her waist as she stood by his chair. "'Course not, sugar. Uncle James and the boys sat in the woods with him real respectful while I rode in to the post office in Oktaha early this morning and wired the sheriff in Muskogee. Since it looked like an old burial he sent out one of his deputies, a fellow name of Morgan. Morgan knew of the place and managed to get down there pretty quick. He studied the situation for a spell, asked us for the particulars, then sent us packing. He said we'd likely never know what happened. We gave him our names and told him where we were from and he said he expected the sheriff would get in touch with us later with more questions. So we came home."

"About how long do you guess he's been there?" Alafair asked.

"Maybe a decade, I'd reckon," James said, "judging by the state of the body. His flesh had turned to dust but his boots were left. A long time."

Alafair thought about this for a moment. "I wonder if his wife and children have been missing him all this time?"

Chapter Eight

It was late that night before Alafair could get Shaw to herself and ask what was bothering him. After James and his sons left for home, Shaw immediately set out to inspect the barns and livestock to make sure that while he was away his foreman and future son-in-law, Kurt Lukenbach, had maintained Shaw's exacting standards. It was an unnecessary exercise considering Kurt's Germanic efficiency. But Shaw was never one to let the youngsters think he wasn't keeping a keen eye on them.

Charlie and Gee Dub accompanied their father in order to receive their work assignments, so Alafair wasn't even able to pump the boys for background information. She spent the afternoon quilting with the girls until the natural light in the house became too dim to stitch without eyestrain. Early in the evening, she sent Sophronia and Blanche to milk the cows and feed chickens while she and Grace picked squash from what was left of the vegetable garden and cut back the frost-nipped vines. There were a few pumpkins left on the vine. Alafair sliced them off for temporary storage on the screened-in back porch. Later they would go up in the attic for the winter, along with the rest of the pumpkin harvest.

The older daughters returned from town as the sun neared the horizon; first, freckle-faced Ruth, her long auburn braid swinging behind her, walked the two miles from town following her day of music and practice with her piano teacher. A little later Martha and Mary drove in together in the buggy.

Her two eldest were both nearing their mid-twenties and recently engaged to be married. Martha was a dark, slender, serious, young woman who had something of a career as secretary to Mr. Bushyhead, President of the First National Bank of Boynton. She had never expressed the slightest interest in finding a husband until two months earlier, when one Streeter McCoy had finally worn down her resistance by offering her true and eternal love and an executive position in the McCoy Land and Title Company.

Mary, on the other hand, was a plump, blue-eyed, blonde who loved to laugh, loved to eat, loved children, and loved Kurt Lukenbach. They had been planning to marry for some months, but Mary wanted to finish her year of teaching the third and fourth grade class at Boynton Grammar School.

The older girls had lately developed the habit of taking over the household chores when they came home from work and school. Mary usually made supper, since she enjoyed cooking. Ruth liked to play with the children, so Alafair was thus relieved of babysitting chores. Martha instructed her mother to sit down and directed everyone else in whatever task was at hand, since that's what Martha did best.

Shaw and the boys, Kurt included, showed up for supper as soon as it grew too dark to work. But there was no opportunity for private conversation. The men were engaged in cleaning themselves up and the women in readying the table and dishing up the meal. Grace decided that her father's lap was the best place to eat supper that evening. Alafair made a move to bodily return the tot to her own chair since Shaw looked as though he barely had enough energy to feed himself, much less deal with a messy three year old. But Shaw assured her that he didn't mind. After all, he'd gone for almost two whole days without a little girl to love on.

Their light supper of potato soup and cornbread proceeded, full of news and chatter from the children. Martha had spent the day at Streeter's office, learning how to go about a title search. Mary had cleaned her classroom, laid in a supply of coal for the potbellied stove in the middle of the room, and written out her lesson plans for the entire upcoming week: one set for the third graders, one for the fourth graders, and a few special notations for the two or three students who needed a little extra attention. Ruth was learning to transpose piano music and had whiled away her entire Saturday on Mozart.

The rest of the mealtime talk was dominated by the discovery of the body in the woods. Alafair listened with interest as Charlie and Gee Dub went over the entire story again, even more thrilling with a second telling. She also noticed that Shaw didn't contribute much. He sat quietly with Grace on his lap, trying to avoid dribbling hot soup on himself while heading off Grace's drips and drops. He seemed interested in the conversation and occasionally smiled at a particularly egregious embellishment of the facts. But unless he was asked directly he didn't engage. And that was not like Shaw Tucker at all.

She finally cornered him after supper as the older girls were cleaning up and the rest of the children had adjourned to the parlor for games and music before bedtime.

He was standing in the yard, just outside the door that led to the screened-in back porch, staring up at the sky. It was already fully night, the moonless sky a velvety black, the stars brilliant points in the clear autumn air.

He looked over at her as she stepped out, alerted by the creak of the screen door. She moved up beside him and drew her shawl close around her shoulders.

"Mercy, it's finally turned downright cold. Winter's on the way."

Shaw resumed his celestial observation. "I expect I'd better plan on some butchering next week. I'll talk to John Lee, see if he'll lend a hand."

"I figured you'd be thinking of that directly. There was frost on the pumpkins for the first time this morning." A momentary silence fell before Alafair launched into the real reason she had followed him outside. "What's bothering you? You've been looking peaked ever since you got back."

He slid her an ironic glance which she couldn't see in the dark. "I was enjoying that hunting trip. Now that Gee Dub is off at college I like it when we can get off together. I wasn't best pleased to have to cut it short."

"There's more to it than that, I think."

Shaw put his arm around her shoulders. He was a tall man and she was not so tall, but they fit together perfectly. The warmth of her body felt good in the chill air. "Oh, you do, do you?"

"I do. The boys all act like finding that body is just a great adventure, but there's something about it that particularly eats at you."

Shaw didn't answer right away. He didn't know what to say. "I just wish we hadn't disturbed that burial. It's not good to stir up things from the past that ought to stay buried. Let the dead rest." He slipped his free hand into his coat pocket, his fingertips resting on the jagged points of vertebrae in the snake bone necklace.

His response gave her pause. Alafair and Shaw had both been raised in the deep woods of the Ozarks. They both knew that the dead weren't necessarily gone. Especially if there was unfinished business to attend to. But she had never known Shaw to concern himself overmuch about these things.

Shaw continued. "We never mentioned it at dinner but our skinny friend didn't just up and die on his own. There was a bullet hole in the middle of his forehead."

"Murder!"

He shrugged off the suggestion. "Like I said before, maybe he's left over from a skirmish during the Rebellion or some Creek tribal dust-up. Even so, I don't like it that maybe we found a murdered man in a hidden grave on land that belongs to Papa."

Alafair slipped an arm around his waist and gave him a shake. "Well, you can be sure Papa McBride don't know anything about it. He's tough as an old game rooster and I don't doubt he'd plug somebody between the eyes if he had to. But he wouldn't do it in secret. Besides, it's none of your affair anymore. Now it's up to the county sheriff to figure out what happened and dispense any justice that needs to be done. We'll be at your folks' for dinner after church tomorrow anyway, so just go ahead and ask your papa if he's got any ideas. Put your mind to rest."

Shaw agreed that he would talk to his stepfather in the morning. Though until he discovered what it was he'd seen in the woods, he suspected that nothing was going to put his mind to rest.

Chapter Nine

Alafair loved November. Much of the hard work of harvest was done and the weather was usually mild. Mornings were crisp and cold. But by noon it was often warm enough to do without a wrap, especially if one were engaged in heavy labor, which Alafair always was.

Not much was left in the garden. There were still a few winter squashes on the vines. The apples had been picked and stored in pits, or dried, or preserved for the winter. Her mother-in-law's native pecan orchard had already been harvested twice. Late-maturing nuts continued to fall, though, and the children were always bringing home baskets, aprons, and pockets-full of pecans they had picked up off the ground as they passed through their grandparents' orchard on their way home from school.

The hardest tasks of November, in Alafair's opinion, came with butchering time. For every one of the twenty-six years they had been married Shaw butchered a hog after the first frost. They would be butchering soon.

For the past couple of years, since two of their daughters had married and set up their own households, Shaw and his helpers had butchered and dressed two two-hundred-pound hogs, which provided enough meat for the entire extended family.

Alafair figured she had cured and smoked enough hams, bacon slabs, and shoulders, cleaned out enough stomachs and bladders and intestines, ground enough sausage, made enough blood sausage and head cheese and jellied enough pig's feet in her life to feed everybody in the Great State of Oklahoma for a year. And it wasn't just the hog-killing she had to deal with every fall. The menfolks' hunting trips provided her with plenty of quail, doves, turkeys, squirrels, and rabbits to cook, and even a rare deer or possum.

Alafair loved animals of all sorts and very much subscribed to the philosophy of kindness and respect for all of God's creatures. But she was a mother with ten children. She wasn't sentimental about what she had to do to feed them. The panther mother who lived in the hills yonder did the same. That was the way of things.

Since their grisly discovery had cut short the men's hunting trip, they had only bagged a dozen or so bobwhite quail between them. Shaw's cut of six quail would not make a big enough meal for Alafair to invite the married offspring over for a feast, but she thought she could make a couple of quail pies that would make a nice contribution to take to Sunday dinner at the in-laws' house. Besides, Shaw was particularly partial to her quail pie.

As it turned out, the wet spring and the long summer had produced some mighty fat birds. Alafair was able to make three large pies full of meat and enhanced with vegetables and herbs from her own garden.

◇◇◇

Grandpapa Peter McBride, Shaw's stepfather, removed the napkin from around his neck and pushed himself back from the table with a contented sigh. "Well, Alafair, that quail pie was a wonder."

"I would say so, honey." Shaw's mother Sally offered her congratulations as well.

Alafair felt her cheeks grow warm. She was used to plaudits for her cooking, but praise from Sally McBride really meant something. "Good ingredients make good cooking."

Charlie had temporarily staunched his hunger and had other things on his mind. "Grandpapa, Buttercup dug up a skeleton when we were out hunting!"

"I'll swan!" Sally exclaimed. "A skeleton!"

"Mama," Grace protested.

Alafair gestured to Ruth. "Honey, take the girls outside and get some sun for a spell while the weather is still nice." Ruth gathered up the children and left before Alafair turned back to her son. "The table is not the place to talk about things like that, Charlie. Let your dinner settle before you start talking about bones and such."

Grandpapa undermined Alafair's scolding with a chuckle. "James told me at church this morning that y'all had some excitement on your hunting trip, but he didn't have time to give me the details. What happened, lad?"

"Well, sir, we found a whole skeleton with his boots on who got buried in a shallow grave in the woods!"

Peter was amused at Charlie's macabre excitement, His eyes crinkled. "You don't say? And where was this?"

"I need to ask you about that, Papa." Shaw intervened before Charlie could answer. "We took the boys out to that section you own over by Oktaha."

Peter was a man who had no trouble mastering his emotions, but his eyes widened and his gaze skittered away. When he looked back at Shaw his expression was carefully neutral. "Son, I'd rather you boys didn't go out there. There's an evil hand over that place."

All chatter at the table stopped abruptly and every head turned toward Peter.

Shaw was taken aback at his stepfather's tone. "I'm sorry, sir. Me and James figured you wouldn't care since you've let the place run to ruin. But it's done, now. What do you mean by an 'evil hand'?"

Peter answered the question with another question. "You found a skeleton, you say? Do you have a notion how long he'd been there?"

"No. Long enough to thin out."

"Where exactly was it that you found him?"

While Shaw repeated the story of Buttercup's discovery, Alafair studied her parents-in-law's reactions. Sally listened intently, bright and interested. Peter's normally open and mobile face was still.

Shaw finished his tale and paused before he asked, "Papa, I don't suppose you know anything about this, do you?"

Peter managed a ghost of a smile. "No, I don't, son. But I do know that some bad things happened out there, though I didn't ken that a lonely death was one of them."

"What bad things?"

It was Sally who answered. "That place is haunted."

The matter-of-fact statement was so unexpected that for an instant Alafair wondered if she had actually heard it. "You don't say?"

Sally McBride reminded Alafair of a wren, small, plump, and brown, with curious, lively, black eyes, and black hair wound into a tight bun at the back of her head. Her mother had been a full-blood Cherokee from a remote hollow in the Ozark Mountains, and Sally's view of the world and her place in it was very much influenced thereby. "There's been a spirit wandering around out in them woods for years. That's why Peter's never been able to rent it out. Everybody around there knows about it."

Alafair glanced at Shaw, who was regarding his mother with a startled expression. She turned back to Sally. "Y'all never mentioned it!"

Sally shrugged. "Peter's heard reports from a couple of folks who've seen it, always at night. It sighs and moans and likes to do mischief to a campsite, if a body is inclined to stay out there overnight. I'm surprised it didn't bother the boys when they was down there Friday night."

Alafair knew that Indians were often gifted with the ability to sense the other world, but Peter McBride had been raised in Irelandm and she didn't know as much about the Irish. Peter had never claimed to have insights, as far as she knew. But judging by the elves, fairies, banshees, and silkies who graced the stories he delighted in telling at every opportunity, the veil between the worlds was mighty thin in his native land. "Any idea who it is?" she asked him.

Peter shook his head.

"Somebody who ain't figured out yet that he's dead," Sally said.

Peter looked at Shaw. "Whoever it is, you may have found his bones, son."

After the kitchen was back in order and the children had made their escape, Sally, Alafair, and Martha wandered over the front yard, inspecting the condition of the herb garden. The garden lined the rock path to the gate and took up much of the area between the porch and the rail fence that surrounded the yard. At this time of year the annuals were long gone, pulled up and dried, and were now hanging in fragrant bundles from the rafters on Sally's back porch. The perennials were mostly dormant and following the recent frost many were beginning to die back. The mints close to the house, however, were still lusty.

"How did Peter come to buy that property off of Hawkins in the first place, Ma?" Alafair pulled a wintergreen leaf off the bush and nibbled it. "There's not even a graded path leads to it. Shaw says there's naught but two ruts running through the woods and the brush for a good two or three miles after you leave the main road."

Alafair couldn't see her face, hidden as it was by the stiff brim of her poke bonnet, but Sally's head bobbed up and down. "I know it. I think Peter liked it that it's way off yonder and they never much cleared the place. Almost all that acreage is native woods. But mostly he was just trying to do a favor for a friend who needed the money. Of course, that's before he knew there was a haint on the property."

"Not much of a stand-up fellow, was he, to sell Grandpapa a haunted farm?" Martha's tone was ironic.

Sally leaned over and broke off the dried tip of a lavender twig. "Naw, but Roane always was a scoundrel, to my way of thinking." She sniffed the herb in her hand then briskly rolled the brittle leaves between her palms, reducing them to powder. "This'd make a nice dream pillow," she observed. She dusted off her hands and resumed her wander.

"Why was Papa friends with him, then?" Alafair had always known Peter McBride to be a pretty shrewd judge of character.

"I wouldn't say he trusted him. But Roane saved his life once when they were in the cavalry together. And it was Roane who told Peter about this property we're standing on and helped him make a good bargain for it. Roane did do the right thing every once in a while."

"You ever seen the ghost, Grandma?"

"I never did, Martha, darlin'. But Peter caught a glimpse of it and spoke with others who have, too. He's not much of a one to be fooled."

Alafair was about to ask if Peter had ever seen a ghost before when Martha nodded toward the road.

"Look, Grandma, yonder comes Cousin Scott and he's got somebody with him."

Two men on horseback had just passed through the front gate and were riding toward them up the long drive that led to the house. The shorter, rounder, jolly-looking man on the tall chestnut gelding was Shaw's cousin, Scott Tucker, town sheriff of Boynton, Oklahoma. Alafair was surprised. They had just seen Scott and his wife and boys at church that morning and the dinner plans he had related to them then had not included a midafternoon social call. The other man, a tall, dark-eyed, morose person with a black mustache almost as thick and handsome as Shaw's, was a stranger to her.

"Hey, Aunt Sally," Scott called as soon as the women turned in his direction. The two men dismounted and hitched their horses to the posts at the watering trough in front of the picket fence before removing their hats and entering.

Sally had come up to the gate to meet them, trailing Alafair and Martha behind her. "Hey, Scott. What brings you and your friend out here on a Sunday afternoon. Y'all et?"

"Thank you, ma'am. We've et." He turned to his companion, who was standing quietly at his side, hat in hand. "Aunt Sally, this here is John Barger, the county sheriff. He's come down from Muskogee on the train this morning because he'd like to have a word with Shaw about that body him and James found. With Uncle Peter, too, since that's his land."

Barger greeted her with a solemn nod. "Sorry to be bothering you on a Sunday, ma'am."

"Sorry you have to be away from your family today, Sheriff. Well, come on in and have some pie and coffee, at least, and y'all men can chat all you want. Martha, would you please go down to the paddock and fetch your daddy and grandpapa into the parlor?"

Chapter Ten

Both Shaw and Gee Dub were a head taller than Peter, yet both had some trouble keeping up with him as he chugged down the hill toward the horse paddock, his purposeful stride aided by an ash walking stick. They could see from a distance that Peter's handsome Tennessee walker stallion was already on its way to meet them. The McBrides' main source of income was from their orchards, but Peter's small herd of Tennessee walker horses was his greatest pleasure.

Being a breeder himself, Shaw was no mean judge of horseflesh. He had seen many a fine animal in his time. But the sight of Red Allen trotting toward them across the pasture with his neat head bobbing up and down in time to his distinctive gliding gait never failed to make the man catch his breath. The stallion was a tall horse, long-necked with sloping shoulders. His long, ivory-colored mane and tail made a startling contrast to his burnished chestnut coat. There was not a horse owner in the county who wouldn't love to own one of Red Allen's strong, smooth-striding offspring. He was one of the most sought-after studs in eastern Oklahoma, and Peter was able to name his price for the horse's services.

Shaw himself was proud owner of two of Red Allen's daughters; his own saddle horse, Hannah, and Gee Dub's beloved half-thoroughbred mare, Penny. Neither mare was a full-blood walker, but both had inherited their father's smooth gait. A rider could stay in the saddle all day and never tire.

By the time they reached the fence Red Allen was waiting for them, his ears pitched forward and his nostrils wide, eager for the treat he knew the old man had for him. Horse and man exchanged a breath before Peter offered an apple on his outstretched palm.

"*Sha, macushla, machree,*" he murmured. Peter had lived in America for more than fifty years. Long enough for his Irish accent to abate considerably. Yet in moments of extreme tenderness—with babies, with his wife in the middle of the night, with his horses—he still spoke in the language his mother had whispered in his ear when he was a child.

Gee Dub reached across the fence to stroke Red Allen's neck and the horse nodded his approval. "I'll be switched, Grandpapa. He must be getting on toward twenty years old, yet he's as full of vinegar as a yearling."

Peter put a tender hand on the horse's muzzle. "Yes, I made a special trip to Tennessee for this one and I do believe that was the year before you were born. He's a fine stout-hearted fellow, he is. You know, boys, last year alone he earned enough in stud fees to pay for the new cider mill I lately put in. It's true he is no youngster but he still does his duty with enthusiasm."

"Too bad you're so persnickety about where he does it, McBride."

The strange voice behind them caused all three men to flinch and turn around. Red Allen started at their alarm and shied away from the fence.

Gee Dub blinked at the man with the sour expression glaring at them them from the back of a bay gelding. The man was as scrawny as a weed and just about as tall. He was dressed in a heavy sheepskin coat and a flat tweed cap and sat stiff and indignant in the saddle. Fierce blue eyes blazed out of a wizened, snub-nosed face.

Shaw's mustache twitched. "Hello, Mr. Doolan."

"Hello, Shaw. It's been a long time." Doolan's greeting was perfectly pleasant but his scalding gaze never wavered from Peter's face.

"Doolan!" Peter seethed. "You've got a nerve! What the hell are you doing on my property?"

"I've come to try one more time to talk sense into you, McBride."

"Forget it."

"Don't be so hard-headed. My money is as good as the next man's. And I'm prepared to offer you more of it than the next man, at that."

"I don't care if you offer me a king's ransom, Doolan. I'll never let this beast stand stud for a mare of yours while I have breath in my body."

The sudden tense atmosphere was too much for Red Allen. He wheeled and trotted away. His fast-walking pace was so eye-catching, his back feet overstriding his front hoof prints as he sailed across the pasture, that the argument was suspended for a moment while the men admired the beauty of it.

"You're a spiteful heathen, McBride." The argument may have been delayed but was no less heated when Doolan resumed. "There's no stud in Oklahoma can hold a candle to yon stallion and well you know it. Talk some sense into the fool, Shaw. I'd have to haul my mares clean to Tennessee to find another half so fine, nor could I buy another of such quality even if I could afford to scour the country to find him."

Shaw threw up his hands and took a step back.

Doolan was undeterred by the lack of support. "You mean to keep my herd second-rate and drive me out of business, McBride."

Peter had had enough. "You're the one who's second rate, Doolan. I can do nothing for the poor beasts you own already. But I'll be damned if I'll do anything to help you get more of them to abuse!"

"For the sake of forty years of comradeship…"

"It took me forty years to find out what kind of man you are. So save your wind. Go back to Okmulgee and that torture chamber you call a horse farm. And mend your ways!" Peter's face was a dangerous shade of red as he shook his cane in the air. "Get out get out get out!"

"You were seeing things! I never abused an animal in my life!" Doolan was already riding away as he yelled back over his shoulder.

Peter looked murderous. Shaw put a hand on his stepfather's arm in an attempt to calm him.

Peter didn't notice. "If you ever come back onto my land without permission again, I'll shoot you, Doolan, you spivey maggot!"

"You're a hard man, McBride." Doolan's voice faded as the bay galloped toward the road.

"Papa," Shaw began, but Peter cut him off with a look.

"I've no desire to discuss it, son. Gee Dub, I'm sorry you had to see that."

"Yes, sir." Gee Dub's response was somber, but the moment Peter turned away the young man gave Shaw a wicked grin that said he had rather enjoyed the spectacle of the ancient warriors breathing fire at one another.

Peter seemed to have quite returned to his even-tempered self when he nodded toward the path to the house. "Oh, look, boys. Yonder comes Martha."

Chapter Eleven

"I was hoping that if I come on a Sunday I could find y'all at home and not off out in the fields. I didn't expect to find you and Mr. Tucker and his boys all together, Mr. McBride, but I'm glad of it. Means I can get back to Muskogee quicker. My wife will appreciate that."

Sheriff Barger took the plateful of apple pie from Alafair's tray. She slowly moved around to offer a piece to Scott, who was sitting next to the sheriff on the red, horsehair-stuffed settee. Shaw, Peter, Gee Dub, and Charlie were arrayed in a semi-circle of armchairs and kitchen chairs in front of the two law officers. Alafair and the other females had been banished to the kitchen, at least for the interim, while the men retold the tale of Buttercup and the bones in the woods. Alafair was taking her time as she served the pie.

"Me and the boys were just talking about what they found on my property, sheriff, so I can't say I'm surprised to see you today. Will you be wanting to talk to my other son, James, before you leave town?" Grandpapa Peter was not James' and Shaw's biological father, but he had long ago forgotten that fact.

"I already been over there this morning, Mr. McBride, and heard what him and his sons had to say. I read the report that Morgan wrote. But it helps me to hear the story over again straight from the mouths of them that lived it. But the main reason I'm here today is to ask you what you know about the history of that piece of land, sir. I've been doing some research, and according to the deed, you bought the property from one Lucretia Hawkins in nineteen and six. Did you know Miz Hawkins beforehand?"

"We were acquainted. But in truth I only knew her because I was friends with her second husband, Roane Hawkins."

"And how'd you know Hawkins?"

"Me and Roane were friends from way back when we were both pony soldiers fighting the Apaches out in the Arizona Territory." Peter's luxurious silvery-white hair, blue eyes, rosy cheeks, and sly Irish charm gave him more than a passing resemblance to a beardless Santa Claus, though this Santa had an iron core under his jolly exterior.

"How'd Hawkins come by that property?" Barger took a bite of pie. The sharp look in his eye as he asked the question told Alafair that he already knew the answer.

Peter's wry smile said that he knew he was being tested. "Miz Hawkins was a Muskogee Creek and half that land was her allotment, Sheriff. The other half was alloted to her first husband, Mr. Goingback. She inherited it when he died."

Barger put his plate on the side table and fished a piece of paper out of his inside jacket pocket. He finished chewing and swallowing his mouthful of pie while he unfolded it and gave it a cursory perusal before spreading it out on the side table between himself and Peter. Scott could see it by leaning across, but Shaw and the boys had to stand before they were able to tell what it was.

"That's a parcel map," Shaw observed.

Barger nodded. "It is. Central Muskogee County. Dated nineteen and ten."

"There's Oktaha, Grandpapa," Charlie said, "and there's your property right there. It says *McBride* right on it!"

Barger tapped the map with his finger. "Right here is where you found the grave, Mr. Tucker. Must be a mile from the farmhouse." He shifted to face Peter. "That's a good-sized parcel, Mr. McBride. You go out there much?"

"No, not often. Once or twice a year, mostly to make sure there are no squatters. I thought of leasing it out but never have come up with a tenant."

"That's lot of property to be sitting idle."

If Barger's tone was accusatory, Peter didn't acknowledge it. "It is. The parcel consists of Miz Hawkins' original one hundred-sixty-acre allotment, as well as her first husband's that she inherited when he died."

"Yes, it says at the county recorder's office that the property originally belonged to a Lucretia Goingback, enrolled member of the Muscogee Creek Nation. I expect she's the same Lucretia Hawkins." He refolded the paper and returned it to his pocket. "How'd your friend Mr. Hawkins come to be married to a Creek woman, Mr. McBride?"

Peter settled back in his chair, resigned to telling a tale that he didn't appear to enjoy. "After Roane and I were discharged from the Army back in '70, we worked together at the Tucker sawmill in Lone Elm, Arkansas. He heard that the Missouri, Kansas, and Texas railroad was thinking to build a spur that'd run right through that wooded country down around Oktaha, so he hatched a scheme to go to the Indian Territory, build a sawmill in that area and get rich."

"When was that, Mr. McBride?"

Peter shrugged. "About '89, '90, around then."

"White folks couldn't buy Indian land back then, I believe," Barger observed,

"No, sir. Roane could sell water to a fish, though. He talked Goingback into going into business with him. They were in the process of clearing the land when a tree fell on the poor Indian chap. The next thing I know, Roane was married to his widow and named guardian of her affairs."

"Could Slim be Mr. Goingback, Grandpapa?" Gee Dub asked.

"No, Gee, Goingback had a proper funeral, I hear."

Barger nodded. "Yes, Goingback is resting peaceably in the Indian cemetery just south of Muskogee. So it wasn't him you found." He turned back to Peter. "Did Mr. and Miz Hawkins seem happy with one another, you think?"

"If you're asking if Roane only married Lucretia to get her land, sheriff, I have to say that I wouldn't put it past him. Roane was a bit of a boyo as long as I knew him. For a while after he married Lucretia I went out to visit with him quite a bit. They seemed to suit each other all right. Me and Roane drifted apart over the years, though, and I hadn't seen him for quite a spell before I bought the property."

"I spent a few weeks out there helping Roane Hawkins clear a space for his sawmill, sheriff," Shaw volunteered. "I remember him as a big, loud, friendly sort of fellow, quick to rile and quick to get over it. I never saw much of her but when she fed us. She was a quiet woman, kind of pretty. She already had a couple of half-grown children with Goingback. A girl name of Jenny, and a boy, maybe seventeen, who worked with us. I don't remember his name, but him and Mr. Hawkins acted like they were close, laughing and joking and all. Lucretia and Roane had two of their own that I know about. The youngest wasn't even born last I saw them. Of course the children had their allotments, too, surrounding their mother's. See, here they are on the map. The two Goingbacks to the east and the Hawkins boys' to the west. I remember Mr. Hawkins joking that when his sawmill got built, between his wife's property and the children's he'd have enough lumber to build a city as big as Chicago."

Barger dabbed his mustache with his napkin, folded the white linen square carefully and placed it on the table in front of him.

He's about to spring something on us, Alafair thought.

"Near as I've been able to find out, not one of those children took up their allotment. It would have been quite an empire if they had. But what I wonder is if this Hawkins was so all-fired anxious to get his hands on all that property in the first place and such a devoted family man, why did he up and run off and leave them without so much as a fare-thee-well?"

Shaw's eyebrows shot up. "I never heard that he did!"

Peter wasn't surprised. He breathed a laugh. "Well, sir, that's Roane for you. As long as he thought he was going to become a timber millionaire he worked that piece like a demon. But when the KATY rail spur didn't happen and there wasn't any way for him to get the timber to market, Roane lost interest pretty quick and took a powder."

"He abandoned his wife and little children?" Alafair was so shocked that she blurted it out. When Barger looked at her she nearly clapped her hand over her mouth, dismayed at having drawn attention to herself.

It was Peter who answered her. "I'm sorry to say that that wasn't the first time Roane had done such a thing, Alafair."

"So you bought the land from Lucretia and not Roane, Papa?" Shaw asked.

"That's right. I hate to tell the tale since the poor woman was so hard done by."

Barger returned to business. "How did it come about that she sold the property to you?"

"Well, sir, just before Roane ran out on her, the oldest son took out on his own. Then Indian Affairs came and took both her half-white boys to boarding school. Not long after that her daughter with Goingback got married. Lucretia had some kin that lived around there but I expect it was lonely for her out there by herself. She came here and asked me if I'd buy it. She needed money to leave and I expect I'm the only person she knew who had some. Besides, with Roane gone she probably didn't much care about the place any more. She was a traditional Creek and didn't think you could own land any more than you can own the air."

Alafair noted with interest that Peter didn't mention anything about a ghost on the property.

"Besides," Peter continued, "I felt bad for her. I knew what Roane was like. But he lived out there so long that I really thought he maybe would stick with her."

"He'd skipped out before, you say?"

"At least twice before that I know of. He left a wife and baby in Boston when he joined the Army. I believe he left someone in Ireland as well, though I don't know if he married her."

Charlie made a little sound, like an embarrassed giggle. Did men really do things like that?

"I assume you walked that property before you bought it."

"I did. I never saw anything suspicious."

Shaw joined the conversation. "Has anybody decided how long the fellow has been out there?"

"We're thinking it's been about ten years, not much less. Could be more."

"So you have a suspicion that he ended up in the ground right around the time that Roane Hawkins ran off? Or are you thinking that Hawkins didn't really run off after all?"

"I can't say, Mr. Tucker. But if I could find Hawkins or Lucretia either one and ask them about it, that would go a long way toward helping us find out who our friend is and how he got there." Barger turned back to Peter. "Where'd she go, this Lucretia?"

Peter picked up his cup, took a sip and set it down before he answered. "Could be she went to live with some of the tribal Creeks. There's a bunch not too far from there, up around Tiger Mountain. That's where her older son went when he abandoned his allotment."

"All right then. And now, Mr. Tucker, boys, why don't y'all tell me again how you came to find the bones."

Alafair had heard this part before. She decided not to press her luck any further and withdrew to the kitchen to update Sally and the girls.

Chapter Twelve

Charlie appeared in the kitchen door. "Grandma, Sheriff Barger asks if y'all would kindly come into the dining room and have a look at some things he brought?"

Sheriff Barger had placed several items in a neat row along the dining table in the narrow, cheerful room that had once been a breezeway between the kitchen and the main part of the house.

There were two black leather boots which had been cleaned, and, Alafair was glad to see, no longer contained the remains of feet. Several dirty and degraded items had been arranged on the table next to a smallish, fringed, leather satchel. Alafair could identify a rose stone, a small bone knife, a tiny tobacco pouch. Most interesting to her was a fairly good-sized piece of cloth material in the shape of a lopsided rectangle, perhaps six inches by eight inches. It was in a bad state after ten years in the ground. There had been a rudimentary attempt to brush away some of the dirt but she could still see protrusions of hair-like tendrils of grass and weed roots. There was no way to tell what the original color of the cloth had been. But there was a distinct repetition of dark shapes on a lighter background. Some sort of pattern. And the remnants of tiny, even lines of stitches across the face of the material.

"That's a piece of a quilt," Martha said just as Alafair thought it.

"Yes, ma'am," the sheriff said. "That's what we reckoned. It was in the bag, wrapped around the other things."

Alafair leaned close and peered at the dark pattern. "What is this?" she asked, thinking aloud rather than expecting an answer. "Looks like…is it birds?"

Barger looked at her with interest. "None of us that examined it back in Muskogee could tell what that pattern is, Miz Tucker. Does it look familiar?"

Alafair impulsively reached for the fragment of cloth but caught herself before she touched it. She cast Barger a questioning glance, her hand hovering in the air, and he nodded. She gingerly picked up the quilt piece and peered closely at it. "Martha, come have a look at this. You have younger eyes than me. Does that look like birds to you?"

Not only Martha responded to Alafair's request, but both her brothers as well. Martha, Gee Dub, and Charlie crowded around for a closer look.

"It doesn't look like much of anything to me, Mama," Charlie offered.

"Just a regular pattern of dark smudges," Gee Dub agreed.

Alafair held it out to Sally, who shook her head. Martha took a step back.

She put the scrap back down on the table. "Sorry, Sheriff. Something about that pattern reminds me of birds. I reckon that's the best I can do."

Barger wasn't displeased. "Well, that's a better guess than anybody else has come up with."

Shaw said nothing. He was standing behind the crowd with his back pressed to the wall next to the door, fingering the bone necklace in his pocket.

Chapter Thirteen

"Ma, unless my eyes were playing tricks on me, I think I've seen the pattern on that piece of quilt before."

Alafair was leaning over a wash tub in the back yard, up to her elbows in soapy water, when Martha made this startling announcement. It was a raw Monday morning, overcast and gray, with a cold, blustery wind chapping Alafair's cheeks and flapping the sheets she had already hung over the clothesline. Martha was dressed for work in a neat Navy-blue skirt. Her square white collar was just peeking out from the top of the belted wool coat she had donned for her upcoming buggy ride into town.

Alafair gaped at her for an instant, then straightened and dried her hands and forearms on a piece of towel she had tucked into the pocket of the apron she was wearing over her heavy cardigan. "You recognized that quilt piece? Are you sure? Why didn't you say something?"

"Well, I had to think about it for a spell first. Besides, what if I'm wrong? I didn't want to say anything in front of Sheriff Barger or Scott before I mentioned it to you." Martha rubbed her red nose with a mittened hand before she continued. "Mama, do you remember that blue and white pinafore you made for me when I was five or six, the one I liked so much and wore all the time until I couldn't fit into it?"

Alafair rolled down her sleeves. "Sure, honey. The one with the..." She swallowed her words and her eyes widened.

Martha nodded. "The one with the birds. Yes, you remember too. Indigo birds on a white background. They had their wings spread like they were flying. You made a pinafore for me and one for Mary, too, if I remember."

"I'll be switched! The way those little dark blobs were arranged on that bit of quilt must have just tickled my memory enough to make me say 'birds' without quite knowing why. Martha, honey, I see what you're getting at, but just because one thing reminds you of the other it don't mean that they really are the same."

"Why did we both think the same thing, then?"

Alafair smiled. "We might both think a stranger looks like Daddy without thinking he really is Daddy."

Martha didn't look quite as sure of herself as she did before. But she persisted. "Whatever happened to those pinafores, Ma?"

"I don't rightly remember. They probably got handed down to the twins. Most of your clothes did. Then Alice most likely wore hers to a nubbin and Phoebe's went to Ruth for a play dress. After that I'm guessing I used them as dust cloths or wove them into a rag rug."

"Or a quilt?"

"I've used many a scrap of you children's worn clothes to make quilts, sugar, but I can't recall us owning a single quilt with indigo birds on it. Can you?"

"Not right off." Martha's forehead crinkled as she mentally inventoried her mother's collection of bedding. "Still. Would you care if I had a look through the chests after I get home this evening?"

"No, honey, you go ahead on whenever you want."

The screen door on the back porch creaked open and Mary's head popped out. "Martha, come on," she called. "It's almost seven o'clock. I've got to get to the schoolhouse."

Martha left and Alafair rolled up her sleeves before resuming her scrubbing. She could hardly keep from muttering to herself as she rubbed. Why had Shaw and his brother taken a notion to hunt birds on that forsaken plot of land out in the middle of nowhere? What malevolent force had led Buttercup to retrieve a piece of leg that had been attached to someone lying quietly buried in the woods for at least a decade? Who was that inconvenient fellow with the hole in his forehead and why was he causing such a bother for folks who never did anything to him?

Chapter Fourteen

Martha kept banker's hours for once and walked home as soon as the bank closed in the afternoon, leaving the buggy at the schoolhouse for her siblings. She barely took time to strip off her coat and scarf and greet her mother before rummaging through the cedar chests and armoires, inspecting every blanket, pillowcase, quilt, sheet, and towel for a patch of blue birds. All the children had returned from school and completed their afternoon chores. Alafair had begun mixing cornbread for supper when Martha finally wandered into the kitchen, her eyes on the floor and an expression of intense concentration on her face.

Alafair couldn't help but grin. "Now you're inspecting the rugs?"

Martha looked up and managed a quirky smile. "All right, I give up, Ma. I reckon those birds are long gone."

Mary turned from stirring the big pot of beans on the stove. "What are y'all talking about? What birds?"

Martha put her hands on her hips. "Mary, do you remember those pinafores we had when we were girls, the ones with the blue birds on them?"

"Sure I do. I hated mine. It was real thick material and I thought it was scratchy."

"Do you remember what happened to them?"

Alafair sighed. "Oh, Martha, let it go."

But Mary nodded. "Yes, mine got all ripped up when I fell off old Pork Chop. It had seen better days by then anyway, so

Mama used what was left of it to make a rag mop. I enjoyed that rag mop more than the dress. I don't know about yours, Martha. I do remember when you made those, Mama. I was with you when you picked out the material at Cousin Hattie's mercantile. That was the first time you ever let me help you choose a pattern and it made a big impression on me. You said that it was 'linsey-woolsey'. I thought that was funny."

"Oh, that's right! You can't hardly get linsey-woolsey any more. It makes good clothes for children because it's tough as canvas."

Mary stirred as she reminisced. "You had some of that material left over, if I remember right. You said you were going to make a baby gown, I think, but never did,"

Alafair slid the cornbread pans into the oven. *Why don't I remember any of this? I guess I've sewn so many little girl dresses in my time that I can't remember one from another. Did I ever make a baby gown with blue birds? Who was a baby when I bought the bird material?*

She began to calculate the years, intrigued by the problem in spite of herself. Martha said she was five or six at the time. Gee Dub was born in the fall just before Martha turned five. Must have been about 1896 or '97.

Alafair paused in the midst of slicing onions. That was the year she'd borne the boy who died after a brief week of life. She had intended to make a baby gown for him but he had been born and died before she got around to it. It was no wonder she didn't remember what happened to that leftover material.

Mary did. "That piece sat up in the top of your armoire for a while, Ma. I think you finally used it to make a quilt."

Chapter Fifteen

Shaw was spending a lot more time grooming Gee Dub's long-legged red mare, Penny, than he ought to, these days. He always left that particular task until the very end of the work day, just before he dismissed the hands and gathered up the boys and headed up to the house for supper. Since Gee Dub had gone off to study agriculture at Oklahoma A&M, Penny was feeling a bit lonely so Shaw tried to make a point of seeing that she was ridden and put through her paces once or twice a week.

Or maybe it was Shaw who was feeling a bit lonely since Gee Dub had left for A&M and ending his day by combing Penny connected him in some way to his absent son.

Shaw could hardly admit it to himself but he hated to see his children grow up and leave. Yet, ever since Martha had drawn her first breath nearly a quarter century before, he had considered his primary purpose on earth to prepare his children to do just that. He and Alafair had done a damn fine job of it, too, without a doubt. He loved being surrounded by his cheerful, contentious, boisterous bunch, the more of them the better.

But first Phoebe had married, and then Alice. Gee Dub had made the decision to go away and study. Mary would be gone in the spring and Martha by next fall. Even Ruth, just sixteen, was making plans to take a music course in Muskogee next year. Every time one of them broke away it left a gaping tear in the fabric of the family. It didn't seem fair to Shaw that he was losing half his children within a three-year span.

Alafair told him that the family was just getting bigger, what with the sons-in-law and the new grandbaby, and many more of both to come. Shaw liked all his daughters' husbands and future husbands and he adored his little granddaughter Zeltha Day. He still had five young ones coming up, and after all Grace was only three years old. How could he possibly complain?

Even so, it just was not the same as when all ten were skipping and running and flying around the farm. He remembered an early summer day several years ago, before Grace was even born, when he and Gee Dub and Charlie came home from town with a hundred pound block of ice in the buckboard. As he pulled up behind the house to unload he found Alafair and all seven of the girls in the back, sun-drying their hair after a mass washing with water from the rain barrel. Alafair and the older girls were sitting in kitchen chairs brushing out their long tresses and the little ones were dashing about with hair flying behind like silken sails. They were so beautiful, all of them there together, laughing and talking, hair of every hue, pale blond and honey, chestnut and auburn, deep brown and sable, shining in the sun. For a moment the sight had rendered Shaw unable to move, and he sat there with the reins looped through his fingers until Gee Dub had poked him.

"Daddy, the ice is going to melt."

Shaw had made a joke and leaped down before the boys could see the tears in his eyes.

Penny shifted and bumped Shaw up against the side of the stall. He came back to the present with a jolt. He had been standing with both brushes still against the horse's flanks and she was impatient for him to get on with it. He obliged, annoyed at his self-indulgent mood.

What was wrong with him lately? First he's seeing ghosts in the woods, then hearing his long-gone father whispering to him, then getting all sentimental over the children. It wasn't manly to be so soft-hearted. Or soft-headed. Maybe it was the change in the weather. Autumn had always made him feel melancholy. Or maybe he should never have disturbed that grave.

"Shaw, you in here?" Alafair's voice was a welcome distraction.
"Over here, darlin'."

He threw a blanket over Penny's back and left the stall to meet
Alafair coming up the long middle aisle that divided the stable.

He blinked at the pale light streaming in through the stable
door. "Well, hush me up! I didn't know it was getting so late. I
was wanting to go over to Ma's. Is supper ready?"

"The girls are putting it on the table now. Charlie and Kurt
are already up to the house. Kurt was going to come get you
but I told him I'd do it. There's something I wanted to mention
to you in private."

He felt a stab of dread. Their private conversations usually
took place after they went to bed, the only time they were alone
in the natural course of the day. If she had something to tell him
that couldn't wait until bedtime it didn't bode well. "What's the
matter?"

"Martha just told me that piece of quilt she saw at Grandma's
yesterday looks to her like it was made out of some material that I
used to make dresses for her and Mary when they were children."

Shaw sagged, relieved and annoyed at once. He shook his
head. "After such a long spell in the ground it didn't look like
much of anything to me."

"Well, I'd agree with you, but when she mentioned it I could
see what she was talking about. The pattern and the shape of the
little figures and even what color I could make out does look a
powerful lot like the material in those pinafores. Mary thought
that I had a hank of that material left over and used it to make
a quilt with."

"I don't understand, Alafair. How could a quilt made of
our little girls' dresses get wrapped around a stranger who was
murdered ten years ago and buried miles away from here? What
did you do with this quilt you made?"

She shrugged. "I don't even remember making a quilt with
bird material."

"Well, then, I expect the girls are misremembering. The
pattern on that scrap probably just reminded y'all of some little

dresses they used to wear a lot. It most likely isn't the same pattern at all. And even if it it is, that don't mean it's off the same bolt you bought."

Alafair crossed her arms over her chest and looked down at her feet as she considered this. "Makes sense," she conceded, looking up.

Shaw opened his mouth to ask what was on the menu for supper, but Alafair wasn't quite finished.

"Do you fear that Barger suspects Grandpapa of knowing something about how that skeleton got in the ground?"

"I don't know what Barger thinks. But I doubt if Papa knows anything about it. I do know that he didn't have a very high opinion of Hawkins. It was probably real easy for him to believe that Hawkins scampered for some evil reason."

"Your Papa bought that property even though he doesn't seem to have wanted it. He certainly hasn't done anything with it in all these years."

"Well, him and Roane were in the Cavalry together and that's a bond for most men. He would help a deserted wife if he could, too. Besides, Papa most likely thought to turn around and sell the farm for a profit. I've known him to do that with other parcels. But maybe it didn't work out this time because the place has a cloud over it."

"I do hope that the sheriff doesn't take it into his head that Grandpapa knows more than he already said. Why didn't he tell Barger about the haint? Maybe the place has been haunted since long before Hawkins ever came along. Maybe that's why he ran away."

When Alafair brought up the ghost, Shaw's face flushed red. "Barger's never going to find out anything for sure about that body. Neither are we, Alafair. It's been too long. I declare, honey, I wish the sheriff would just drop the whole thing. Whatever happened to that fellow, it was long ago and whoever done it is long gone. What good does it do the living to stir up the past?"

Alafair studied his face. Shaw was not telling her everything about that hunting trip, she was certain of that. Something had happened to him that had not happened to the others. For a moment she pondered whether or not to press him on the matter. Had it been one of the children who was so obviously troubled she wouldn't have hesitated. But Shaw was a different story altogether, and he had had about enough of the topic. She decided that patience was the best tactic for the moment. She took his arm. "I'm sure you're right, hon. I'm sorry I mentioned it. Come on in, now. Supper's on the table."

Chapter Sixteen

Normally Shaw was asleep almost before his head hit the pillow. Even though he was still and quiet, his back turned toward her, Alafair knew he was awake. The roil of his thoughts was palpable. She turned onto her side and pressed up against his back. She didn't need to ask what was on his mind so didn't bother to ease into the topic.

"Why didn't you tell him?"

She put an arm over Shaw's side and felt him take a breath. "Tell who what?"

The night was dead silent. The windows were closed against the chill, and besides, it was too late in the year for the riotous frog and insect noise of a summer night. Even the children's sighs and breaths were muffled by piles of bedclothes. Yet Alafair lifted up on her elbow and put her mouth next to his ear to whisper something too secret to be said aloud even in such quiet.

"Why didn't you tell your Papa about the thing you saw?"

Shaw felt a jolt like someone had punched him in the chest. He rolled onto his back and found himself nose to nose with her. "How did you know?" He spoke so loudly that Alafair shushed him.

Her breath warmed his face as she murmured her answer. "You said you wished you hadn't of disturbed that grave. Add that up with the fact that your mama told us the Goingback place is haunted. And considering that you've been acting like you've seen a ghost, I put one and two together and come up with three."

He continued in a strained whisper. "Have you told anybody else? Does Mama know?"

"No, I didn't have time to mention it to her before Scott and Barger rode up and then I forgot about it. That is until later this evening. After supper I got to studying how you've been so shook up since you got home from that hunting trip. Whatever is on your mind, you don't want to talk about it."

For days, Shaw had been carrying the memory of the strange visitation like a weight, fearful that if someone found out what he saw they'd doubt his sanity. He'd been doubting his own sanity. But now that Alafair knew, he felt a rush of relief wash over him. He made a move to sit up. "We'd better go ask Ma and Papa to tell us everything they know about this ghost."

Alafair put her hand on his shoulder. "I expect we'd best wait until tomorrow, honey. It's a bit late." She sounded amused.

Shaw flopped back down. He could have felt embarrassed at his unreasonable eagerness to get to the bottom of this if he had not been so relieved. Perhaps he wasn't crazy after all.

Alafair nestled down under the covers. "Now, tell me what you saw." She laid her head on his shoulder and listened as he recounted his tale of the disembodied legs and the shadow in the trees.

Chapter Seventeen

Sally and Peter weren't alarmed when they heard the front door open in the middle of the morning, even though they weren't expecting visitors. They had so many relations that they had long ago lost count, and none ever bothered to knock when they came to Grandma and Grandpapa's.

The couple was in the kitchen at the back of the house. Peter was just pulling on his coat. Sally was canning pumpkin. She had already put up quarts of plain pumpkin purée over the previous weeks. The batch she was working on now was seasoned for pies, and the whole house was fragrant with the smell of cinnamon and clove, nutmeg and allspice. Thanksgiving was right around the corner, after all.

Sally gave the big pot of simmering pumpkin a final stir with her long-handled wooden spoon before she wiped her hands on her apron and headed out to see who had come calling.

"Ma?"

Sally smiled at Peter when she recognized Shaw's voice. "In the kitchen, son," she called. "Come on back."

Peter hung his coat back on the peg beside the door and sat down, prepared to visit. Sally returned to the stove and slid the coffee pot back over the fire before moving a covered ceramic pie plate from the pie keep to the middle of the long kitchen table. She was pulling saucers out of the hutch when Alafair appeared in the door with Shaw right behind her.

Peter grinned. "Well, I declare! What are you children doing out and about his time of day? Sit yourselves down and have a piece of pie."

Shaw's gaze darted around the kitchen, hunting for the source of the enticing odor. "Pumpkin?"

"Not yet." Sally removed the cover on the pie dish to reveal three-quarters of a two-crust apple pie. She cut and plated three enormous slabs and handed them around the table. "There's cream in the pitcher on the windowsill yonder." She went to the stove and poured coffee into mugs and distributed them before seating herself across the table from her son and his wife.

"Gee Dub get off to Stillwater all right?" she asked.

"He did." Alafair spooned the unsweetened heavy cream from the pitcher over her pie. Not that it wasn't rich enough. The crust was so short, crisp, and flakey from the lard that Sally had made it with that it barely held together. But this was what Alafair called a "Peter pie." Peter McBride had a terrible sweet tooth and any dessert that Sally made to please him was so sweet that it set a normal person's teeth on edge. In fact there was so much sugar in this pie that the apples had dissolved. *Applesauce* pie, was more like it. And to top it off Sally had sprinkled granulated sugar over the top crust. Alafair was amused to note that the super-sweetness didn't seem to bother Shaw any more than it did Peter.

Shaw shoveled in another mouthful before looking up at his mother. She was sitting across from him with her mug in her two hands, her apron stained with pumpkin puree and smelling of nutmeg, watching him, patient as always.

He swallowed his bite and looked at Peter. "I'm surprised to find you home this time of day, Papa."

"I'm betwixt the apple barn and the stable at the moment, son. Some fellow from Shawnee is coming in this afternoon to talk to me about having Red Allen stand to stud for a walker filly he owns. I told him to meet me here at the house. I don't expect he'll be here for a couple of hours, but you're welcome to come with us if you want."

Shaw suddenly lost his appetite and pushed the plate away. "Thanks, but we'll not be here that long. Me and Alafair got to talking last night and she reminded me that you had said the old Goingback place is supposed to be haunted. Papa, you told us that you didn't know who the haint is supposed to have been when he lived. But we were wondering if the folks that live around there have a story about somebody dying in those woods. Was there a battle there, or a fight, or a killing back in the past? If there was, it could give us a hint as to who we dug up last week."

Peter shook his head. "Not that I ever heard about, son. The only tales I heard from the good citizens of Oktaha told of lights in the forest, lights in that old house. Before she left, Miz Hawkins told me that strange things were happening and she was afraid. I figured it was wastrels who had heard of a woman alone out there and took advantage to do some thieving."

Sally stood up and returned to the stove in order to stir her bubbling purée. "Don't you remember the story Jack Cecil told us, Peter?"

"Oh, I had forgotten that, Sally, dear."

Sally glanced back over her shoulder at Shaw and Alafair. "Jack took his boy Joe out there camping, oh, four, five years ago. Said bits of their food kept disappearing. A knife went missing out of a knapsack. They woke up one morning and everything in the camp had been rearranged. Not ruined or broke, mind you. Just moved around and set back down real neat. Joe told his daddy that he had heard somebody whispering in the night but when Joe stuck his head out the tent to see who it was, no one was there."

Shaw's heartbeat picked up. He determined to have a talk with his sister Josie's husband Jack Cecil at his earliest opportunity. He shook himself. "Well, animals could have got to their food. And I saw for myself how deep and wet the woods are. I'd say swamp gas and moonlit fog for the lights. The other thing sounds more like a vagabond who likes to play tricks than a ghost."

"Maybe," Sally admitted. "Jack thought so at first, 'til he passed through Oktaha on the way home. Him and the boy stopped off at the market there, and when they related their tale to the proprietor, he told them that there had been something in the woods out that way for years."

Alafair took a sip of her coffee. After the pie the strong, bitter brew was delicious. "How many years? Before Hawkins got there or after?"

"I don't know, sugar."

Whether it was before or after the disappearance of Roane Hawkins, Shaw was relieved to hear them confirm that the disturbance had been there for years. He was not the one who set it loose by disturbing its grave.

Alafair put her hand on Shaw's arm. "Shaw, if the grocer told Jack about the ghost I'm sure the sheriff heard the same tale when he went to asking around in Oktaha after y'all discovered the body. If anybody in Oktaha had an idea of who folks think could be haunting those woods, Sheriff Barger probably knows about it by now."

"You've seen it, Papa?" Shaw asked.

Peter shrugged and poked at his pie with his fork. "Maybe. Just once have I stayed all the night there. That was not long after Miz Hawkins moved away. The house was still standing, then, and I rolled out my sleeping bag on the floor. It was a bitter cold night, I remember. I heard something outside and went to investigate. There was no one around the cabin but I thought I saw a figure slipping into the woods and called out. I still had it in my mind that vandals were about, you see. But it was dark as Hades. Perhaps I saw something and perhaps I didn't. " He smiled. "Your mother assures me I was hearing things, but I could have sworn I heard a voice say my name."

That last sentence caused the hair on Shaw's arms to rise. "You ever been out to that place, Ma?"

"Once, not long after Peter bought it." Sally didn't turn from her stirring. "Miz Hawkins had already moved away. It was daytime, so I never saw any roving spirits. I thought it was a nice house when I saw it."

"It was on its last legs when we were out there. I was afraid to let the boys explore it for fear it'd fall in on their heads. When was it that Miz Hawkins asked you to buy her place, Papa?"

"I don't remember exactly, but the Sheriff said it was in '06. It's on the deed transfer. It was about this time of year. Lucretia came riding up here to the house in a broken-down old buckboard and told me that Roane had skipped and she was looking to sell. I followed her back out there the next morning and stayed a couple of days looking over the property before I agreed to buy it off her."

"I remember he told me it was a nice, big, wooded parcel, with a house and water," Sally said. "He was back out there once or twice to complete the sale. I never thought much about it again." She cast a casual glance at Shaw before replacing the lid on the simmering puree. "I suppose you saw the haint, son." It wasn't a question.

Peter nearly choked on his coffee. "Did you now, Shaw!"

Shaw knew it shouldn't have, but his mother's statement took him aback. He exchanged a look with Alafair, who didn't seem at all surprised. "Well, I saw *something*, Papa, and I'd appreciate to know what it was." The situation suddenly struck him as ironic and he laughed. "So much for trying to keep a secret around you two gals."

Sally shrugged. "You're awful curious about that ghost. I've never known you to show much interest in the other world before now."

"I'd like to go back to Oktaha and ask around about the haint. I wish I could do it right now, but I plan to butcher tomorrow. I've got John Lee coming over to help out, and the hogs are already fasting. I can't put it off."

"You'd better not," Alafair admonished. "I've been cooking for days to get ready. Ruth and Charlie are staying home from school tomorrow, and Phoebe and Alice both will be over during the next week to help me put up sausages and render lard. Nobody will be gallivanting off to Oktaha for a good while."

Chapter Eighteen

After the first frost Shaw had placed a bucket of water just outside the back door. When an almost imperceptible skin of ice formed on the water for three or four mornings in a row, he decided that the weather had finally turned cool enough to butcher. He had already decided which pigs were going to meet their fate. The two porkers had been isolated in their own pens for some weeks.

Shaw always approached butchering time with mixed emotions. He loved late fall and the end of the heat and hard work of summer and harvest. He loved tending to all his animals, raising happy and healthy beasts. He felt no guilt when time came for them to die, but he had to admit he did feel regret. Still, he concentrated on the task at hand and made sure they met their ends in as humane a fashion as possible and as they had lived, without fear.

Early in the morning after breakfast, just as dawn made its first streak on the horizon, Shaw loaded his .22 pistol and herded Charlie out the door. He missed Gee Dub at times like this, when there was a big and unpleasant job to do. Gee Dub was a calm and efficient presence, working quickly and quietly when he wasn't cracking jokes. Charlie had always been something of a gnat, buzzing around, easily distracted and often more an annoyance than a help. Shaw had to admit, though, that Charlie had buckled down considerably in the last year or so since his older brother had gone off to Stillwater. He had turned fourteen.

He had always been a scrawny little bundle of motion, but lately he had shot up and filled out so much that sometimes Shaw caught himself wondering who was the strange youth living in his house and eating up so much of his food.

As they made their way toward the confinement pens, Shaw found himself wishing that he had brought a cane to herd the dawdling Charlie. Charlie's way of dealing with the onerous job before them was to avoid it as long as possible.

Shaw, on the other hand, had a different philosophy. "Come on, son. Let's get this over with."

He rounded the barn and caught sight of John Lee Day, his daughter Phoebe's husband, sitting on a sanded-off stump with Kurt, waiting for them. John Lee was a small, neat-figured young man with a wealth of coarse, unruly dark hair, and solemn, over-sized black eyes. All four men were dressed in their raggediest clothing: overalls with broken straps, faded woolen shirts with multiple mendings and missing buttons, frayed trousers patched at seats and knees, old boots with holes in the toes and run-down heels or no heels at all. This was going to be a hard, messy job, and whatever they had on would not be fit to wear ever again.

The "slaughter house" was simply a ramada, a small, roofed shelter next to a very large American elm fitted with a block and tackle over one limb, located a few yards behind the barn and toward the woods. The shelter covered no more than a packed earth floor, a long, sturdy table, and a very large iron cauldron. The smoke house was only a few steps away.

It was a frigid morning and their breath fogged the air. They immediately hung their coats on hooks in the shelter, far removed from the action. Adrenalin and sheer brute toil would keep them plenty warm.

Each hog was quickly dispatched with a bullet in the brain, then hauled up with a block and tackle to hang head down from a sturdy limb of the elm tree, where the real work of preparing the carcass began.

The entire process of putting up the meat for two two-hundred pound hogs was going to take much of the upcoming week, so Alafair had been baking and preparing for easy-to-cook meals for several days. Charlie and Ruth had been kept home from school to help, but Alafair had sent Grace to Phoebe's house and the younger girls were in school. Martha was at work and Mary should have been as well. Shaw expected that she had volunteered to help out because she was interested in spending time with Kurt rather than from any desire to clean hog intestines. Other grown children and children-in-law would appear at intervals throughout the week to assist in the work.

By noon the group was so inured to what they were doing and so depleted by the physical toll the work took on them that they ate Alafair's vegetable soup and cornbread like a squad of soldiers after a battle.

The younger girls came home from school, changed clothes, and joined the family for the rest of the afternoon as they sat around tubs of hot water, washing intestines and stomachs for sausages and head cheese, turning them inside out, scraping out the fat for rendering. When the light began to fade, Shaw rigged a portable shelter around the hog carcasses and left them cooling overnight in the chill November air, the innards soaking in salt water, before the men trooped inside to clean up and go to bed. Alafair made "bear soup" by heating milk and pouring it over bowls of left-over cornbread for supper, but everyone was too exhausted to eat much.

Chapter Nineteen

The sun hadn't even tickled the horizon when Shaw stumbled outside first thing the next morning with a lantern in hand, half awake, to check on the cooling hog carcasses.

He left Alafair in the kitchen heating up the stove for breakfast and went out the back door with Charlie Dog trailing behind. Crook appeared, all charm and good humor, wagging his crooked tail in greeting. The three of them proceeded to the processing shed in a companionable knot. Buttercup was being held incommunicado. Last night Shaw had noticed Crook sniffing around her, distracted and stupid with love. Shaw recognized the signs and immediately locked her in the tool shed. He wasn't prepared to deal with a litter of puppies at the moment so Buttercup would be spending a week or so in her own private convent.

The butchered hogs were still hanging suspended from the ceiling beams, protected from night critters by a jury-rigged shelter of Shaw's own invention. It was made of chicken wire and a grid of sturdy poles driven into pre-drilled holes in the hard dirt floor. It wouldn't stop a bear, he expected, but few had been around in past years. It was good enough to make a raccoon or fox stop and scratch his head, though. And the best part was that he didn't have to lug the hogs around before they were cut up into manageable pieces.

As they approached the shed Crook put his nose to the ground and began to snuffle around in circles. This was normal hunting dog behavior and Shaw barely noticed. But when Charlie Dog fell back and emitted a low growl, Shaw paused and lifted his lantern. The pink carcasses caught the light through the wooden cage. Everything looked the same as it had last night. The only movement he could see was the pale fog of his own breath in the lamplight. He looked down at the yellow shepherd now sitting at his feet, ears pricked. The dog seemed alert but not alarmed.

"What is it, boy?" Shaw's voice was barely above a murmur.

Charlie Dog looked up at him, always happy to be acknowledged. His fluffy tail swept the dirt a couple of times. Shaw snorted. Whatever had gotten his back up, the dog had forgotten about it already. Crook was nowhere to be seen. Perhaps an animal had checked the situation during the night and Crook was on its trail. Either that or he had slipped off to see if he could find a way to sneak into Buttercup's cell for a tryst.

Shaw lifted the peeled tree limb used to bar the makeshift door of the portable cage and went inside. He held the lantern high and circled the dead swine, patting them up and down to make sure they were well cooled. When he circled around the back of the second hog he froze, his hand still extended, hardly believing what he was looking at. He moved in so close that his nose was almost touching the meat and moved the light up next to his face. A long rectangle of fatback and loin had been cut out of the carcass.

He stepped back and drew a sharp breath.

What is this?

He stood holding up the lantern, staring at the raw gape. It was jagged and uneven, but not as though an animal had ripped it out with its teeth. More like an inexpert butcher had sawed at the meat. Whoever had helped himself to a slab of pork had replaced the bar on the door and had made sure to leave everything in the shed as he found it. Shaw didn't feel particularly frightened. If the thief had been intent on real harm there was no evidence of it here. He wasn't happy that an intruder had been wandering around on the property and he hadn't known a thing about it. He suddenly thought of the moccasin-clad feet that had made free with their campsite and was struck by an unreasonable pang of annoyance at Crook. Why hadn't that durn beast barked?

Now he was alarmed. Had someone followed him home? He held the lantern down close to the ground, searching for footprints, but could see nothing. He stepped out of the cage, closed it back up, and sat down on a stool to think about this development. Charlie Dog sidled up to him and Shaw draped his arm over the dog's back.

"I don't want to scare Alafair and the children," he said. It was helpful to ponder aloud and Charlie Dog was a good listener, even if he was short on advice. "I expect our visitor helped himself and left, but I'd just as soon be careful. I'll tell Kurt and John Lee what happened and see that they keep their eyes peeled. Better tell Alafair, too, and have her keep the young'uns close to the house for a few days. I'll ride into town when I can and let Scott know we've got a thief about in case he wants to warn the other farms around here." He gave the dog a squeeze. "Crook and Buttercup are love-struck and worthless right now, so I'm expecting you to look out for everybody until we're sure we're safe."

He stood up. "Alafair will be expecting us for breakfast. Let's take a look around first and make sure that back bacon is the only thing the sneak took last night."

Chapter Twenty

When Shaw finally got back to the house, a couple of fingers of sunlight were poking up over the horizon. His inspection of the barn and outbuildings around the house had turned up no further evidence of an intruder and he was feeling more reassured that it was a passing vagrant who had been carving on the swine carcass.

Breakfast was in full swing. Kurt had joined the family and John Lee was at the table as well, along with his wife, Shaw's fourth daughter, Phoebe, and their baby Zeltha. Charlie and Ruth were both staying home from school again today to help finish the butchering. But Mary was dressed for teaching duty and was already herding the younger girls toward the door for the trip into town. Martha was at the stove frying thick slabs of homemade bread in bacon grease. Judging by her attire she was taking the day off from work to help her mother render lard and make sausages, blood puddings, and head cheese. Alafair was sitting in a kitchen chair with a squirmy Grace clamped between her knees as she brushed the girl's black pageboy.

Every eye turned Shaw's way as he entered. The warm kitchen was cheery with lamplight and fragrant with the smell of fresh bread, oniony gravy, and bacon. His mood lifted at the chorus of greetings from his family and he smiled.

Zeltha appeared from under the kitchen table with a cry of "Wa!" and crawled toward him. He lifted her into his arms and sat down in his place at the head of the table. His granddaughter was just over a year old and not yet walking or talking. It seemed to Shaw that she was small for her age and immature, especially compared to his hearty crew, every one of whom had been on his or her feet by fourteen months. But she was an exceptionally sweet and pretty child with thick black hair like John Lee's, and large, kind, hazel eyes like her mother Phoebe's. Or like her Grandpa Shaw's. Besides, she zipped around perfectly well on hands and knees and Shaw knew for a fact that "Wa" meant "Dearest Grandfather."

Martha set a plateful of bacon before him, along with fried bread topped with fried eggs and potatoes on the side. Phoebe removed Zeltha from his lap so he could eat in comfort and Charlie passed him the syrup to pour over everything on his plate.

The children were on their way to school and Phoebe had left for home with the toddlers in tow by the time Kurt, Charlie, and John Lee all finished eating at once and stood up from the table. They were just moving toward the back door when Shaw spoke.

"Hang on for a minute, boys."

The three young men paused and eyed him. Shaw sopped the last of his gravy with a piece of bread and swallowed it down before continuing. Out of the corner of his eye he could see that Alafair and Martha had stopped scraping dishes and were watching him as well.

He pushed his plate away and sat back in his chair. "Seems we had us a sneak thief break in during the night and carve himself off a slab of pork."

The boys exchanged a glance, but only Kurt exclaimed. "I heard nothing!" Kurt slept in the tool shed, one end of which had been partitioned off to create spartan living quarters. His room was situated a scant ten yards from the ramada where the hog carcasses hung.

"I'm not surprised," Shaw said. "The fellow must be pretty good at slinking about unseen and unheard. He got inside the cage, hacked himself out a piece of meat, and closed everything up like he found it. It was still dark when I went out there this morning, but I couldn't find any footprints."

"Sounds like a tramp," Alafair offered, "who makes his way by helping himself to whatever he can find on farms he passes by."

"That's what I figure," Shaw agreed. He felt an odd relief that she would offer this perfectly logical explanation.

"Did he take very much?" John Lee asked.

Shaw shook his head. "No, just enough for a couple of meals, I reckon. But what he did take was choice. Charlie, you go start the fire under the cauldron. Kurt, head on out to the shed and fetch the saws and knives." He looked at his son-in-law, who stood gazing at him out of solemn black eyes awaiting his assignment. "John Lee, it's finally about to get light enough to see. Have a look around and see if you can find any other signs of mischief. Maybe a stray print or anything else that would give us a clue about where the vagabond went."

As the boys hurried off to their tasks, Shaw turned to Martha and Ruth, both still at the table. "Darlin's, when you slop the hogs and feed the chickens, take some breakfast to Buttercup, please."

The girls moved to obey, but Martha shot her mother a surreptitious glance before she put on her coat and left with the scrap bucket in one hand and an empty tin pan in the other.

As soon as they were alone Alafair folded her arms over her chest. "Are you thinking of your haint?"

Her comment wasn't meant to be funny but Shaw couldn't help but laugh. Alafair never did beat about the bush. "That was my first thought," he admitted. "But I'm more inclined to believe your tramp story."

"And that's sure enough who stole the pork." She was firm about it. "There's no other way to look at it. I never knew a ghost to eat fatback."

He walked across the room and gave her a hug and kiss. She not only could read his mind, she knew just how to set it at ease.

He retrieved his hat from the rack by the door and plopped it on his head. "I'll be outside carving hams for a spell, sugar, and will be too busy to worry about thieves or departed spirits, either one."

Chapter Twenty-one

Shaw and the boys spent the day carving the cooled carcasses into hams and loins, bacon, ribs, roasts, and shoulders. By mid-afternoon the meat had been shelved or hung on hooks in the smokehouse. Shaw was kindling the hickory wood fire in the center of the little room when John Lee found him. Shaw brushed the ash off his hands and directed John Lee outside away from the rapidly spreading smoke, where they could talk. He barred the smokehouse door and secured it with an iron padlock, then put the key in his pocket before he turned to see John Lee with his chilly hands muffed in the bib of his overalls, patiently waiting for him to finish.

Shaw spoke first. "Did you find any trace of our thief?"

"I didn't, Pa. Nary a footprint. There's a place in the yard where there's no grass, though, where it looks to me like the ground has been brushed. Our tramp likely rubbed out his prints. Maybe tied leafy twigs to his heels like I've seen some Indians do. He knows how to cover his tracks, I reckon. I didn't find any broken branches in the woods, neither. But without a trail to follow I don't know where he went into the trees, so just 'cause I couldn't find any that don't mean they ain't there."

"You didn't find a camp? If he took pork loin for his breakfast he had a campfire. He sure didn't eat that meat raw."

"I didn't see one. I didn't smell one, neither."

Shaw thought about this. John Lee was thorough and observant, and if he couldn't find a sign of the intruder, then there probably wasn't a sign to find. He dismissed the young man to help Kurt finish packing some of the bacon in a barrel of salt before going by himself to check the root cellar close behind the house.

He lifted the plank barring the door and walked down the half-dozen steps into the dark, earthy-fragrant interior. The cave-like room carved out of the dirt was lined with shelves and piled high with sacks of beans and potatoes, jars of vegetables, canned fruits, jams, bags of nuts, barrels of apples. Had the contents been disturbed? None of the sacks appeared to have been opened. How could he tell if a potato was missing, a jar of blackberry jam or a handful of beans? Would it do him any good to inspect the corn crib? Had an ear of dried corn disappeared? He retrieved an extra padlock from the tool shed and secured the cellar door.

Whoever the intruder was, he wasn't a vandal. He had not been bent on destruction but had only helped himself to a meal. Shaw doubted the vagabond posed a danger, although he couldn't know the man's mind. It was best to be careful. He decided to wear his gun belt for a spell, just as a precaution, while he was outside working. He walked back toward the house through Alafair's large truck garden, his eyes sweeping the rows for any sign of disturbance. The garden was mostly gone. Alafair had already brought in the pumpkins and squash, the last of the season's harvest. Only the potato vines were left, and they were dying back quickly since the cold snap.

He stopped on the back porch long enough to break the skin of ice on the wash bucket and wash his face and hands with yellow-grey, homemade lye soap. Dozens of glass jars and masonry crocks of newly-rendered lard, white as snow, were stacked in pyramids on one of the long wooden benches that ran along the sides of the screened porch. He retrieved a flour-sack towel from the twine clothesline Alafair had strung across the porch for rainy days or emergency child-spill laundry and vigorously dried himself. By the time he opened the back door into the kitchen his face was glowing a healthy red.

Warmth enveloped him like a blanket. The kitchen had become a meat processing plant, hot, raw, and spicy smelling, full of the laughter and chatter of females. Alafair and her girls were making sausages, each woman busy at her task. Sophronia was having a high time forcing chunks of raw pork through the iron meat grinder that was attached with a clamp to the end of the kitchen table. Alafair stood next to her at the center of the action, pounding dried sage and thyme in a mortar and supervising at the same time. At her side, daughter Alice leaned over a tub of ground pork and minced fat, mixing in the spices with her bare hands. At the other end of the table Blanche was feeding the finished mixture through a sausage stuffer. As she pressed the plunger into the canister the meat was forced out into a length of hog intestines that had been washed so often and scraped so thoroughly that it was transparent. Ruth sat in a chair and carefully pulled and guided the filling tubes of sausage. Every five or six inches she gave the meat-filled tube a twist, creating a long string of links which she wound around into a circular pile on the table. Martha was at the stove frying sausage patties in a cast-iron skillet. When she had a goodly number of fried patties on her platter, she stacked them into ceramic pint jars and poured hot fat over all. After the jars of sausages were sealed they would be turned upside down and stored standing on their lids in the root cellar.

Alice, up to her elbows in ground pork, looked up at Shaw and smiled. "Hi, Daddy!"

Shaw grabbed a handful of cracklins from a big bowl on top of the pie safe and popped one into his mouth. "Hi, honey. I didn't see when you came in. Is Walter here?"

"No, the barber shop is open today and he didn't figure he ought to leave. But Mama told me that if I wanted a share of sausages or some head cheese this year I durn well better come help her put them up." She winked a pale blue eye at him when her mother snorted.

Alice, the third of the Tucker brood and wife of barber Walter Kelley, was the closest thing the town of Boynton had to a socialite. She was tall and exceedingly pretty, and usually dressed to the nines. But today she was clad as scruffily as the rest of the family, her blond hair wrapped up in a frayed and faded scarf.

Alafair wiped her hands on her apron. "You want something to eat?"

Shaw popped another cracklin into his mouth and shook his head. "Don't let me bother you gals. I just came in to fetch something from the bedroom. I'll be out of your hair directly."

He half expected that Alafair would ask him what he wanted. But to his relief, she was busy enough that she left him to his own task. He bestowed several forehead kisses as he made his way into the bedroom to retrieve his gun belt from a hook on the wall and his .44 revolver from a strongbox at the top of the armoire. He only took the time to scoop out a single handful of cartridges from the box in a dresser drawer and put them into his coat pocket before making his escape out the front door.

Chapter Twenty-two

Shaw and Peter stood together on the covered front porch of the McBride house. Alafair and Sally were already half-way across the yard, heads together, deep in conversation and walking toward the Tuckers' buggy parked at the front gate. Shaw and Alafair had made a quick trip to the parents' house to deliver a brown paper- and burlap-wrapped package of fresh head cheese, along with a ham joint and a long string of sausage that Peter would smoke in an applewood fire. It was a bright, clear afternoon, but cold. Shaw put his hands into the pockets of his sheepskin coat. He could feel the knobby protrusions of the snake-bone necklace under his left hand and the curve of his revolver handle under his right. Alafair's eyes had zeroed in on the gun belt about five minutes after Shaw had put it on, but she had said nothing.

"You think Scott'll get your pork thief, Shaw?" Peter asked.

"No. I expect he's long gone. Every few years there's a rash of vagabond thievery on several farms and seldom does the culprit get caught. By the way, whatever happened with that fellow from Shawnee that came by here the other day to contract a stud fee? Did y'all come to an arrangement?"

Shaw was surprised when Peter scowled. The older man was usually elated when he was able to put Red Allen to a likely mare. "I did not. Turns out he was a faker. That rascal Doolan had paid the scallawag ten dollars to pretend he was the owner of the red walker mare Doolan wants to breed."

"You don't say! Well, that's pretty clever if you ask me."

Peter was not amused. "Not clever enough. I got my suspicions when he slipped and said his farm was in Okmulgee and not Shawnee like he'd told me before. So I asked for the filly's papers, and he turned shifty. That's when I got it out of him."

Shaw's mustache twitched. He could imagine how Peter "got it out of him." Some combination of threats to sue and a couple of fancy moves with that knob-headed stick he liked to carry. "So you sent him packing?"

"I did." Peter was peering into the distance, thinking his own thoughts.

"Papa, I know you don't like to talk about it, but I'm wondering what happened between you and Doolan. As long as I've known the both of you—and that's a mighty long time—y'all were the best of friends. Until a few years ago. What could he have done to turn you against him so?"

Peter slid him a brief glance but was silent for so long that Shaw thought he wasn't going to answer. But Peter finally spoke.

"He was my friend, Shaw. As good a friend as ever was. But he's lost my good opinion and he'll never have it back, even if he sprouts the wings of an angel and flies away to heaven. I'll have no truck with a man who's cruel to a beast."

Shaw looked doubtful. "I'm surprised to hear that. I'd have never pegged Mr. Doolan as the kind of man to mistreat an animal."

Peter blew a small breath that was half-way between a snort of exasperation and a sigh. "I'd have never thought it of him, either. Not Doolan, of all men. Yet I caught him red-handed at the County Fair back five years ago. It was the middle of the night and I went to check on Red Allen in the horse barn. I found Doolan with that walker gelding he used to have. Osage Dancer. Remember him?"

"I do. He was a roan with two white stockings. That horse had a fine high gait and won many a pacing competition."

"There was a sad reason for that high gait. Doolan was putting mustard oil on Dancer's feet the night before the Walker competition."

Shaw was so taken aback that he struggled to find an appropriate response. "He 'sored' that handsome critter?"

If a man owned a naturally talented Tennessee walker and worked with it long and hard, he could turn the horse's in-born high stepping gait into a dramatic prance called a "big lick." Unfortunately some less scrupulous owners weren't willing to go to the trouble to train the horse in order to enhance its natural pace. Instead, they would use a variety of cruel methods to make an animal's feet so sore that it could barely tolerate the pain. Every step hurt, so as it strode the horse would lift its front hooves off the ground as fast and high as it could.

"He ruined Osage Dancer's feet," Peter said. "The horse had to be put down and Doolan was barred from competition for five years. The five years are almost over. I expect that's why he's come around again. He's looking to breed another champion, and I've got the best stud in the state. It was me who turned him in, so Doolan thinks I owe him." Now that the tale, so long dammed, had been broached, it flooded out. "If it was up to me he'd be barred from ever owning another horse for the rest of his life. I thought he loved the beasts as dearly as do I. Until that moment in the barn I thought him a gentle man, the one man I would turn to for a kindness. He denied it without a blush, Shaw, but I saw him do it plain as day. It was more important to him to win the ribbons and the cups. Champions warrant higher prices, don't you know."

The distress in his stepfather's voice told Shaw how hurt and betrayed Peter was. How would you feel to know that you had so badly misjudged a man's character for forty years? Naive? Foolish?

Peter continued. "Ever since that day I'll not sell an animal to anyone who won't sign a paper swearing he's never sored a horse and never will. And if I find out otherwise, I'll take the beast back."

"Come on, Shaw!" Alafair had been standing with Sally next to the buggy at the gate for several minutes, now, and was eager to be on her way. "Lots to do yet before the day is over."

Shaw lifted an arm by way of acknowledgment but didn't move. His sigh fogged in the chilly air. Sometimes he despaired of human nature. "I'm sorry I asked, Papa."

"It's a misery to lose a friend in such a way, son."

Chapter Twenty-three

After Shaw and Alafair got home they joined the family in cleaning the tools and tubs and sluicing down the slaughter area. Then everyone dispersed to do his or her regular daily chores. John Lee went home to tend to his own farm and family while Shaw spent the remainder of the day with the horses and mules in the paddocks, stables, and fields, parceling out chores to Charlie and Kurt.

It felt good to be clean. Shaw had scrubbed himself from tip to toe after everything was done and then built a fire in the yard and boiled the ragged, bloody clothes of everyone who had been involved.

The light was nearly gone when he finally took the time to fetch his butchering knives for sharpening on the grindstone in the barn. He was bone weary, but to neglect one's tools would be the height of irresponsibility. He trudged across the yard with his box of knives in his hand and his revolver on his hip, determined put the half-hour before supper to good use. In the crisp evening air he could smell the inviting aroma of stew burbling away on the kitchen stove.

The temperature was sinking rapidly with the sun by the time he lit a kerosene lantern and hung it on a post in one corner of the large, dim space of the barn. He opened a drawer in his worktable and retrieved an Eveready flashlight, a birthday gift from Gee Dub. Shaw wasn't overly impressed with the new-fangled device, since a lantern cast a much brighter light and lasted infinitely longer than the battery-powered flashlight. But he did find the directed light to be useful for inspecting close work in a dark environment. He put the Eveready on the table next to the dull knives and sat down at the grindstone with a cleaver in his hand. Charlie Dog had followed him into the barn, which was unusual. The yellow shepherd was getting old and didn't take cold weather as cheerfully as he did when he was a pup. Besides, when Alafair and the girls were in the midst of making supper, Charlie Dog never missed an opportunity to gobble a scrap of food that may have fallen on the floor, accidentally or not.

Shaw was amused and maybe a bit gratified that the dog wanted his company. "What's on your mind, old fella? You don't mean to say that none of the children are in the mood to sneak a treat for you?"

Charlie Dog panted at him by way of a comment before lying down so close to Shaw's right leg that he could feel the dog's heat through his trouser leg. It felt good. Man and dog kept a companionable silence as Shaw honed his instruments amidst showers of sparks and the grating whine of the spinning stone.

Shaw had just placed the sharpened cleaver on a side table and reached for a long boning knife when a flurry of barking, followed by a long howl, pierced the silence. Buttercup, still imprisoned in the tool shed, had scented something. Crook's answering bay arose from some distance away. Charlie Dog's head came up, his ears pricked. Shaw straightened and looked toward the open door of the barn, following the dog's intent gaze. Charlie Dog's hackles rose and his lip curled.

"What is it, boy?" Shaw asked the question in a wary whisper. Charlie Dog was generally friendly, yet he was protective of his extensive family and had an eerie ability to sense ill intent in man or animal.

The dog growled just as a long shadow fell outside the open barn door. Shaw stood up with the boning knife still in his hand.

Sudden and quiet, a dark shape appeared in the doorway. The last gray light of day was behind the figure, rendering his features invisible to the startled man inside. From the tunic-like shirt, the dark fall of long hair, the knee-high hide moccasins, Shaw could tell at once that the apparition was an Indian.

Charlie Dog went crazy. He leaped at the figure, his jaws snapping, but Shaw grabbed his collar before he could do any damage. The Indian didn't move. The rifle in the crook of his arm was decorated with three red stripes painted on the stock and a turkey feather suspended from the lever. All Shaw could think was that the children would be inconsolable if the dog was shot. He spoke sharply to the animal who reluctantly backed off, rumbling his unhappiness in his throat.

The Indian said nothing. Neither did Shaw, for a long moment. He stood with his hand on Charlie Dog's collar, his heart at a standstill, hardly able to credit his own eyes. Shaw knew plenty of Indians and nobody dressed like this any more unless it was a special occasion, not even Shaw's own traditionalist Cherokee uncles deep in the woods of the Ozarks. If it hadn't been for the dog's reaction, Shaw would have wondered if he was hallucinating.

Shaw spoke Cherokee moderately well since his uncles refused to speak anything else, but the few Creek words he had picked up over the years had fled. He resorted to English. "Name yourself."

The Indian didn't respond, though he cocked his head when spoken to. Shaw thought he was going to have to wrack his brain for some Creek phrases but tried again in English. "What do you want?"

When the creature finally spoke his voice was low and resonant. "You unburied them bones."

Alafair was sitting in a chair in the corner of the kitchen playing with Grace and feeling excessively happy. Alice was home for supper tonight. She was the family's great pie-maker and had brought three of sweet-potato which were now sitting on the window sill. Her supper duties done to her satisfaction, Alice was in the parlor with the younger girls, doodling on the piano and singing for the amusement of the boys. While Mary stirred the stew and Ruth made cornbread, Martha was chipping ice off the block in the top of the icebox in order to top off the ice bucket. It may have been close to freezing outside but that was no excuse not to have sweet iced tea with supper. John Lee, Phoebe, and Zeltha had gone home, but Kurt was there, and he fit into the family like he was born into it. That almost made up for the fact that Gee Dub was far away at college and wouldn't be home again until the Thanksgiving break at the end of the month.

Alafair was startled out of her reverie by the sound of the dogs barking outside. The hunting dogs were always howling at something, but Charlie Dog was usually unflappable. The children were too much occupied to take note of the noise. However Alafair immediately thought of Shaw, alone in the barn. She stood and shooed Grace into the parlor to join the singing before walking out onto the back porch and peering across the yard toward the hulking shape of the barn silhouetted against the gray sky.

Chapter Twenty-four

He was gone like smoke.

Shaw barely got a glimpse of a dark shadow, low and close to the ground, as it shot across the open barn door and into the night, emitting a hair-raising howl. Crook was after the stranger. Shaw's heart leaped and began to thud in his chest. Which was a relief, considering that he thought he was having a seizure an instant before.

Anger flooded him. He had finally come face to face with his haint. It was a man and not a ghost. Shaw could deal with a man. And by God, he was going to.

Charlie Dog was twisting like an eel, snarling and trying to escape his master's clutch on his collar. Every hair on the dog's body was standing on end, making him seem twice his normal size.

"Sit!" Shaw's command came out louder than he intended. Charlie Dog deflated and sunk down to the floor. Shaw drew his .44 and checked the ammunition before grabbing his flashlight off the work table, all the while instructing the dog in a terse undertone.

"You go back to the house and stay with Mama and the children. I aim to track that hellion. I'd like to lop off his nose just for scaring the wadding out of me. But I'll just bring him back to the stables and chain him to the wall in an empty stall until we can get Scott out here to arrest him in the morning."

Shaw and Charlie Dog trotted out into the night, the man turning toward the woods and the dog toward the house. Shaw didn't cast him a second glance. He had no doubt the animal would do exactly as he was told. Shaw was vaguely aware of a woman's figure standing by the back door, outlined by the dim light coming from the kitchen. Alafair had come outside to see what the racket was. He pushed the thought out of his mind and concentrated on the task at hand.

◇◇◇

In the faded light Alafair could barely discern the shape of a man moving so fast that he was practically skimming the ground, chased by a snarling apparition that she did not at once recognize as Shaw's mellow coon dog. Her hair stood on end and she started toward the barn, where Shaw was supposed to be sharpening knives. She had only taken a couple of steps when he appeared around the back corner of the barn, following the fleeing figures at a smooth lope.

Alafair drew up short and released a huge breath that she hadn't realized she was holding. The gap between the strange man and the dog was narrowing by the time the two disappeared into the woods behind the house, followed closely by Shaw. She could see that he had objects in both hands. Some kind of cylinder in the left, and by its shape, a gun in his right. A nose nuzzled her leg and she looked down at Charlie Dog.

"I reckon that was our sneak thief, boy." Her inflection made it more of a question than a statement. She didn't want to be scared but a knot of fear rose up in her throat just the same. She put her hand on the top of Charlie Dog's head.

Shaw had to be furious indeed in order to follow an armed fugitive into the woods in the dark. Not-thinking-straight furious. She hurried up the porch steps and into the house to apprise Kurt of the situation.

Chapter Twenty-five

Shaw was more than familiar with the copse of woods behind his house, but when he entered the trees it was so completely black that he couldn't have found his way ten feet without the aid of the flashlight.

He could hear Crook in the distance, his barking lengthening into a periodic bay. Crook was made for this kind of hunt. Raccoon hunts always happened at night. Crook would follow the scent until he neared his quarry, then go after it like Beelzebub himself. The only way a coon—or a man—would be able to escape being torn to shreds would be to go up a tree. And if he did, the dog would keep him up that tree until Shaw arrived, or Doomsday, whichever came first. Shaw followed the dog through the woods until he couldn't hear the sound of the chase any more. He slowed down, picking his way through the trees. It was eerily quiet. Even his own footfall didn't make noise since the thick carpet of fallen leaves was damp and spongy.

It was fully night, now, and fog began to rise from the forest floor. As he tracked his ghost through the mist, just as he had at the hunting camp, he was struck by a sense of *déjà vu*. As cold as it was, a sheen of sweat arose on his forehead. He shone his light low, at his feet, his revolver clutched in the other hand.

Somewhere ahead of him, Crook began to *bell*—that peculiar, resonant howl that said he was on his quarry. Shaw had to stop himself from running toward the sound. He moved as quickly as possible but trod carefully. With the pistol in his hand, a fall could be disastrous.

The dog was baying and barking hysterically and Shaw heard a growl and snap of jaws. Suddenly he wasn't worried about being seen. He shone the light straight into the woods before him and started to trot, desperate to get there before the dog ripped the man's throat out.

Just ahead Shaw heard Crook yip, then squeal in pain. He stopped in his tracks and held his breath. Silence.

All caution abandoned, Shaw crashed through the woods, his legs swallowed by floating shreds of mist, knee-deep. He found Crook at the base of tree, whimpering, writhing and trying without success to stand. A spreading dark patch on his right foreleg turned a lurid red in the light of Shaw's Eveready.

Oh, Lord.

He holstered his pistol before kneeling down and carefully running his hand over the dog's body, checking for other injuries. Crook yelped when Shaw examined the leg, then licked his master's hand to apologize for being such a bother. The leg had been cleanly snapped, the bone protruding through the skin. The Indian had given the dog a vicious kick or clubbing. Shaw put his flashlight down in the leaves. He was leaning forward to lift Crook in his arms when he felt the press of cold steel on the back of his neck.

"Stand up." The voice was low, male, young. "Leave that shooter be."

Shaw didn't argue with him. He stood slowly.

"Throw up your hands."

Shaw made no attempt to look at the man behind him. But he took note that even if his captor was dressed like a Creek, he didn't sound like it. Crook growled and Shaw laid a gentle boot on the dog's flank to keep him down before speaking to the Indian. "What do you want? I don't have your bones any more. What do you want from me? What are you looking for?"

"The white-haired man."

Shaw said nothing to this.

"Where is the white-haired man?"

The rifle barrel was still pressed against his neck. *It's a mistake to touch me,* Shaw thought, *and let me know your position.* "I know a passel of white-haired men, partner. Which one in particular do you seek?" He'd keep him talking until he felt the man relax his attention, then drop and take him down at the knees.

"The one who made the bones. I've been looking for him a long time. Where is the white-haired man?"

"Not at my house. I don't know who you are or whose bones we found, or how they got in the ground. Nor who the white-haired man is who put them there. Leave my family alone."

The young voice sounded adamant. "You lie. You know where he is."

"You're wrong, fella." Shaw fell into the low, sing-song tone he used with skittish mules. "You're on a wild goose chase. You'd better get yourself back to wherever you come from lest you miss this white-haired man when he shows up. Who are you, anyway?"

The half moon broke through the overcast and sent fingers of stark moonlight piercing through the bare branches of the trees. The fog had covered the figure of the wounded dog at Shaw's feet.

"I am Crying Blood."

The sharp ping of a rifle bullet grazing a tree trunk interrupted the conversation. Shaw didn't take the time to be startled. He whirled around and knocked the rifle away with his left hand then gave the haint a right uppercut to the jaw that knocked him off his feet. Crying Blood hit the ground like a dead weight. Shaw was so blind with rage that he straddled the body and pounded him a few more times before he realized that his effort was wasted. The Indian was out cold.

The clouds closed over the light.

"Shaw!"

The sound of that familiar voice shocked him. "Alafair, is that you?"

A dark figure in a coat, skirt, and a cowboy hat appeared, holding a rifle.

"Shaw, thank Heaven! I heard y'all. Did I get him? Kurt! Kurt, they're over here!"

He grabbed her shoulders. "Dang, woman, you could have blowed my head off! What are you doing here? I told you…"

She dismissed his outburst for what it was, adrenalin and relief. "There's no need to swear, Shaw. And I wouldn't have fired except for that shaft of moonlight. I seen him plain as day. I guess you aren't dreaming things nor are you being haunted, either. What did he say to you? What does he want?"

"Pick up that flashlight for me, honey, and give me some light." Shaw bent over with his hands on his knees, trying to catch his breath as Alafair shone the light into the unconscious man's face. He took his first good look at the person who had been making his life miserable for the past week.

"He's just a kid," Alafair exclaimed. "Why, he's no older than Gee Dub, if that." His hair was blue-black in the artificial light and long, black lashes curled out from smooth lids. He looked deceptively innocent even though half his face was painted with red ochre. He had declared war on somebody.

Kurt's tall, thin, shape appeared through the trees, a darker shape in the darkness of the woods. "I heard a shot! Are you all right, Miz Tucker?"

"Shaw got the pork thief, Kurt. He's a boy!"

The fugitive's youth did nothing to make Shaw feel charitable. When he stirred and opened his eyes, Shaw grabbed his collar and heaved him none too gently to his feet. Crying Blood made a feeble effort to fend him off, but Shaw slapped him across the face so hard that he nearly fell again.

"Behave!" he spat. He drew his pistol and pressed the barrel against Crying Blood's cheek. "I could kill you right now and stuff your carcass down a fox hole and nobody'd ever find you again."

Alafair was less concerned with Crying Blood's welfare than with Shaw's state of mind. His fury caused her to take a step back. "Shaw," she began, before a keening whine cut her short. "Mercy me! Is that Crook? Did the villain shoot him?'

The dog's plight drew Shaw's attention. "No, looks like he kicked him, or walloped him somehow and busted his leg pretty bad. Kurt, train that shotgun on this yahoo and don't let him twitch a toe." Kurt stepped forward and raised the shotgun, quiet and purposeful, and motioned for the Indian to move back. Crying Blood blinked at him and shook his head, trying to clear it. He got his feet under him and managed to step away.

Shaw knelt back down to attend to the wounded dog and removed his bandana from his back pocket. Shaw continued to talk to Alafair in an undertone as he gently bound the dog's leg, aided by the already dimming stream of light from the Eveready. "He said he's after a white-haired man who put those bones in the ground, and he followed me home so I'd lead him to this fellow."

"White-haired man?"

He cast a malevolent glance in the Indian's direction. "I don't know who. I'm guessing some old man killed whoever we found buried in the woods and this crazy Indian has got it into his head that I know something about it."

Alafair addressed the young man. "You know who the dead man is, and you think my husband can lead you to his killer?" The boy said nothing, so she tried a different tack. "What's your name, son?"

Shaw answered for him. "He called himself Crying Blood, Alafair. Don't be talking to him. He's right round the bend, who-ever he is." He picked up the dog as carefully as he could and stood.

Alafair stroked Crook's silky ear. "Oh, poor old Crook. Poor old boy," she crooned. "I know it hurts."

"You got him covered, Kurt?" Shaw asked.

"Yessir."

"Bring him along. Alafair, you go first."

Kurt gave his captive a violent shove in the direction of the house. "Walk."

Crying Blood did as he was told. He was still unsteady on his feet, but Kurt had no sympathy. He planted his foot on the seat of the boy's pants and kicked him forward. Crying Blood staggered but didn't fall. He threw a poisonous look over his shoulder.

"Go on," Shaw urged. "Make a break for it. I wish you would."

"Let's send Charlie into town to get Scott right now," Alafair urged as they picked their way through the woods.

"No, wait until morning."

She could tell by his tone that Shaw had already determined what he was going to do. In fact, she knew him well enough that she could tell by his stride, the way he cradled the dog, the crackle of electricity in the air surrounding him, that no matter what he had decided there was no use arguing with him now.

She accepted the situation with a certain fatalism. "I hope you aren't planning to shoot him for hurting your dog and stealing a hunk of fatback."

Her question caused him a twist of irony and he emitted a humorless laugh. He spoke into the darkness, loud enough for Crying Blood to hear. "If I was going to shoot him, it'd be for scaring the liver out of me."

Chapter Twenty-six

When they cleared the woods and approached the barn, Kurt made Crying Blood clasp his hands behind his head and seized the back of his shirt to guide him toward the barn, all the while keeping the shotgun aimed carefully at the back of the Indian's head.

Shaw traded burdens with Alafair, taking her rifle and giving her the wounded dog. He followed Kurt and their prisoner to the barn, leaving Alafair to go to the house and deal with the their many progeny, who were all standing together in a a roiling mob just outside the back door of the house. They descended on her like a swarm of bees as she approached, buzzing with questions. Martha had raised a lantern in one hand, the better to assess what was happening. The light illuminated the faces of Alafair's three eldest, Martha, Mary, and Alice, standing shoulder to shoulder and eyeing their mother with concern while the younger ones fussed over the dog.

Mary, in the middle, was holding Grace in her arms. "Looks like y'all got him."

Alafair nodded and raised her voice to be heard over the hubbub. "Daddy and Kurt caught our pork thief. He's just a hungry youngster, so no need to be scared. Crook went to bite him and got kicked. Looks like he has a broken leg, but he'll be all right. Fronie, back up. You're crowding him, here." She walked up the back steps with the children in orbit around her, talking all the while. "Y'all should have gone ahead and eaten supper.

It's dark already and you children need to get to bed. Mary and Alice, go on and feed the young ones. Alice, if Walter's going to come get you soon, you'd better get some food into you. Here, Charlie, you take care of Crook. Martha, you can help him with a poultice and splint, can't you? Make him a bed here on the porch. I'm going out to the barn and see how Daddy and Kurt are doing with their prisoner."

Kurt hauled Crying Blood into the barn and threw him into an empty stall.

Shaw leaned his rifle against the wall and lit a couple of kerosene lanterns before he took a lariat from its hook. "Son," he said to Kurt, "you keep that shotgun pointed right between this fellow's eyes and don't take your eye off him for a second." He entered the stall, careful not to block Kurt's line of sight, and pushed the Indian to the ground. He knelt down and tied the young man's hands to the slats in the stall gate. Crying Blood grunted involuntarily when Shaw gave the knots around his wrists a final vindictive tug before standing up.

For a long moment, they assessed one another. Shaw was breathing heavily, from emotion rather than exertion. The young Indian's jaw was red and one of his eyes was swelling, but he was calm. He cast a glance at the tall man with the funny accent who was aiming the 12-gauge at him, gimlet eyed. He decided not to make any sudden moves.

Crying Blood spoke first. "Who are you?"

Shaw was so taken aback at the question that he nearly choked. "Who am *I*, you birdbrain? Who the blazes are *you*?"

Before the boy could answer, Alafair sailed into the barn with a bucket of warm water in one hand and bandages and a small, square, blue glass bottle in the other. She took in the situation at a glance. Shaw was right on the edge. "I told the children you caught our haint." Her tone was calm, almost conversational. "Looks like you roughed him up a mite, too. Kurt, put that gun down. He can't do any harm trussed up like that." She set the bucket down and put a gentle hand on Shaw's arm before lowering herself to her knees in front of the captive.

She dipped a cloth in the warm water and began cleaning the cut under Crying Blood's eye.

"When's the last time you ate, child?" She asked the question in her best motherly voice.

Shaw emitted a noise that may have been akin to a laugh. Trust Alafair to try and diffuse the tension, even if the last thing he wanted to be was reasonable. Her presence did calm him, however, and he felt his shoulders relax. He motioned to Kurt to do as she asked.

Crying Blood was regarding her as though she were a creature from another planet. He didn't answer her question.

Shaw hunkered down next to his wife. "He asked me who I was, if you can believe it. Now, why do you expect some crazy Muscogee boy who dresses like Tecumseh himself is stalking somebody he doesn't even know?"

"Maybe he thought you were whoever he's looking for," Alafair speculated as she dabbed. "And now he gets a look at you he sees that he's wrong."

Shaw's mouth quirked as he considered this. "Well, Alafair, a little while back, as he was poking me in the neck with a rifle, he mentioned that he was looking for a white-haired man and I don't expect I fit that description."

A look of annoyance flashed in Crying Blood's eyes, as though he suspected he was being toyed with and didn't appreciate it.

Alafair draped the bloodied rag over the side of the bucket and pulled the cork out of the small bottle. She poured a bit of reddish liquid from the bottle onto a square of white cotton. "This is iodine, son," she warned. "It's going to sting,"

Crying Blood yelped and jerked away when she touched his cut lip with the iodine and Alafair grabbed his jaw to hold him steady as she doctored. The boy's discomfort gave Shaw perverse satisfaction. Some small retribution for the discomfort Crying Blood had given him. He sat back in the straw and crossed his legs.

Now that he had calmed down some, Shaw was sorry that he had pounded on the kid. But he couldn't take it back. When he spoke again, Shaw's voice had lost its rage. "You've been giving me fits, boy, ever since I come back from Oktaha."

He was glad that Alafair was here. No young thing could resist her peculiar magic and Crying Blood seemed to be no exception. His eyes never left her face as she washed the war paint off his cheeks in a businesslike manner. She cast Shaw a glance as she dropped the wash cloth back into the bucket.

"Honey, his hands are turning blue." Her tone was intimate, a comment just between the two of them. "Surely it wouldn't hurt anything if he was tied with his hands lower than his head."

Shaw didn't reply. He wasn't in the mood to be charitable. It took a moment of internal struggle before Shaw overcame enough of his pique to admit that she was probably right. Alafair moved to the side as he carefully loosed one of the Indian's hands and retied it to a lower slat, then did the same with the other.

As he tied he spoke to the boy, low, like he would to an animal. "You're the one skulking around our camp the other night. I recognize them moccasins. What were you doing out in the big middle of lonesome?"

The boy's only response was a stubborn stare. But years of fatherhood had taught Shaw a thing or two about how to deal with a sulky teen. "I can't figure out how you managed to get around three hunting dogs and sashay around the camp as free as you please."

The stony expression gave way to a self satisfied smirk. "A hunk of squirrel and a kind word. Them dogs was easy to charm."

Alafair could tell that the boy was relieved to have his hands readjusted by the way his body relaxed. "But not when you presumed to skulk around here."

"That yeller dog set them off." He hesitated and cast a rueful glance at Alafair. "I'm sorry I hurt that hound. He'd of had me for sure, elsewise."

"Why did you take it into your head to follow me home?" Shaw asked.

"I don't care nothing about you. I want the white-haired haint."

"Maybe we can help you find him," Alafair said.

His suspicious mien said that he didn't believe her for a minute.

She tried another tack. "Why don't you tell us the whole story, youngster?"

Both Shaw and Alafair recognized Crying Blood's look of disdain for the hopeless ignorance of his elders. They had seen it on their own children. Alafair was tempted to laugh.

Shaw was tempted to slap the expression off his face. He restrained himself with an effort. "I don't have the littlest notion what you think you're about!"

Alafair could tell by Shaw's rising volume that his frustration at this back and forth was about to get the better of him. She placed a discreet hand on his thigh. "Leave it for a little bit, Shaw. Why don't you come up to the house with me and have a bite to eat? Kurt will watch him, won't you, Kurt?"

Kurt had been watching the proceedings with intense interest from the open stall gate, his stringy frame slouched against the slats. He had traded the 12-gauge for Shaw's .22 Winchester, which was cradled in the crook of his arm. He directed his answer to Shaw. "Yes, sir, I can, Mister Tucker. He won't go nowhere while I am looking on him."

Chapter Twenty-seven

"I been trying for a year to find that farm where y'all was hunting. Ira only took me out there the once and I couldn't remember much about where it was or how we got there. But I knew I had to find it again."

The boy was stuffing his mouth with cornbread and stew as he spoke, which made it hard for Alafair to understand him. A diet of stolen fatback and whatever field critters he could snare had obviously left Crying Blood on the edge of starvation. He was not a bad-looking boy, she thought, though small and undernourished. He had the cheekbones and black hair of a Creek, but otherwise, he looked more White than Indian with round, grey-green eyes and a long-nosed, narrow face. His cheeks were still round with youth. Alafair lowered her estimate of his age to not more than sixteen, and not a very well-grown sixteen at that. In his old-fashioned Creek garb he looked more like a boy playing at dress-up than any kind of a threat.

His swollen lip and rapidly purpling shiner didn't seem to bother him much. Neither did the fact that Shaw had shackled him to the wall with a length of chain, some old handcuffs, and a couple of pieces of harness leather. He was managing to shovel in the stew in spite of a limited range of motion and a sore mouth. The stew seemed to have loosened his tongue as well.

Alafair was sitting on an upturned crate at the far end of the stall, close to the open gate, leaning forward with her elbows on her knees, watching the boy demolish his meal and asking what she hoped were innocuous but leading questions. She wanted to have a closer look at that eye, but Shaw had forbidden her from getting too close to him now that he had some use of his hands. She could feel Shaw standing behind her, his body heat, his suspicion, his curiosity. He had his rifle at his side, she knew, cautious as always. They had sent Kurt to bed.

"When was the last time you ate, young'un?" she asked again.

"A while, I guess," he admitted, as he sopped up the last of the gravy from the bowl with a hunk of cornbread.

Shaw almost made a remark about a recent meal of pork, but decided that the boy would probably be more forthcoming without sarcastic remarks from the man who had just beaten him up. He bit his lip and left him to Alafair's tenderer approach.

"I guess you've been living rough for a spell," she said.

"Yes, ma'am." He paused to lick the empty bowl. "I been looking for the white-haired haint for a long time now."

"You want some more stew?"

He shot a glance upward at Shaw before he extended his bowl toward her, eager. "I'd be beholden."

She ladled stew out of the covered pail at her side, picked another crumbly piece of cornbread from the basket in her lap, and laid it on top of the bowl. She let him wolf down a few bites before venturing another question. "Who's Ira?"

"He was my brother."

She didn't miss the fact that he spoke of his brother in the past tense. "Is Ira dead, honey?"

Crying Blood didn't look up from his meal. "They said it was an accident that he fell off his mule and broke his neck. But I saw. Old Billy was a mild critter, but something spooked him and he bucked Ira off. Then a thing with long white hair came out of the bushes. It walked like a man, but it had a face like an evil spirit. That's how I know he's a haint. He grabbed Ira up and twisted his neck. Then he disappeared like he was never there. It was night, and rainy, and I was pretty far off. And nobody believes a kid, anyway. But I know what I saw."

Alafair and Shaw exchanged a glance. *Now we're getting some-where.* She tried another question. "Why did this fellow kill Ira, do you suppose?"

Crying Blood's eyes grew round. "I think he seen us when Ira took me there to that farm. I think he followed us home and waited till he could do Ira in."

"But why?" she persisted.

"Hell, I don't know—'scuse me—I don't know for sure." His spoon hesitated on its way to his mouth and he looked over her head at Shaw. "I hardly remember anything from when I was little. I remember my brother. A couple years ago, he took me to that farm and told me it was ours 'cause we were Muscogee. He said nobody lived there because there was a haint walked the place. But then after we got home, Ira came to me all scared and told me he'd seen it. That it'd followed us home. He told me it wanted to kill him, and it did. That ghost, he'll get me, too, if I don't get him first."

Alafair offered yet another piece of cornbread and he took it. "Where is your home?"

She had hoped that he was on a roll, but that was one inquiry too many. He cast her a glance as he ate but didn't answer.

She tried a different question. "How long have you been waiting out there to see your ghost?"

He considered his answer, then decided there was nothing in it that could give him away. "Just a few days, but I never saw a sign of him. Then a bunch of White folks showed up and commenced to bird hunting." He had begun by speaking to Alafair, but now he turned his attention to Shaw. "I couldn't hardly wait for y'all to leave so I could get on with it."

Shaw was unable to keep quiet any longer. "Well, then, why did you follow me? Why do you think he's here, this white-haired man, or haint, or whatever he is?"

Crying Blood's gaze swiveled enough to look at him. "I did, 'cause he did. When y'all cooked that rabbit he finally showed up. I heard him. He said your name."

Shaw's brows knit. "He said my…" The sentence died on his lips as he suddenly remembered—a single, icy, sigh of wind, ruffling the remaining dry leaves on the trees, the sound like a voice. *Shaw.*

"I know he's here," said Crying Blood.

Alafair and Shaw stood close together just outside the barn door. The sky was overcast, so even though the moon was full it only shone as a round, grey, luminescence in a black sky.

The empty food pail was slung over Alafair's forearm, the dishes that Crying Blood had licked clean were in her hands. Shaw cradled his rifle in his arms. He was still wearing his worse-for-wear Stetson pulled down low on his forehead. The brim shadowed his face and made it invisible in the gloom of the night.

She was on her way back to the house. Shaw had come out of the barn with her, intending to watch her make the trip through the barnyard, the truck garden, and the back yard through the darkness, just in case the boy was right and someone, or something, else had accompanied him back from Oktaha and was spying on them right now.

Alafair balked, loath to leave Shaw on his own in the shadowy barn with his captive. She had urged him to let her wake Kurt, but he had refused. What danger is one chained-up teenaged fake Indian, he had asked?

"You don't believe there's a haint after him?"

She couldn't make out his face, but she could hear his snort of disdain. "What do you think?"

"What about what he said about hearing it call your name?"

She could see his head turn as he looked away from her. "Hearing things," he said. "The wind in the trees. Hearing things."

"You think he's crazy?"

"I reckon that he was told the story of the ghost on that farm and when his brother got killed in an accident he conjured up this tale in order to make sense of it. In the morning Scott will figure out where he belongs and get him back to his folks."

"What about the bones you found? Do you suspect they belonged to his brother?"

"Honey, he said his brother died just a couple of years ago, and Slim has been in the ground for a lot longer than that. I think we've got two different things going on here. I doubt if one has anything to do with the other."

Alafair's brows knit. Shaw had always been a realistic and practical man who dealt with things as he found them. But there was something about his reasoning that smacked of avoidance and denial. She opened her mouth to speak, but he beat her to it.

"You go on back up to the house, Alafair. I'm bunking in the barn. I don't intend to leave that slippery youngster out here unguarded tonight."

"But…"

He put his hand on her shoulder. "Send out some breakfast with Charlie when he comes to milk in the morning." He gave her a gentle shove in the direction of the house.

Chapter Twenty-eight

Shaw checked the boy's bonds. He had created a pallet for him out of clean gunny sacks and an old horse blanket over the straw. Alafair had wanted to bring him a quilt. Even though Shaw wasn't feeling quite as murderous as he had when he first caught Crying Blood, he still wasn't in the mood to make the troublesome lad too comfortable.

Without Alafair's soothing presence, the atmosphere between captor and captive was tense at first. Shaw took Alafair's vacated seat on the upturned crate, rifle across his knees, and Crying Blood hunkered in the corner of the stall, shifting at intervals to ease his bonds. Shaw had hung one solitary kerosene lantern on a hook near the gate and the two eyed each other silently by its dim light.

Shaw waited in vain over a long hour for the boy to go to sleep, but he didn't appear to be so inclined. Shaw was surprised. Young people could generally drop off under practically any circumstance, and he was pretty sure that Crying Blood hadn't found himself in such comfortable surroundings in some time.

Shaw himself was tired to the bone and exasperated almost beyond bearing; at his exhausted body, at his unruly imagination and unreasonable fear, and above all at this pesky child.

"How old are you, young'un?" The sound of Shaw's voice breaking the silence surprised even himself. Crying Blood raised his head but didn't reply.

Shaw persisted. "Fourteen, fifteen? Or more like thirteen, maybe. You look pretty scrawny to be much older."

This was an affront that Crying Blood couldn't tolerate. "I'm fifteen."

"Fifteen. I've got a son close to your age. He'd make about two of you, though."

"I'll be sixteen come spring. That's what the Reverend Edmond says, anyway."

Aha! Shaw smiled in spite of himself. "Reverend Edmond, you say."

The boy grimaced at the realization he'd given himself away.

"You reckon the Reverend Edmond is wondering where you are?"

The kid's bottom lip pushed out into a pout and he looked away.

Shaw crossed one ankle over his knee and regarded his prisoner for a moment, suddenly feeling much better. He tried another angle. "Well, I hope you enjoyed the barbeque you made out of of my fresh-killed hog, at least."

The grey-green eyes widened. "I didn't eat it. I took that meat for bait. I meant to lure him with it."

"The white-haired haint? Your ghost likes meat?"

"Yeah, he likes the smell of meat a'cookin'. The only time I've ever been able to glimpse him is when there's meat over the fire."

Shaw's improved mood evaporated. "You've seen him?"

"I have. Just a glimpse, out of the corner of my eye, like. I could see that white hair in the moonlight. He only comes out at night, you see. That's what Ira told me. That's 'cause he's a spirit. He still likes the smell of meat, though."

Shaw shook his head, fighting his rising annoyance. For an instant he had thought the boy's tale was more than fantasy. Still, Crying Blood was talking, after a fashion. Shaw made an effort to sound reasonable. "Well, if this white-haired fellow is already dead, how are you aiming to kill him?"

Crying Blood sat up, eager. "I went to see an *owalu* over by Eufaula. He looked in the fire and saw a man whose breath had left his body but his flesh had forgot that it was dead. He told me that until this flesh was back beneath the ground where it belongs, the world is out of balance. So if he's naught but flesh, I expect I can just shoot him." The boy shifted awkwardly and maneuvered his bound hands enough to retrieve a pigskin pouch from the pocket of his britches. "He told me not never to go to sleep without I burn some of this."

Shaw took the pouch and opened the drawstring top with two fingers. Before he even looked inside, he could tell by the redolent aroma that it was full of cedar wood shavings. He didn't ask what it was for. Everyone knew that cedar smoke repelled ghosts. "I reckon you'd better keep this, then." He stretched forward and put the bag back into the boy's hand. "Before you sleep we'll throw a pinch in the lantern. Why did this ghost-man get the idea to kill your brother and you?"

"I'm not exactly sure. Maybe it was because we trespassed on his haunting place. Or maybe something happened long ago." Crying Blood's gaze wandered off. "We had a mama once. Ira told me she give us away to keep us safe. Maybe it's something to do with that. Ira says I was too little, but I wasn't. Sometimes I think I remember her face. It's like a dream in my mind."

Shaw listened quietly, trying to maintain his skepticism but feeling himself being drawn into Crying Blood's tale. Boys. He knew from bitter experience how easily a young man could buy into a myth to explain a world that made no sense to him. He nearly suggested that together he and Crying Blood could do some investigation and discover what really happened to Ira, but he stopped himself. He had sons of his own to raise.

"You got any other kinfolks?" he asked. "Somebody is probably wondering where you are."

Crying Blood slouched back into the straw and shrugged. "Naw, not as I know of." His expression was ironic. "The Reverend Edmond, he taught me to be a Christian and tried to cure me of wickedness. I wanted mighty hard to be good, but I reckon it just never did take."

The lad was blinking with fatigue now, and Shaw threw the horse blanket over him. "Never mind, then. You can tell the rest of your story to the sheriff in the morning."

Crying Blood curled up in his little nest and pulled the blanket up to his chin. One greenish eye regarded Shaw sleepily.

"I'm sorry I hurt your dog, Mister," he murmured. "I like them dogs."

Shaw stood up and turned down the wick in the lantern hanging on its hook by the stall gate. "Just go to sleep."

Chapter Twenty-nine

Shaw sat on the crate with his rifle over his knees, struggling to stay awake, for over an hour, or two hours. He lost track of time. He withdrew his watch from his coat pocket and peered at it in the dim glow of the lantern. It was close to midnight. He was going to be useless in the morning. He decided to give himself another hour then wake Kurt to relieve him. Just for something to do, he briefly considered filling the feed boxes for the cows and the pregnant mares who were housed in the barn. He could hear their occasional snuffing and shifting in their stalls. But he decided against doing the chore ahead of schedule lest he discombobulate the animals. He stood and walked up and down the broad, open expanse of the barn for a few minutes, then sat back down on his crate.

It didn't take but a few minutes for him to begin to doze, drifting between wake and sleep, and then dream. He dreamed he was chasing the haint through the woods, mixing up both hunts in his mind. He could smell the damp leaf litter, see the wisps of fog entangling the boles of the trees, his legs. He heard the hound baying, the snap of the dry tree branches as he plunged past. He felt the cold press of the rifle on his neck and his hand twitched and tingled as he relived the smash of his fist against his foe's jaw, his hand closing around the rifle barrel before he jerked it away from his captor and flung it to the ground.

He awoke with a start. The boy's rifle. He had forgotten all about it. As far as he knew it was still lying in a pile of wet leaves in the woods behind the house. Had Alafair picked it up? Kurt? He didn't remember.

He wiped the sleep from his eyes and stood up, removing the lantern from its hook and leaning over to check his captive. The boy was sound asleep, dug down into the blanket and gunny sacks like a nesting pup.

Shaw closed the stall gate, dropped the lock and secured it with a padlock. He took the lantern with him when he left the barn and walked through the dark barnyard, around the tool shed to Kurt's room. He didn't bother to knock before he went in.

The furnishings of Kurt's little apartment consisted of two squeaky cast-iron cots with straw mattresses, a rickety table and two equally rickety chairs, a flat-topped iron Franklin stove with two burners, a gun rack over the door, a wooden shelf and half a dozen pegs on the wall to serve for a closet.

The shutters on the single glassless window were closed and barred. The room was dark as a cow's insides. Shaw propped his rifle at the foot of the empty cot by the door and picked his way across the room by lamplight. Kurt was sprawled out in his long johns, lying on his stomach, cradling his head on his arms. Shaw had to shake him.

He rolled over, squinting, but instantly awake. "Yes, sir?" His blue eyes looked colorless in the yellow light of the lantern.

"Reckon you can take a turn watching our prisoner? I can't keep my eyes open." Shaw sat down on one of the chairs as Kurt rolled out of bed and pulled his trousers on over his union suit.

Shaw felt himself sagging with fatigue. His knees were aching, his hand hurt, his eyes felt gritty. He was having trouble concentrating. Kurt, on the other hand, seemed perfectly refreshed and full of energy after his few hours of sleep. Shaw was suddenly struck with envy for the big, healthy German. He almost laughed aloud at himself. He had already had his turn at being twenty-five and immortal.

"Say," Shaw began, as Kurt sat down to pull on his boots, "did you pick up the rifle with the three red stripes, the one I wrested from the kid out in the woods?"

"No, sir. I'm sorry, I did not think of it. You wish I am fetching it?" Kurt's English was much improved since he had first come to work here, but sometimes Shaw had to ponder a moment before he understood exactly what Kurt meant.

"You know, that's probably a good idea. I don't care to leave a loaded weapon unattended. Do you think you can find your way back there in the dark?"

"I think yes, sir."

Shaw fished the flashlight out of his coat pocket. "Take this. I put in a new battery, so it'll work good as long as you don't leave it on too long and use up the juice. And take your shotgun with you."

Kurt was dressed by now. Shaw waited patiently as he grabbed his hat and coat off the tree by the door, took his shotgun off the rack, retrieved a couple of shells from a drawer in his bedside table and slipped them into his coat pocket. They walked together for a little way down the path before Shaw turned toward the barn, and Kurt went his own way toward the woods.

Chapter Thirty

It was four-thirty in the morning, still cold and black as the dark side of the moon, when Sally brought Peter the news about Red Allen.

"Leroy's in the kitchen," she began. "Red Allen is gone."

There was no heat in the bedroom, but the chill was forgotten as Peter tried to process what his wife had just said. "What do you mean, gone?" He knew it was a stupid thing to ask even as he said it.

Sally was standing in the bedroom door with coal tongs in her hand. She had been firing up the stove for breakfast when their grandson and part-time stableboy Leroy had burst into her kitchen with the news. She didn't have to bother with an answer when Leroy himself loomed up at her shoulder, his face red and his black hair sticking up every which way. "I went to feed him and his stall is empty, Gramp!" The teenager's words tumbled all over one another in his excitement. "Somebody took him! The stall gate was closed and Red Allen's rope halter ain't on its hook!"

Peter hustled Sally and Leroy before him into the parlor where he flung himself into a chair and pulled on his boots. "Did you look for him, Leroy? Are there tracks?"

"No, Gramp. As soon as I saw the stall was empty I come a'running to get you."

Sally managed to light a lantern and shove it into Peter's hand before he and the boy ran out the back door. Peter held the lamp at arm's length and followed at the best pace he could manage as his grandson tore across the yard and down the path to the stables.

Leroy was dancing with impatience in front of the empty stall when Peter finally puffed in behind him.

"Look, Gramp, he's gone!"

The expression that crossed Peter's face when he saw the empty stall caused the boy to swallow his words. Peter's complexion had gone puce in the lamplight. But when he spoke he sounded perfectly reasonable. "Leroy, saddle up Tiger, there, and ride to the Sheriff's office. Roust up Scott or Trent or whoever's on duty and get 'em out here."

"Yessir." Leroy moved smartly to do as he was told.

Peter had no doubt what had happened. He should have known that Doolan wasn't about to take no for an answer. He swore under his breath. When he was soldiering out West, horse-thieves got hanged. He was still staring at the empty stall and longing for the days of rough justice when Leroy reappeared at the stable door, leading Tiger by the reins.

"What are you dallying for, lad?" Peter barked.

"You'd best come see this." He dropped the reins and beckoned for Peter to follow him outside.

Sweet Jesus, Peter thought as he followed the boy around to the small corral at the side of the building. *If Doolan has harmed that horse I will kill him with my bare hands.*

The lantern light glinted off an ivory mane as they neared the fence and Peter's breath caught. Red Allen was standing with his head over the rail, nodding with contentment and looking quite satisfied with himself. Peter stopped in his tracks and laughed a laugh that was more like a sob of relief.

Leroy took the lantern from his grandfather's hand and stretched over the fence to illuminate the horse's nether regions. "Look, Gramp. This stallion has been at a mare."

The horizon was just turning from black to grey when Leroy came back to the house to let Sally know what was happening.

The young man sat down at the table and Sally put a plate full of fried eggs and syrup-covered biscuits in front of him.

"Is the horse all right, sugar?" she asked.

"Yes'm. I've washed him down and stabled him and fed him. He's none the worse for wear."

"How's Grandpapa?"

"Fit to be tied. He found some tracks. Now he's sure that somebody brought a mare in on the sly last night then took Red Allen out to her in the corral. He's gone to fetch the sheriff himself." Leroy reddened. "Gran, I didn't know Grandpapa was acquainted with such language."

Chapter Thirty-one

The big double barn doors were closed and locked, but as Shaw approached he could hear the animals lowing, whinnying, bumping and knocking against their stalls. Perplexed, he opened the door to the smaller side entrance and was immediately struck with the smell—a gamey, dark, animal smell. A bear, a lion? No, he knew those scents. There was no mistaking the iron tang of blood, though.

He caught his breath and chambered a round in his rifle before he slipped in.

He could see from ten yards out that the bar across the gate of Crying Blood's prison stall had been splintered and the hasp, padlock still affixed, was hanging askew. He quickened his pace as he moved across the floor.

Dang it, he knew he should never have left that slippery son of a gun unguarded. The question of how the boy had managed to break the lock on the outside niggled the back of his mind, but he fully expected to find the stall empty when he threw open the door and stepped inside.

Crying Blood lay on his back, the horse blanket thrown to one side, eyes wide open and staring at the ceiling. He wasn't seeing anything, though. A crude wooden lance thrust through his heart had pinned his body to the ground and sent his soul to heaven.

Shaw staggered back like he had been kicked in the chest, almost dropping the lantern. He must have cried out, for a minute later, as he stood just outside the open gate gasping in shock, Kurt appeared at at run, stuffing a shell into the breach of his shotgun.

"Was ist los?" He skidded to a stop, alarmed at the look of horror on Shaw's face. Shaw gestured toward the broken gate, still too breathless to speak. Kurt took the lantern and peered into the stall.

He jerked his head out. *"Lieber Gott!"*

Shaw gulped. "I should have... I should have..."

Kurt put the lantern on the ground and placed a hand on Shaw's back. "Look, Mr. Tucker, there is prints! Bare feet in such cold!"

Shaw took himself in hand and straightened. "Whoever done this is still around. Throw a saddle on a horse and slap leather, Kurt. Get Sheriff Tucker out here as fast as you can."

Kurt was half-way back to the tack closet before Shaw finished speaking. Shaw picked up the lantern and searched the barn from top to bottom before going back into the stall. He leaned over the dead boy and examined the scene by the dim light.

The boy had seen who killed him, if the wide open eyes were any indication, but he didn't look afraid, or even surprised. There was no sign of a struggle. Shaw tried to imagine what had happened.

The boy must have heard the wood splinter when the lock was broken. The murderer entered the stall holding a lance, but the boy didn't cry out or try to stand up. He rolled over onto his back, threw back the blanket and looked at his killer. Did they speak?

Crying Blood either had no time to react or he had no fear. Whichever, he had died quick. A pool of dark blood had oozed out from under the body, but there wasn't much blood on his shirt. The lance had gone right through his heart.

God have mercy. I should have remembered to burn a pinch of the cedar, Shaw thought. He squatted down and brought the lamp close. The light illuminated something white peeking out at the throat of Crying Blood's tunic. Shaw should have been shocked or frightened or awed when he saw what it was, but he wasn't feeling much of anything as he fingered the knobby protrusions on the small snake bones that made up the youngster's necklace. It was identical to the one Shaw still carried in his pocket. The tender young skin of the boy's throat felt supple and alive, though no pulse warmed it. Shaw touched the still face, closed the staring eyes, then lifted one out-flung arm. Crying Blood was clutching something in his hand. Shaw pried open the fingers and removed what looked at first like a dead leaf, but felt like a snatch of half-rotten, brown burlap. He stood up and cast a look around but didn't immediately see that anything else in the stall was much disturbed. The murderer could be long gone by now. But Shaw was struck by a cold fear that he was lurking somewhere near.

He only paused long enough to wedge the broken door shut before hurrying back to the house to guard his sleeping wife and children.

Chapter Thirty-two

Alafair was so troubled with dreams that she hardly slept at all. It was still a long time before dawn when she finally gave it up as a bad job and rolled out of bed, careful not to wake Grace, who had taken advantage of her father's absence to jump into her parents' big bed. Alafair hadn't had the will to eject her. Even if Shaw reclaimed his spot during the night, Grace didn't take up enough room to be a bother.

She pulled on a wool skirt and a heavy shirt and tiptoed though the parlor with her shoes in her hand. Charlie slept dead to the world on his bed in the corner. She went into the kitchen and sat down on a chair to pull on her shoes, removed her hat and coat from the coat tree by the back door. She slipped onto the back porch to light a lantern and speak to the invalid Crook.

Charlie had made a hospital bed for Crook out of an old crate, some straw, and a blanket that had seen better days. Charlie Dog was stretched out next to his friend's pallet, and when Alafair opened the back door both dogs raised their heads and wagged their tails at her.

She gave both of them a head scratch and a friendly word before kneeling down to check Crook's broken foreleg. It looked better. She had set it the night before—a traumatic procedure for all concerned. Grace had hidden under her bed rather than be present for the operation.

The leg was splinted on two sides and tightly bound. When they first brought him home Crook kept trying to stand on it. Alafair was glad to see that he had given up that idea and was lying on his side, resigned to a period of inactivity. He was happy to see her, for the distraction from boredom if nothing else, and allowed her to gently unwrap the comfrey poultice she had bound directly over the wound.

"There now, Crook, that's a good boy. Have you been gnawing at your bandages, you rascal? Didn't I tell you quite particular not to do that? Well, looks like you haven't done any damage. Looks good!" Satisfied, Alafair wiped her hands on a towel and stood. She was informing the dogs of her intention to make a trip out to the barn to see if Shaw and his captive had fallen asleep when she heard something on the night. Both dogs snapped to attention. Alafair swallowed her comment and listened, but the sound didn't recur. Yet she knew she wasn't imagining things. It had sounded like a human voice. A man's voice. She opened the screen and was just about to walk out into the yard when Shaw's cry of "Stop!" froze her in her tracks.

She hadn't seen him running toward the house through the dark, rifle in hand.

"Don't come out!" By this time he was on her. He seized her upper arm with such force that she would sport finger-shaped bruises for days afterwards, and hustled her back inside. "Honey, I went to wake up Kurt and while I was gone somebody snuck into the barn and killed Crying Blood." He was speaking fast, urgent. She made a squeaking noise, but his words rushed over her. "The killer had to have been watching and seen me leave the boy all trussed up alone in there. He's like to still be around and I don't know but what he has more evil mischief planned. Unlock the gun case and arm yourself. I sent Kurt headlong to fetch Scott."

They were in the kitchen now. Shaw was no longer propelling Alafair along. She was purposefully heading under her own steam toward the gun cabinet in the parlor. All she had managed to glean from what he said was that there may be danger to her children lurking about. She would take time to process the rest later.

She ran into Charlie's sturdy form, a long-john clad wall blocking the door between kitchen and parlor.

"Somebody killed Crying Blood?" he asked. Horrified. He hadn't even managed to get a good look at their intriguing captive, practically the same age as he, now murdered.

An unstoppable tide of parental concern pushed him backwards into the parlor. "Get dressed," his father ordered. "Fetch me a box of shells from the chifforobe and be quiet about it. Don't wake up any of the girls."

Too late. Alafair caught sight of a ghostly figure standing in the bedroom door. Martha, in her white flannel nightgown, long, dark, hair spilling over her shoulders, one hand on either door jamb, the only one of the sisters to be wakened by the disturbance.

Charlie was already struggling into his trousers. "I want to go with you, Daddy…"

"No!" Alafair said over his request.

Shaw put his hand on Charlie's shoulder. "You load up Gee Dub's Winchester, son, and stand guard over your sisters and Mama."

◇◇◇

In the end, Martha and Charlie stood armed sentry as their siblings slept and Alafair went with Shaw back out to the barn. She insisted on going as much for Shaw's sake than for Crying Blood's. There was nothing they could do for the boy now. They couldn't even arrange his body decently until the sheriff was able to examine the scene of the crime.

The moment Alafair saw Crying Blood lying dead in the straw, she burst into tears. Her grief over the unjust and gruesome end to a young life almost unmanned Shaw. He held her in his arms while she sobbed, unable to keep the tears from spilling down his cheeks.

Her storm subsided after a few minutes and she pulled back enough to look up at him. She put her hand on his face. "It wasn't your fault, honey."

His eyes widened. She always knew what he was thinking. "I shouldn't have left him alone, even for a minute."

"What decent man could credit that someone would do this?"

He almost smiled at her question. She had always had a better opinion of humankind than he. "I didn't believe him, Alafair. I didn't believe what he said about the white-haired man."

She grasped his arms and gave him a shake. "Nobody can look into another's heart and know for sure whether they're telling the truth or not. Except maybe the Lord Jesus himself. And the last time I looked you weren't quite of that ilk. I'll tell you what, and it's the same thing you'd tell the children. The only man who's responsible for this awful act is the man who done it."

"I know," he said, but she knew he didn't believe it.

Well, talk never did feed the bulldog. "You've got to do whatever it takes to see that he pays." Even as she said the words, she was aware that he would not take her advice the way she meant it; to help the law find the murderer. In his mind his guilt would not be expiated until he himself put things right. So be it. Men had their own ways, and she had more faith in Shaw's abilities and good sense than any other man she knew.

Chapter Thirty-three

"He probably transported a mare in heat down here from Okmulgee on the train yesterday. I'm guessing that he holed up with her somewhere until the middle of the night. Then he led that mare onto my place, went into the stable bold as brass and took Red Allen out of his stall. Then he put the two of them together in the exercise corral and let nature take its course."

Scott listened to Peter's rant with one ear while he scooped coffee out of a sack and into the tin pot, then placed the pot on top of the pot-bellied stove that stood in the corner of the Sheriff's Office. He was trying to pay proper attention, he really was. But twenty minutes earlier he had been sound asleep in his warm bed next to his warm wife. That was before his young deputy, Trenton Calder, had pounded on his front door like the devil was after him. Scott had pulled on his clothes in the dark and practically run to the jailhouse after Trent told him that Peter McBride was there in a frightful state of mind, waiting to report a crime.

The sight of his uncle's mottled red face had alarmed Scott. It took a minute for him to understand the gist of the tale, since the old man was beside himself with fury. At first Scott thought someone had killed Peter's valuable walker stallion. Then it seemed the horse had been stolen. Now it was becoming clear that the only thing that had been stolen was Red Allen's vital essence, and the sudden deflation of his alarm left Scott feeling flat.

Not that the theft of Red Allen's vital essence was a small thing. The horse commanded impressive stud fees. But no one was harmed, and it was six o'clock in the morning, and Scott was having a bit of trouble concentrating.

"You're sure it was Doolan?" Scott was staring at the coffee pot as though the intensity of his gaze could make the water boil faster.

"Of course it was Doolan! It hasn't been a week since he was here trying to buy Red Allen's service. And in all my life I never knew a man who so refused to be thwarted. He'll do anything to have his way!"

Scott gave Peter a sidelong squint. "Well, soon as the depot opens up we'll go ask the station master if anybody got off the train recently with a mare in tow. Maybe we'll get lucky and find Doolan and his mare waiting on the platform to catch the ten o'clock back to Okmulgee."

Peter didn't think Scott was taking this as seriously as he should. "He's smarter than that, lad. He's likely to meet the train up or down the line somewhere. Why, I wouldn't put it past him to walk the mare the whole twelve miles between his farm and mine!"

Scott grabbed a cloth, opened the door of the stove's firebox and shoved a couple more pieces of coal into the flames. *Boil, damn you, coffee.* "Well, the culprit wasn't that smart, whoever he was. If he had returned Red Allen to his stall instead of leaving him in the corral after the deed was done, you might have been none the wiser."

"You don't know Doolan, Scott. He wants me to know. He's throwing it in my face. But if we don't catch him before he gets his mare back to his place, he'll cover his tracks and we'll not be able to prove it was actually him who done it." Peter was shifting from one foot to the other with frustration.

Hopping mad, Scott thought. "Uncle Peter, the sun will rise in an hour or so. We can go hunting for him better in the light. Why don't you sit down and have a cup of coffee? Try to calm down. I'll telephone all the train stations between here and

Okmulgee as soon as they open. Trent, walk down to the station right now and have a look for anything suspicious."

Trent was leaning on the wall next to the front door, watching the action with a bemused look on his face. When Scott spoke to him he nodded and pulled on his coat, though it was obvious that the errand was only to make the old fellow happy.

Trent didn't get the chance to leave. He had just put his hand on the doorknob when Kurt Lukenbach's gelding pounded up Main Street and came to a skidding halt in front of the jailhouse.

Chapter Thirty-four

Shaw Tucker's barn was dim and chill. Both the front and back doors were wide open, but it was still some time until sunrise and the two or three kerosene lanterns hanging from hooks on the support beams provided the only light in the cavernous interior. Scott and Peter stood solitary watch, waiting for Kurt to return from town with Mr. Moore, the undertaker.

For the present, Scott had gleaned all the information he could from the scene. He had left Trent in Boynton with instructions to assemble a posse and bring them out here as soon as they could see to make their way. There would be a manhunt this morning after all. Shaw and Alafair he had dismissed to the house with instructions to stay there until called. If he could have persuaded Shaw not to join the posse he would have. Under the circumstances he knew better than to waste his breath.

Crying Blood still reposed in the hay, his slight body covered with a sheet that Scott had turned back from the boy's face. The shaft that killed him had been removed from his chest and carefully wrapped for later scrutiny. His eyes had been closed and his skin had an unnatural, waxy tone. Otherwise, he didn't look dead.

Peter McBride said nothing for a long time, his face as still as the dead youngster's.

Scott wasn't looking at Crying Blood. He was watching his uncle. When he had uncovered the boy's face, Peter's only reaction had been to take a single step forward. That was half an hour ago. Peter had yet to utter a sound or make another move.

When Kurt burst into the office with his terrible tale, Peter appeared to have instantly forgotten about his intruder and insisted in coming along with Scott. He had expressed concern about Shaw's state of mind, about Alafair and the children, worried that a murderer was on the loose.

Natural reactions, Scott thought. But there was nothing natural about this chill, immobile silence that went on for so long.

Scott was just taking a breath to speak when Peter finally broke the spell.

"He's but a child." He uttered the words so softly that Scott barely understood.

"He is that. He told Shaw he was fifteen."

Peter didn't look up. "Shaw said he called himself Crying Blood. Where have I heard that before?"

"Uncle Peter, you heard Shaw say that he thinks this young'un followed him home from your place near Oktaha…"

But Peter interrupted. "You know, Scott, your daddy was my commanding officer when I was a pony soldier at Ft. Yuma."

Scott blinked, wondering what this had to do with anything. "So I've heard…"

"He was just a shavetail, Lt. Tucker, green as grass. But he had more than his share of character. Yes, he did. Still does, too.

"We were all three in his unit, me and Doolan and Hawkins. Quite a bunch of roaring boys, we were, and hardly worth shooting. Always on report, in the stockade or on kitchen duty. One thing about us Irishmen, we knew how to peel potatoes. Paul Tucker took a shine to me for some reason and gave me more of a chance than I deserved. It wasn't the heat or hardship or terror of soldiering that finally made a man out of me, Scott. It was him. See, I'd never had the example of a man with character and once I'd got his measure I didn't like to disappoint him. He invited me to look him up in Arkansas after my hitch was done. He gave me a job in the Tucker family sawmill. T'was he who introduced me to his brother's widow. Changed my life, he did. Made my life."

"Uncle Peter, why are you telling me this now?"

Peter went on as though Scott hadn't spoken. "Doolan and Hawkins came with me to Arkansas. They both worked at the Tucker mill for a while, too. We all ended up out here in the Indian Territory eventually. Me and Hawkins drifted apart even before he took a powder. Then it was just me and Doolan, 'til I learned my old friend hid a cruel heart." He heaved a sigh. "Funny, I haven't thought of Hawkins or Doolan either one in years. And all of a sudden the past looms up like a monster out of the fog."

Scott was feeling oddly alarmed now. "Uncle Peter, what's going on? Do you know who this boy is?"

Peter finally raised his head. Looked Scott in the eye. "I swear to you that I've never seen this child before in my life." He put his hat on. "There's nothing else I can do here. Scott, tell Shaw I had to leave but I'll be back directly as I can."

Scott gaped at the old man's retreating form. "Where are you going?"

Peter didn't look back. "I have business in Okmulgee."

Chapter Thirty-five

The men spread in a line across the field, wary and still, shotguns at the ready. This time the hunt had nothing to do with birds. This time their prey was a man.

Skimmingmoon's bloodhounds were working the field, back and forth in a zigzag pattern, noses to the ground. They had picked up the scent the moment they had been allowed to sniff the bit of rough cloth that Crying Blood had torn from his murderer's body. At the pale beginning of dawn they had led the posse straight through the woods that covered part of Tucker property and several acres of the Day and Eichelberger places. Shaw was impressed by the hounds' skill. They led the hunters directly to three almost invisible campsites. If Scott hadn't sifted through the leaf litter which covered the tiny open areas that the dogs insisted were important, they would never have found the traces of ash from the camouflaged cooking fires. Crying Blood's camps, Shaw wondered, or his murderer's? In whichever case, the murderer had been there as well.

By mid-morning the hounds had led the men completely out of the trees and into a brushy, uncleared field on the Eichelberger property.

As soon as the dogs crossed onto his property, Eichelberger himself had been invited to join the hunting party, which brought their number up to an even ten: Shaw, his brothers James Tucker and Howard McBride, his brother-in-law Jack Cecil, and Kurt had all volunteered immediately. John Lee had started out with them at dawn, but Shaw had sent him back to look after things when it became apparent how far from home the hunt would lead them. Charlie had come along, much against his mother's will. But the boy was a well-grown fourteen and apt to get it into his head to go off half-cocked and do something foolish. Shaw thought it better to have him at his elbow where he could keep an eye on him. Sheriff Scott Tucker had brought his deputy, young Trenton Calder, and of course Mr. Skimmingmoon was out in front with his bloodhounds. Odell Skimmingmoon not only owned the best man-trackers in the county, he was full-blood Muscogee Creek, which Scott reckoned could come in handy on this particular hunt.

The morning was crisp and dry and was shaping up to be sunny and warmer as the day progressed. Shaw was relieved that there had been no mist at dawn.

The hounds were intent as they moved directly across the brushy meadow and into a fallow corn field. The yellowed stalks had long been pulled up, bundled, tied, and stood like an empty village of miniature tepees that ran from the edge of the lea all the way to the road into town. The dogs didn't hesitate when they reached the boundary fence. They crossed the road and moved straight onto the Naylor place.

Naylor joined them as they moved across his farm, then dropped off when they regained the road on the other side of this section. The hounds never paused. They sniffed a few yards up and down the bar ditch then headed due north. The posse was moving fast now, trotting to keep up with the bloodhounds.

There were eating up ground, sticking close beside the graded, graveled highway leading to Lee, Ridge, and Haskell. They passed the Francis Brickworks north of Boynton. One mile. Two. It occurred to Scott that they were now out of his jurisdiction. But as long as the dogs stayed close to the road he continued on, too intrigued to stop now.

At about two miles and a half, the dogs finally veered off and entered the tiny cemetery next to the African Methodist Episcopal Church a few yards off the highway. They had outstripped the posse, all but Skimmingmoon who followed close behind them.

Scott hefted himself over the fence and called out to Skimmingmoon, breathless. "Call 'em off, Odell."

Skimmingmoon didn't look back. He gave a brief, piercing whistle and the dogs turned in their tracks. One by one, the hunters climbed over the fence and gathered around the sheriff in the middle of the cemetery.

Scott pushed his hat back with his thumb, still winded.

Time was I could run for a mile and never break a sweat, he thought, rueful. *I'm going to have to cut back on the biscuits and gravy.*

He eyed his posse members standing in a group around him and assessed each man's condition. Charlie and Trent were still fresh and impatient to get on with it. Stamina. One of the benefits of youth. Kurt, James, and Howard stood quiet and curious to hear what Scott had on his mind. Scott was perversely pleased to see that Jack Cecil looked as ragged out as he was. Eichelberger was older than any of them by two decades, but he was too mean to feel tired, Scott reckoned. Who could tell about Skimmingmoon? He had folded his arms and was awaiting instructions, impassive.

Shaw looked dangerous.

Scott cocked his head and regarded his cousin before he spoke. "Looks to me like he's going toward Haskell."

"We're hot on his heels, Cousin Scott…" Charlie interjected.

Scott responded before the boy could finish the thought. "I'm just a town sheriff, Charlie. I've got no authority out here. I already wired Barger about this mess this morning. It'll be up to him to continue this manhunt."

Trent Calder wasn't willing to wait for permission to carry on. "But the killer's afoot, same as we. Surely we can corner him and hold him 'til the sheriff can get here."

Scott eyed his red-haired deputy. "You'll notice we ain't exactly found him yet, Trent. We could be on his trail until Christmas."

"You think he's headed home, Scott?"

"Wherever that is, Mr. Eichelberger. He ain't headed in the direction of the Goingback place. Not unless his route goes right 'round the world."

Skimmingmoon surprised Scott by offering a comment. "Maybe he ain't the same fellow the boy was hunting out by Oktaha."

"Oh, he's the same one, all right." Shaw's voice held no uncertainty.

Scott turned to look at him. "Shaw, I'm going to leave it up to you. You want to keep after him or shall I leave it to Barger?" They regarded one another squarely for a moment before Scott added, "We don't have much of an idea what's really going on here, Shaw. Could be he's leading us on a wild goose chase, trying to draw us away from home. Could even be there's more than one of them. I'd just as soon y'all not leave your farms unguarded until we sort this out."

Shaw bit his lip, torn between emotion and sense. He flicked a glance toward Charlie. "Let's go back, Scott," he said. "For right now, anyway. Can we see which way he went at least?"

Scott nodded at Skimmingmoon, who signaled the two flop-eared hounds sitting quietly at his feet. The dogs leaped up and pressed their noses to the ground. Back and forth they sniffed, up and down the cemetery, round and round. One examined a weathered tombstone with interest. One concentrated for a moment on the steps of the little white church.

After fifteen minutes both animals returned to their places beside Skimmingmoon. *Sorry*, their droopy expressions said.

"Lost the scent!" Charlie was shocked.

"Look around, boys," Scott said. "Check inside the church. Then we'd best be getting back so I can let Barger know what happened."

James fell in beside Shaw as he moved off to inspect behind the grave markers. "Funny the trail ends in this old cemetery, Shaw." His tone was casual. "Maybe we are chasing a haint after all."

Chapter Thirty-six

"Grace, scoop some dinner into Crook's pan and then let's go see how Buttercup is doing."

It was getting toward afternoon, and even if a vile murder had been committed the chores still had to be done. John Lee, Phoebe, and Zeltha had come over before dawn to stay with the family. Alafair had sent a poke full of clothing along with Ruth, Blanche, and Sophronia when they went to school that morning so they could stay in town at Alice's house until it was safe to come home. Alafair couldn't make the elder girls move into town. Mary refused to leave Kurt and Martha refused, period. Mutiny. Her payback for raising women with their own minds.

When the older girls left for work in the buckboard, carrying the younger girls and their kit in the back, Mary rode shotgun, a loaded twelve-gauge across her knees. Alafair felt all right about that. All of her children learned their way around a firearm as soon as they were old enough.

Alafair had done the children's outdoor chores herself, egg gathering, milking, slopping the pigs, feeding the animals in the barn. John Lee took care of the mules and horses in the stable and fields, leaving Phoebe to the cooking and childcare.

Phoebe and the tots kept under cover in the house. But a three-year-old girl who is used to roaming free doesn't do well after spending hours cooped up inside. By the time the shadows were growing long, Phoebe was ready to throttle her stir-crazy baby sister Grace, and Alafair thought a brief outing might be in order.

Alafair held the skipping little girl by one hand and a rifle in the other as they walked across the yard with Charlie Dog at their side. They went through the fallow garden and through the barn. Crying Blood's body had been removed and now lay in repose at Mr. Moore's mortuary in town. The bloody straw and blankets had been burned. Alafair had placed raw eggs in the corners of the stall where the boy had breathed his last to absorb the lingering taint of evil from the atmosphere.

Buttercup was ecstatic to see them. She was on a lead made from a piece of rope tied to a hook on the back wall, long enough to give her free run of the tool shed, but secure enough to keep her from running out the door when anyone came in. Buttercup was an energetic youngster and chaffed at her imprisonment. Sometimes during the day they could hear her frustrated barking from the house. Alafair felt sorry for her, but not sorry enough to let her loose. She had no desire to be dealing with puppies right now. She ordered Charlie Dog to stay outside, far from the Jezebel within. He meant to obey, but when she opened the door Buttercup's come-hither scent overwhelmed him and he attempted to nose past her. Alafair blocked him with a foot and pushed him out, exasperated, but amused, too. Charlie Dog may have been aged, but there was life in the old boy yet.

Buttercup's greeting was so enthusiastic that she almost knocked them over. Alafair grabbed at the dog's collar before she could send Grace sprawling.

"Down, doggie," Grace scolded, "or you won't get no dinner!"

"Sugar, looks like Buttercup is feeling boisterous today. You put the pail down and stand back over there. I'll feed her."

Always amenable, Grace ran to Shaw's tool table where she had spotted a toy wagon with three wheels that was awaiting repair, while Alafair poured the rest of the scraps into the dented pie pan that served as Buttercup's dinnerware. The dog rolled around on the dirt floor and batted her eyes and Alafair laughed. "It won't do you any good to flirt with me, you hussy. Don't worry, little gal. You'll only have to be in here 'til you lose interest in the fellows. Another couple of days, looks like."

Buttercup's interest was captured by her supper, for her nose was in the pan before Alafair had finished filling it.

Charlie Dog was waiting for them patiently, apparently no longer troubled by amorous feelings, and fell into step as they made their way down the path. It was a beautiful afternoon, sunny and so warm that a sweater was all that was needed. The scent of smoldering hickory wood rising from the smokehouse chimney perfumed the air. The weather was wonderful, but the dry air and clear sky foretold a very cold night. Alafair and Grace walked back to the barn, enjoying the sunshine, in no hurry to get back to making scrapple.

Shaw and the posse had been gone since dawn. If they had run their quarry to ground, Shaw would have sent Charlie back to let her know. If the dogs had not been able to pick up any trail at all they would have been home by now. She both feared and hoped that lack of word meant that they had not been able to catch up with the killer and he would never be seen again.

Charlie Dog took the lead as they walked back toward the house. They hadn't gone ten yards when Alafair saw movement on the front porch. Three men. She seized the back of Grace's coat collar and stopped, wary.

She was just about to sweep Grace up when the little girl cried, "Daddy!"

One of the figures walked down the front steps. She recognized Shaw's stride and felt the tension drop out of her shoulders.

They met at the front gate. Before he spoke, Shaw lifted Grace up over the white picket fence that surrounded the yard. "Alafair, James and Howard and the rest of them went on home, but I asked Scott and Odell Skimmingmoon to stop a spell. Charlie Boy is inside locking up the guns, and Phoebe is whipping us up a bite to eat."

She glanced at the two men sitting side by side on the porch swing, watching them. Scott gave her a jaunty tip of the hat and she waved.

"Did y'all find him?"

"Afraid not." Shaw shook his head, exasperated. "Odell's dogs tracked him all the way to the A.M.E. church north of the brick plant, then lost the scent. He give us the slip somehow."

"North!"

"Yeah. He doesn't seem to be headed back to Oktaha."

"Do y'all think he's gotten away?"

"Who knows? That's why I asked Scott and Odell to stop, so I might could pick their brains and find out what happens next."

Scott and Skimmingmoon rose when she walked up the porch steps ahead of Shaw. They stood aside to allow her to go into the house first.

Chapter Thirty-seven

She picked up granddaughter Zeltha, who had pulled herself up and was standing with her nose pressed up against the screen door, avidly watching her elders on the porch, and carried her into the kitchen where Phoebe was already throwing together ham sandwiches and brewing coffee. Before arranging themselves around the table the men removed their hats and coats and hung them on the coat tree. Except for Skimmingmoon, who kept his hat firmly on his head. Alafair set Grace and Zeltha in the middle of the parlor, easily visible from the kitchen, to play with the doll house Shaw had created for the girls out of an old crate. It didn't bother her that anyone who went from kitchen to parlor would have to step over the children. There wasn't anyone present who hadn't had a lifetime of dealing with children underfoot.

Charlie came in and sat himself down next to his father, confidently counting himself among the men, since he had done a man's job by hunting with the posse. Shaw glanced at him but didn't send him away. Alafair noted that he sat up a little straighter then, but kept quiet rather than take the risk of drawing attention to himself. She poured another mug of coffee and put it down in front of her youngest son. He shot her a grateful look and doctored the bitter stuff with plenty of cream and sugar before he took a slug.

Alafair and Phoebe went about their business, ears stretched, as the men talked.

"Barger will have issued a bulletin by now," Scott was saying, "so I expect most of the law around these parts already have an eye out for any stealthy or suspicious stranger who comes through. I'd like it if I had any kind of description of the culprit to pass on."

"He has white hair," Shaw said.

Scott cocked an eyebrow. "Maybe. I'll report that the victim thought he was being chased by a white-haired man, though we can't know for sure."

"An old fellow, then," Skimmingmoon offered. "Going north."

"Or somebody who had a bad scare, or the fever," Alafair put in.

Charlie leaned forward. "Or a Swede!"

Scott laughed. "Or an albino. What we need to do is start with our mysterious victim before we can figure out anything about our mysterious killer. I have to find out who this boy was and what his story is. Shaw, tell me everything you can remember about him—what he told you about himself, how he talked, any notions you got about him even if you don't see how it can reckon in." He looked back over his shoulder. "Alafair, you too."

Alafair turned away from the cabinet to face them and flung her dishtowel over her shoulder. "Well, he didn't say much when I was there, Scott, though not for lack of me trying to pry it out of him. He did mention that he once had a brother name of Ira who had fell off a mule and broke his neck."

Scott's blue eyes widened. He dug through his coat pockets for a moment before drawing out a small notebook and a stubby pencil. "Well, now, that's a useful piece of information!" He licked the pencil lead and wrote *Ira* on a blank page.

Alafair continued. "He said everybody thought it was an accident that Ira got killed, but he saw a white-haired man spook the mule and then wrench Ira's neck after he fell off. That was why he was after him, for murdering his brother."

Scott didn't look up from his scribbling. "Did he ken why this fellow killed Ira?"

"He didn't rightly know," she said. "He told us that a couple of years ago Ira took him out to look at Mr. McBride's hunk of property and told him they had a right to it since they were Creeks." She glanced at Shaw, expecting him to take over the conversation. He was staring at Scott with his lips firmly closed, allowing her to do the talking.

Scott looked up at her. "Anything else?"

She pondered before finishing. "He said the mule's name was Billy."

For a moment, the only sound in the kitchen was the scratch of Scott's pencil. He raised his head and fastened his gaze on Shaw. His expression was speculative. Shaw's silence had not escaped his notice. "How do you figure the boy ended up here?"

"I don't know," Shaw said.

"He must have followed you home from Uncle Peter's place."

"Seems likely."

"Why you, I wonder, and not James?"

"I don't know," he repeated. "He did mention that he seen me dig up them bones." Scott drew a breath to question him further, but Shaw headed him off. "When him and me were out there in the barn, alone, in the middle of the night, he let slip that he had talked to an *owalu* down by Eufaula and that somebody by the name of Reverend Edmond had tried to make a Christian out of him."

Scott's head bobbed up and down as his pencil flew over the page.

Skimmingmoon perked up. "An *owalu*, you say?"

Shaw nodded. "Maybe he thought he needed a medicine man tell him how to put his brother's spirit to rest. I figure that's why he was dressed like he was."

"He may have dressed like an old-time Creek," Alafair interjected, "but he didn't have an Indian way of talking, Scott. He sounded White."

They were interrupted by a shrill protest from Zeltha over Grace's bossy ways. Phoebe slipped quietly into the parlor and the shrieking stopped abruptly.

Skimmingmoon picked up the conversation. "There's a Creek boarding school over to Eufaula. If he lived there for a spell they would have knocked the Creek out of him." He didn't sound bitter. He was simply stating a fact.

"Crying Blood looked to me be at least half White," Shaw observed.

Skimmingmoon gave him a sharp look. "What did you call him, Shaw?"

"When he talked to me last night, he called himself Crying Blood, Odell. He said, 'I am Crying Blood.'"

"You've heard of him?" Scott asked.

Odell Skimmingmoon lifted his cowboy hat with one hand and scratched his head with the other, his broad, brown face thoughtful. He replaced the hat and readjusted it to his satisfaction before answering. "*Crying blood* ain't a name, Shaw. In our Muscogee way, the Master of Breath created the world to be in perfect balance. But when a great wrong is done, like a death before its time, the world gets out of whack and it's got to be put back in order. If you kill somebody, then his kinfolks are going to be looking to put things right. You spilled blood and that blood cries for…"

Alafair's hand went to her throat. "Revenge?"

Skimmingmoon's eyebrows knit. "No, ma'am, not exactly. Not punishment for a wrong. Not a feud like the White folks do, where y'all kill each other off 'til there ain't nobody left. Once a life has been took for a life, or paid for in some other way, then everything is straight again and the world is back in balance."

Scott slapped down the cover of his little notebook and put it back in his pocket. "Well, I think I've got a place to start, now. I'm going to issue a description of our young victim in case anybody is looking for him. Then I'll telephone the constable over to Eufaula, see if he ever heard of a Reverend Edmond. By hook or crook, we'll get this figured out. Alafair, I'm sorry, but I'll forego your hospitality this afternoon and get back into town. Shaw, it could be that the killer did circle back on us and is still around here, so keep your eyes peeled."

"I intend to."

Scott took his leave and headed toward the stable to retrieve the horse on which he had ridden to the farm early that morning.

Alafair turned toward Skimmingmoon. "Well, Odell, you might as well eat a bite. Phoebe's made enough ham sandwiches to feed the U.S. Army."

After ham sandwiches, quarts of coffee, and sweet potato pie, Odell and Shaw spent a couple of hours following the bloodhounds on a second sweep through the woods behind the house. The hounds followed the same trail they had at dawn, leading them to the edge of Eichelberger's property before Skimmingmoon called them off. Still no trace of Crying Blood's murderer.

Chapter Thirty-eight

Shaw took Grace and Charlie with him when he went to the barn to feed and groom the mares; Charlie for the help and Grace because she insisted. Since she was blowing through the house like a tornado, Alafair was happy to let her go with her father.

And Shaw was glad for her bright, uncomplicated company. He took her hand as he passed back and forth through the barn, keeping the child close to his side as he methodically checked each stall one by one, the occupied and the unoccupied, reassuring himself that the fugitive had not doubled back on the posse and made his way back here. The yellow shepherd trotted behind, untroubled. Comforted by Charlie Dog's attitude, he left Grace to play with the barn cats while he worked.

Shaw could see out of the corner of his eye that Charlie was shadowing him as he went about mucking out stalls. The boy was keeping his distance, casually attending to his own chores. But whenever Shaw looked directly at him his gaze would drop.

Shaw figured that Alafair had put Charlie up to hovering about, keeping an eye on him, which he found amusing. Charlie was not a subtle spy.

Still, Shaw was grateful for help with the animals this evening. He was constantly distracted by every unusual mark in the dust, every suspicious twig or stone, every flash of color. Had that rake been moved? He didn't remember that feed sack being in just that spot.

He found himself facing a corner of the stable with a half-full bucket of oats in his hand, staring at a long scratch in the wall that resembled the letter "c," not entirely sure how he had come to be standing there.

He glanced back over his shoulder to see Charlie in the near stall, staring at him over the back of one of the pregnant mares.

"What do you see, Daddy?"

Shaw turned around and walked back toward him. "Nothing, son. I just can't get my head to work today." He dumped the oats into the feed box of one of the occupied stalls.

"I can't stop thinking about the murder, either!" Charlie took his father's statement as permission to broach the subject. He didn't sound frightened. The grisly death and hunt for a mysterious and ghostly killer was more exciting than horrifying to a fourteen-year-old who hadn't actually seen either. "Do you think he's gone, Daddy?"

Shaw rubbed the ears of Alafair's riding mare, Missy, as she nosed her feed. "Son, I'm getting mighty tired of worrying over manhunts and Crying Blood and all of it. All I want is to have some supper and a night's sleep and go to pondering on the problem again in the morning. Now, if you've finished brushing that mare, let's you and me take Grace back up to the house. Then we'll go around while there's still daylight and see that all the outbuildings are locked up tight for the night. That way when your ma starts pumping you for information tonight, you can tell her that Daddy was calm and thinking straight." He gave his son an ironic quirk of a smile and Charlie grinned, caught.

Shaw turned toward the corner where the barn cats liked to lounge. "Come on, honey." But where was Grace? He straightened. Grace had been there half a minute before. His radar eye zoomed in on the girl's figure, hunkered down with her back to her father, in the corner of the empty stall where Crying Blood had died not twenty-four hours before. It had been cleaned out down to the bare clay floor, except for the four raw eggs Alafair had placed in the corners that morning.

"Grace!" Shaw's tone was sharp and Grace swiveled around to look at him, wide eyed. *Have I done something wrong,* her expression said?

"Get out of there, sugar, leave them eggs along. That's no place to be playing." Grace recognized her father's tone. Argument would avail her nothing. She assumed a put-upon expression, but stood and stuffed something into the pocket of her little cotton coat before she trotted to Shaw's side,

"What you got there, cookie?" He had pulled enough disgusting things out of children's pockets to make him wary. "Show me."

Grace's pique disappeared as she dug into her pocket, eager to show him her treasure.

It looked like a piece of green rope, and his eyebrows knit. Grace held it up for him to see.

It was looking at him.

His breath caught and he took a step back.

Grace was still standing there holding her hand out, when Charlie walked up behind her, interested enough in his sister's find that he didn't notice that all the color had drained out of Shaw's face. "It's a snake! Where'd you find a snake in this weather, dinky?" Grace had never been afraid of creepy-crawly things, a useful trait for a farm girl.

She pointed with her free hand. "In that stall yonder. Look, Daddy, she's cold. Can I keep her? "

Charlie bent down and allowed the snake to slide out of Grace's grip and wind around his hand. He brought it up to his face for a closer look. "Well, I'll be jiggered! It's naught but a little old garter snake. What's she doing gadding about at this time of year! She ought to be snuggled up all warm in her den with all her garter snake friends."

"Her name is Cinda," Grace informed him.

Charlie snorted. "Is it, now? Snakes like to eat eggs, you know, but them eggs that Mama put out would be a mighty ambitious meal for this little critter."

Grace threw her arms around Shaw's knees. "Can I keep her, Daddy?'

The snake was about a foot long and less than the diameter of a finger. From its perch on Charlie's hand it lifted its oval head, and two yellowish eyes regarded Shaw dispassionately. His instinct was to scoop up his girl and get out of there as fast as he could go. He put his hand on Grace's head and struggled to get hold of himself. When he spoke, he was surprised that his voice sounded as calm as it did. "No, sugar. A snake shouldn't be about in this cold. Charlie, you and Grace take that critter outside and let it go so it can find its family and sleep the winter away. Then go back to the house," he called to their backs as they moved to do his bidding. "Tell your mama I'll be in directly."

The instant the children were out the barn door he rushed to the empty stall. But there was nothing to see but four speckled brown eggs, one in each corner. He put his hand in his pocket to reassure himself that the snake bone necklace was still there.

Shaw was locking the smokehouse door when he heard Alafair call the children for supper. He glanced to the west. The sky was clear, with only a few stray clouds already stained orange by a sun not more than a finger-width above the horizon. The sun would be down in less than twenty minutes. Shaw withdrew his watch from his coat pocket and flipped open the cover. Five o'clock. He had spent the rest of the afternoon and evening trying his hardest to concentrate on feeding the livestock. To no avail. He and Kurt had managed to fill the stock feeders in the back pasture, but Shaw couldn't keep his mind on his business. He had nearly forgotten his odd encounter with a snake just before he found the bones. And now his fey little daughter had also discovered a snake in November, a creature who shouldn't be anywhere at all, in a place where a boy had just died.

He had almost fashioned a logical story in his head about this young, English-speaking, Creek man who had followed him home in hopes of finding the white-haired man who had shot his relative. But ghosts calling his name—*why had he been so reluctant to tell Scott about that?*—and snake vertebrae necklaces, and snakes showing up where they had no reason to be, had knocked all the logic out of the situation for him. Who was sending those snakes and what were they trying to tell him? Something about the murderer? How in the name of everything holy could a flesh and blood man have eluded those bloodhounds. Could he fly?

Shaw shook his head to dislodge the disturbing thought. No, he had seen the weapon that killed Crying Blood with his own eyes. A human hand had wielded it, no supernatural creature.

Chapter Thirty-nine

Alafair met him on the back porch when he got back to the house. "Scott's back. He's in the parlor," she said.

Shaw's eyebrows lifted. Scott was a close relative. That he was waiting in the parlor and not having supper in the kitchen with the rest of the family meant he was bearing official news.

"He didn't tell me anything." Alafair answered the question in his eyes as she took his coat.

Shaw brushed past her into the house. Charlie was on his heels, but Alafair was too quick for him and grabbed his arm. His face fell.

She tried not to smile. "You wash up, Charlie-boy. Talk to Crook. He's lonely. Daddy'll let us know what's up directly."

Scott stood up when Shaw came into the parlor and immediately launched into his topic. "I've been talking to Sheriff Barger on the telephone. I told him about our manhunt, the Reverend Edmond and all. He was right interested. And as it turns out he had a bunch of interesting information for me, too."

They sat down across from one another, both men on the edge of their seats. Scott continued. "First of all, the skull you found had a slug rattling around inside. So our slender friend was definitely murdered. Second, Deputy Morgan has been asking around Oktaha about the Goingbacks. He found out that there was a tale going around some years ago that Roane Hawkins may have had a hand in the death of his wife's first husband.

Maybe so he could marry the widow and get his hands on the land. Nothing was ever proven, of course. Then when Hawkins took a powder and Lucretia sold the land to Uncle Peter and left, that pretty much ended the rumors."

"I'll tell you what, Scott, ever since I heard that Hawkins disappeared I've had it in my head that the skeleton is Roane Hawkins himself."

"No. Whoever ended up in the ground it wasn't Hawkins. According to the doctor in Muskogee who examined him, it seems the bony *hombre* in the grave you found was an Indian."

Shaw was startled. "How could he tell?"

Scott shrugged. "Something about the shape of the skull. It's all too modern and scientific for the likes of me. Not only was he Indian, but judging by his teeth and bones the doctor thinks he was young." Shaw opened his mouth to speak but Scott held up a finger and continued. "And you were right that he was wearing cavalry boots."

"An Indian in cavalry boots? Somebody Roane Hawkins knew from when he was in the Army?"

"That was thirty years earlier. Slim is too young to have been in the Army with Hawkins and Uncle Peter, I think."

Shaw hesitated before he responded. "Well, Cousin, I don't know have enough information to guess who the skeleton used to be, but as for Crying Blood, consider this. Papa said that Hawkins and Lucretia Goingback had a couple of children of their own…"

Scott completed his sentence for him. "…who got taken away from her by the B.I.A."

But Shaw wasn't quite done. "…to an Indian school…"

The sheriff considered this before he finished. "…in Eufaula?" He leaned back in his chair and stretched his arms along the rests. "I don't know, Shaw. Just before I came I asked Kate Smith at the telephone exchange to ring up the boarding school out there. They told me that a Reverend Edmond used to work there years ago. He still pastors a church in Eufaula. But the lady I spoke with said she didn't remember any children by the name of Hawkins living at the school. I'm planning on traveling over there in the morning to see if I can find this Edmond and see if he can tell me anything about our dead boy. If I need to, I'll stop by the boarding school and have a look at their records. I came by tonight to ask if you want to go with me."

"What for?"

Scott shrugged. "I figured you'd be interested, considering how the young'un died."

Shaw chewed thoughtfully on his bottom lip before he answered. "Unless you need me for a second pair of ears I'd better stay around home. Are you taking the train?"

"No. It'd take me all day to ride up north to Muskogee on the train then wait around and catch the connection south to Eufaula, do my business, and same thing back. Jack Cecil offered to let me drive down there in his Ford."

"What, that Model T he got last year? That's a sturdier automobile than most I've seen, but I've got to tell you if it was to rain tomorrow it'd be faster for you to walk to Eufaula."

Scott laughed. "I know it. It don't look like rain, though, and that road south is in pretty good shape last I rode it."

"Good luck, then."

"I'll go with you." At the interruption Shaw and Scott twisted in their chairs. Alafair was standing in the kitchen door. Neither man was surprised to see her.

"I declare, Alafair," Scott said. "Ever since you went up to your sister's in Enid a while back you've just took it into your head to go gallivanting all over the state!"

She reddened. "Well, if Shaw isn't going, I'd like to, if I won't be in the way. After all, I'd like to find out about that poor child as much as anybody. The younger children are in town with Alice and Grace can stay over at Phoebe's. Martha and Mary can do for you fellows for a day, Shaw."

Scott directed his answer at Shaw. "It's all right with me if she wants to go. I've found her to be a good judge of character and fairly observant. Besides, I could use the company on that long drive." His gaze shifted back to Alafair. "I expect you won't be in the way as long as you let me do the talking."

She gave Shaw a questioning look. He was not one to try and tell her what to do and she was not much of an obeyer if he did. But if he had objections Scott would not overrule him. An anxious moment passed before he responded.

"I think that's a good idea."

Her eyebrows shot up. She had expected grudging acquiescence from him at best. What was he thinking? His expression was so calculating that she almost reconsidered. Was he trying to get her out of the way for some reason? But her desire to meet the Reverend Edmond and perhaps to see from where Crying Blood had sprung overcame her misgivings.

"All right, then," Scott said. "If you want to go, be at the jailhouse at dawn and we'll hit the trail."

She nodded. "Come on into the kitchen, then, boys. Supper's on the table."

Chapter Forty

Just before dawn, after morning chores were done, so many family members had business in town that Shaw had to ferry them all in the buckboard, the only vehicle on the farm that was big enough to hold everyone at once. The first stop was at Phoebe's house on the adjoining farm to drop off Grace. Then into Boynton to leave Mary at the schoolhouse to prepare her classroom, Charlie and Martha at Alice's house, where the three younger girls had already spent the night. The plan was that when time came, the children would walk to school together and Martha would go to work at the bank. Alafair was pretty sure that as soon as the parents were out of sight, Martha would walk downtown to Streeter McCoy's apartment upstairs over his business office and make breakfast for her intended. As long as Martha didn't become an object of gossip Alafair didn't care. Martha was twenty-four years old after all, and the young people would be married in a few months anyway.

Once the children were distributed, Alafair and Shaw drove to the jailhouse. Jack Cecil's black Model T Ford was already parked next to the boardwalk. Shaw pulled the wagon up next to the automobile and threw the reins over the hitching post in front of the building.

It was amazing to Alafair how autos had proliferated around town in just the last couple of years. It wasn't so long ago that an automobile chugging down Main Street was an occasion for wonder, drawing people out of stores to gawk and causing horses to shy. Now, no one raised an eyebrow and most animals were inured to the noisy machines. In fact, there were usually as many cars as buggies parked on the street when the shops were open.

Shaw's brother-in-law Jack Cecil was his older sister Josie's husband. Jack was Vice President of the First National Bank of Boynton, a large, sleek, good-natured man who was not just a shrewd businessman but a kind and generous human being. One had to be careful about expressing a wish or desire in Jack's presence, for Jack would see that it was fulfilled whether you really wanted him to or not. Only months before, Scott had approached the town council about acquiring an automobile for official business. When the council balked Jack had offered his own vehicle for Scott to use whenever he needed it. Alafair expected that Scott found reasons to need it. He was quite an enthusiastic driver.

They left town, heading south just as the sun crowned the horizon. It was a cold, cloudless morning, good for traveling. Alafair was bundled up to her eyes in a duster, boots, gloves, and a stiff-brimmed, felt hat secured to her head with a wool scarf. Shaw couldn't help but smile as they rattled out of town over Boynton's red brick streets, Alafair bolt upright in the seat next to Scott, hanging on to the door frame for dear life. When she got home this evening she was going to be wind-blown, gritty, bumped, and jostled to within an inch of her life. *She always has been up for an adventure*, he thought.

And she was out of the way.

He turned his buckboard in the opposite direction out of town, toward home. Before he reached the turnoff that led west, he steered the team up the long driveway of his parents' two story, dove-grey farmhouse.

His mother was in the dining room. She was sitting at the big mahogany table with several other ladies of a certain age, all eating biscuits and honey and chattering like birds. He beckoned to her from the parlor door and she rose to meet him in the foyer, drawing the stained glass French doors closed behind her.

He snatched his hat off and pressed it to his chest. "Sorry to bother you, Ma."

"I'm always glad to see you, sugar. Today's my Bible study breakfast but we ain't quite got started yet. Come on in and have a bite. Say howdy to the ladies."

"I'm afraid I'll have to forego that pleasure today, ma'am. I was just wanting to have a word with Papa."

Sally's expression sharpened. "He's not here, son. Does this have something to do with that poor child who got murdered out to your place?"

"It does."

"Honey, he's not back from Okmulgee yet."

Shaw looked startled. "He's not?"

"Well, no. After he got home from your place yesterday morning and told me what happened, he said that Scott wouldn't have time to be thinking about his piddling problem. I went straight over to your house to help Alafair for a spell, but your Papa told me that he had business in Okmulgee that couldn't wait and lit out. I figured he'd determined to either go to the law in Okmulgee or have it out with Doolan directly. Said he'd be back in a day or two. What's going on, Shaw?"

"I haven't seen him since that morning. Scott said he was acting funny before he left, talking about him and Hawkins and Doolan being in the Army. Seems odd he'd take off like that."

"It's an odd situation, son, the business with Doolan and the business out at Hawkins' old place both happening at once. It probably got him to reminiscing. As for him going after Doolan when he did, I expect that since Papa didn't know who the boy was he didn't figure there was anything he could do to help you. And he didn't want to pester Scott with his troubles."

Shaw looked doubtful, but he said, "That's more than likely it. Well, I guess I'll just wait 'til he gets home to talk to him, then. You go on back to your guests, Mama. I'll see you later."

Sally hesitated, considering whether to probe further. She knew her son well enough to realize that this murder of a young person right under his nose would be eating at him terribly. But she also knew that platitudes weren't going to help him. At the moment that was all she could offer. Best to let him be. She squeezed his arm. "Me and Papa will come out to see you after he gets back from Okmulgee."

He gave her a pale smile. "I'd like that."

She left him in the foyer, and he turned to leave. He was just raising his hat to his head when his eye lit on the oval portrait of his mother and stepfather, hanging beside the front door. He knew the picture well. They were sitting side by side staring at the camera, both looking slightly amused by the whole thing. His mother was dressed in the black, high-necked, mutton-sleeved dress that she had worn for every dressy occasion he could remember, until it literally fell apart on her. Peter was looking sharp in a three-piece suit, celluloid collar, and a cravat with a pearl tie pin. His hair was combed straight back, shiny with pomade. The portrait was made over a dozen years before, but even then Peter's thick mane was white as snow.

Shaw looked down at the floor, feeling slightly ill. It absolutely could not be. Even if Peter was the white-haired man Crying Blood was looking for, he was not the boy's murderer. But ever since this nightmare began Shaw had had an uncomfortable suspicion that Peter McBride knew more about what was happening than he let on.

He set his hat firmly on his head. He couldn't wait. Not for Peter, not for Scott, not for Barger. He couldn't say exactly why but he knew this ghost was his to lay down. Alafair was not here to talk sense into him. Now was the time to do it.

Shaw drove the buckboard directly into the barn, unhitched and corralled the mules, and saddled his black mare, Hannah. He strapped on his sidearm, slid his rifle into its holster on the saddle and slipped a couple of boxes of cartridges into the saddlebag. A blanket roll, matches, knife, a tarp, Gee Dub's flashlight, a small tin bucket and spoon. He wrapped some leftover cornbread and a hunk of cheese in some butcher paper, a handful of cracklins, and one of Alafair's cast iron skillets, a small one with feet, called a *spider,* especially for cooking over a campfire.

He pulled a clean, white, muslin, draw-string bag out of the bottom drawer of the sideboard, filled it with a couple of scoops of coarse salt and took it with him to the smokehouse. He picked a fatty piece of barely smoked pork loin, sawed off a hunk and put it into the bag of salt along with several rashers of bacon. He locked the smokehouse door behind him and walked back to the barn, where he mounted up and rode out to the pasture to find Kurt.

Chapter Forty-one

The day was bright and cool with a whisper of breeze out of the north. Not a cloud marred the blue November sky. The road was dry but not too dusty, since it had been recently graded and oiled for some distance outside of Boynton. The first three miles of the trip were fast and smooth and Alafair was thinking that automobile travel was a mighty pleasant way to go. As they got further from town she modified her opinion. The country highway was worn into deep ruts by heavily laden wagons and trucks and pocked with potholes of every imaginable size, shape, and depth. Scott had to slow down to a crawl to get over the bumps and ridges he couldn't avoid by driving around them, sometimes with two wheels on the road and two in a weedy ditch or on the brushy shoulder.

Eufaula was less than twenty-five miles south and a bit east of Boynton as the crow flies. But no crow ever flew the zig-zag route Scott and Alafair had to drive in order to get from where they were to where they wanted to be. They were able to drive pretty much straight south for ten miles or so and make good time, too, if you didn't count those three miles between Boynton and Council Hill where the road dwindled down to nothing more than two bare dirt wagon wheel gouges in the middle of what looked like a wide footpath. Things improved between Council Hill and Hitchita, except for the fact that now the road was leading them west. But Scott assured Alafair that once they got to

Hitchita they would be able to pick up a fair route straight east to Checotah, then a really good road due south into Eufaula.

Alafair had ridden in automobiles before, but always in town. She had certainly never done any cross-country travel in one. It was interesting, she thought, even if somewhat frightening. Especially when they came upon a straight and relatively smooth stretch of road and Scott accelerated to a heart-pounding twenty-five, even thirty, miles an hour. As bumpy as it sometimes was, she found that she was enjoying her auto trip much more than she would have if they had been making this long trip in a horse-drawn conveyance.

The Model T performed like a champion. They only had one flat tire on the way down, just outside of Hitchita. Scott pulled off the road and rummaged around in the back of the auto, mumbling to himself and making a lot of clanking noises. Alafair sat where she was, staring straight ahead and trying not to think about the fact that they were currently stranded in a vast, rolling, brushy, tree-strewn wilderness in the middle of she-knew-not-where.

Eventually the mumbling and rattling stopped and the auto began to jostle. Her curiosity got the better of her. She opened the door and stepped out to see the sheriff squatting next to the passenger-side back tire, cramming a pile of thick wood blocks under the frame.

She was briefly distracted by how good it felt to stand up and stretched until her spine cracked. She made a circuit around the Ford, stamping the blood back into her feet and legs, enjoying the clean, fresh breeze in her face. When she made it back around to Scott he was wrestling off the tire cover to expose the inner tube. For a moment the two of them regarded the pathetic state of the deflated piece of black rubber tubing sagging from the wheel. Alafair suffered a sudden flashback to the past week and all the hours she had spent stuffing meat into miles of sausage casing.

"Is there anything I can do to help you?" she asked.

He pointed to the little pile of tools and equipment he had amassed at his side. "You can hand me that pump. "

He took it from her, attached the hose to the valve stem, stood and began pumping vigorously. He chatted as he pumped. "I didn't see what we run over that poked a hole in us, did you? I hope I can find this puncture and patch it easy. I only brung three extra tubes with me. That's all Jack had on him and I didn't have time to stock up on any more beforehand." He stopped and listened for a hiss. When none was forthcoming, he retrieved a canteen from his accoutrements, wet down the half-inflated tube and squatted down to closely eyeball the offending tire.

"There it is!" He pointed to a couple of innocuous-looking bubbles on the rubber surface. Alafair took one of the square rubber patches from the package and helped Scott apply the adhesive and position it over the puncture. When he was satisfied that there were no more leaks, Scott shook a handful of talcum powder from the can into his palm and began to spread a thin coat over the deflated tube. He smacked his hands together, raising a cloud of talc, before he seized the air pump and began fully inflating the tube.

Alafair leaned up against a fence post and watched the up-and-down motion of his arms for a long moment. "Why'd you agree to let me come along?"

Scott glanced up at her. "Why'd you want to come?"

"Because of that boy," she said. "I feel bad about that boy. He was somebody's child. It could be that you'll find his mama today and break her heart. But what if there ain't no mama nor daddy or no one at all? Every hurt child deserves to be cared for and every dead one deserves to be mourned. I want to do the best I can for him, even now that it's too late."

Scott didn't look up again. "I had the same thought." He unscrewed the hose from the tire valve and checked the wing-bolts to make sure they were tight before he added. "Besides, maybe I'll find his mama, like you said. And if you was there, that'd be nice for her."

After he had manhandled the cover back over the tube and gotten his equipment stowed away, they climbed back into the car and pulled out onto the road. The whole enterprise had taken less than twenty minutes.

They mostly made small talk as they drove east. Alafair laughed at Scott's description of his wife Hattie's hissy-fit when she found out their youngest had eaten every morsel of the apple-sauce cake she had made for the church pot-luck on Wednesday night. Alafair relayed her husband's mix of delight and dismay that he had just sold four young mules to the Farmers' Co-op and had to have them trained and broken to harness by the beginning of the year.

"Why do you expect Shaw didn't want to come today, Alafair?"

"Well, like he said, he's right busy lately and all this to-do on top of the butchering has put him behind."

"He was willing enough for you to come."

They barely skirted a pothole and Alafair grabbed the door frame to keep her head from bouncing into the convertible roof. "I expect he'll grill me like a fish when I get home."

Scott smiled. "You mean you're his spy?"

"I reckon."

Scott watched the road for a mile or so while Alafair watched him. She could practically see him arranging his next comment in his head.

He finally put it to her. "Does Shaw know something about this murder that he ain't telling me, Alafair?"

Aha! Her presence on this trip wasn't entirely due to Scott's compassion for the bereaved. "You think he's keeping something from you?"

"I think he's been acting mighty odd."

For an instant Alafair pondered whether or not to tell Scott about Shaw's ghost. Scott was family after all, and it wasn't as though Shaw had done something wrong. If it had been one of the children in question Alafair wouldn't have hesitated to tell Scott everything. But Shaw was a different story. *If he's not eager for folks to know what he saw,* she thought, *he must have some reason that makes sense to him.* She was far too loyal to try and second-guess him.

"You'd be acting odd too," she said, "if some kid followed you home from a hunting trip and then got himself speared to death in your barn."

Scott's mouth twisted, in a grimace or a smile, Alafair couldn't tell. "You're right there. I just don't want him to get into trouble. Especially if there's something I can do to help."

Alafair was touched that he put it like that. "Don't worry, Scott. You know Shaw. He'd rather eat dirt than not do the right thing. Besides, I'd never let him get into trouble if I could help it."

Now Scott did smile. "That's why God gave us men wives, Alafair, to keep us on the straight and narrow. You just make sure he don't end up eating dirt."

Chapter Forty-two

When they finally reached the sizable town of Checotah, they stopped for a break. They needed it. It felt to Alafair like God had created a crazy quilt out of the country as they travelled east. Miles of flat, straight road through endless cotton fields and large cattle ranches would give way to long, nerve-wracking climbs and roads that seemed to twist in knots through forested hills. Then just as she would decide that the Ford wasn't going to make it and they'd never get out of this alive, they would break out into the open, coast down a long incline, and off they'd go, straight as a plumb line through cultivated fields.

After a cup of coffee and the use of a kind hotelier's facilities, Scott was able to locate a gasoline pump in front of a livery/blacksmith/garage and top off the Ford's gas tank, pleased that he was able to forestall the use of the emergency gasoline he had brought along in a large metal can strapped to the car above the tail bumper.

Immediately past the MK&T switch station they caught the old Ozark Trail south. The country was beautiful, the well kept and well travelled highway cutting through impressive stands of tall hardwood. Occasionally the winter-bare branches almost met over their heads. Smaller, lace-branched redbud trees dotted the sides of the road, reaching for the sunny open spaces unoccupied by their taller neighbors. *This must be an eye-popping drive in the spring,* Alafair thought.

"Are we going to go through Oktaha?" Alafair had to raise her voice to make herself heard over the wind and engine noise.

"No. It's close, though." Scott pointed without taking his eyes off the road. "It's just that way, about five miles due west. This is all Creek Nation allotment land on either side of the highway."

The highway opened up, bare, straight, and flat again, just before they crossed the long, iron-girded bridge over the North Fork of the Canadian River. This time of year the river itself was little more than a sluggish red stream that meandered aimlessly down the middle of its wide bed. Alafair craned her neck to see over the bridge's rails as they crossed. When she looked up on the other side she could see Eufaula in the distance.

Scott's plan was to stop at any likely business to ask for directions to Foley Street, but that became unnecessary when they spotted the Foley Hotel occupying pride of place right in the center of Main, marking the corner of its namesake street.

Past First Street, Foley quickly turned into a tree-lined residential area. Scott crossed Second Street before pulling up in front of a small, white, clapboard house surrounded by a wrought-iron fence and turned off the engine.

Neither moved, momentarily overcome by the sudden peace that came with the cessation of the Ford's noise and vibration.

Alafair was the first to break the silence. "Law! I feel like I've been dragged through a briar patch by the big toe! I hate to think that we have to make that same trip backwards so we can get home!"

Scott suppressed an urge to yawn. "Well, we'd best get to it." He reached over the seat back and retrieved a brown leather grip from the floorboard.

"What you got in there?" Alafair asked. She had spied the grip on the floor when she was fetching tools for Scott to repair the punctured tire.

He tossed her a glance over his shoulder before he stepped out of the Ford. "Something I hope will help the Reverend clear this mess up for us."

Chapter Forty-three

Gee Dub Tucker had walked about a half a mile from the Boynton train station through town and down the dirt road leading toward home by the time his sisters Martha and Mary pulled up beside him in their buggy. He tossed his duffle in the back, hauled himself up beside Mary on the bench and gave each of them a brief hug, gratified in spite of himself at their expressions of delight at seeing him.

"I declare, Gee," Mary said. "We didn't expect you home for another week at least! If we'd known you meant to come in today, somebody could have met you at the station."

"I just took a notion. I was supposed to have a field class today, but the instructor cancelled it and I don't have another class until Monday afternoon. Besides, Ruth wrote me about the excitement y'all been having around here, so I decided I'd see for myself what was going on. Did Dad catch the tramp who carved a hunk out of his porker?" He hesitated, nodded at the shotgun in its holder on the dash in front of Mary. "You expecting to fend off bandits between here and Boynton?"

Martha snapped the reins and the horse picked up speed, jarring Gee Dub's spine as the buggy bounced down the rutted road. "Oh, it's just awful what happened. The thief was just a boy. Daddy trussed him up in the barn until he could take him in to Scott the next morning, but during the night somebody broke into the barn and ran him through with a spear."

She glanced across Mary at Gee Dub, gaging his reaction to her news. He was not one to waste words in pointless exclamation, but his dark eyes were regarding her intently, his face still and one eyebrow raised. The two women took turns filling him in on the details: Crook's broken leg, the murder of Crying Blood, the banishment of their younger sisters to town, their mother's trip with Cousin Scott to find the Reverend Edmond in Eufaula. Martha was finishing the tale just as she pulled up in front of the barbed-wire gate that marked the entrance to the Tucker farm.

Gee Dub climbed down, swung the gate open and stood waiting until she had driven the buggy through, then closed and secured the gate again. He trudged up to where she had halted to wait for him, lifted himself back into the seat and readjusted his cap before he looked at his sister and spoke. "How's Dad taking all this?"

It was Mary who answered. "Not so good. He's blaming himself for leaving the boy alone for a few minutes. Long enough for someone to creep in and kill him. I think he's pretty riled that nobody can seem to find a trace of the killer. I'm sure glad you're here, Gee. It'll perk Daddy up considerably to see you."

Martha reined in front of the house to deposit her passengers before driving the buggy to the barn, but no one had time to alight before Kurt trotted around the side of the house, his blue eyes crinkled with worry, and waved his arm over his head to get their attention.

Gee Dub paused with one foot hovering in the air between buggy and ground. His eye went immediately to the holster on Kurt's hip. Guns everywhere. The situation was far more serious than he had imagined earlier that morning when he had boarded the train in Stillwater to come home.

Kurt came to a halt next to the passenger side and reached across Gee Dub to take Mary's hand. But when he spoke it was to his future brother-in-law. "Gee Dub, I am glad you are home. Miz Tucker is gone with the sheriff to Eufaula, and I did not know what I should do. No one is here and I did not want to leave the farm, but when Charlie come home from school a while ago I sent him to John Lee to talk with him."

"Kurt!" Mary interrupted his narrative. "What's going on? Where's Daddy?"

Kurt's gaze switched from Gee Dub's face to Mary's. "He is not here, *Leibling*. He left on horseback a few hours ago and told me to stay here for you and Miz Tucker. I think he is going to try and find the man who murdered Crying Blood."

The siblings piled out of the buggy and stood together with Kurt in a tight bunch, silent for a moment while each tried to make his or her own sense out of this development. Gee Dub looked over at Martha, the eldest, who for all of his life had been the natural chief of the numerous tribe of Tucker children.

She, however, was looking at him.

Two pairs of dark eyes locked, the oldest daughter's and the oldest son's. Martha spoke first. "Mama and Scott won't be back until this evening. When she gets home and hears what Daddy's done she'll have a conniption."

"She'll grab a firearm and go after him, I know she will!" Mary struggled not to sound as panicky as she felt. "Kurt, did Daddy tell you where he plans to find this killer?"

"He would not tell me much, but that I should let Miz Tucker know and he expected to be gone for a day or two."

Gee Dub suddenly knew the answer as surely as if he had been told. "He's going back to Oktaha."

Martha looked up at her younger brother, now a head taller than she, and nodded. "You've been there. You know where he's headed. Go get him, Gee. Bring him back here before Mama lights out after him."

"Kurt, would you saddle up Penny for me? Then ride over to John Lee's and let him know what's happening. Martha and Mary, I reckon if y'all stay in the house with that shotgun 'til one of the fellows gets back here, you can blow the head off of anybody who tries to sneak up on you." Gee Dub was striding across the yard by this time, his sisters on his heels. Kurt was half-way to the barn. Gee Dub began to shuck off his coat. "Just let me get out of these college duds."

"I'll load your Winchester," Mary said to his back as he crashed into the house.

Chapter Forty-four

Alafair and Scott had removed their long, linen dusters and left them in the back of the auto before they mounted the porch of the little frame house and knocked on the door. Alafair observed that Scott had dressed as carefully as she in order to call on the Reverend. She had on the brand new plum-colored dress and hat that Martha had bought for her, over her objections, on their recent trip to visit relatives in Enid. Scott was wearing his good black three-piece suit and the black felt fedora he only removed from its hat box in the top of his closet for special occasions. She expected that the two of them had different reasons for taking care with their wardrobe, though. He was making an official visit as a representative of the law. She had dressed to call on the bereaved.

The man who answered the door was dressed to receive company, in a dark suit and neatly bowed string tie.

"Reverend Edmond?" Scott asked.

The man gave them a tired once-over from behind the screen door. "Yessir. Are you Sheriff Tucker from over to Boynton?"

Scott's eyebrows peaked. "Yes sir. I'm Scott Tucker and this here is Miz Shaw Tucker, wife to my cousin. You were expecting me?"

"Come in." The reverend pushed open the screen and stood aside to allow them to enter. Alafair examined the parlor while the reverend took Scott's hat and ushered them to two padded armchairs positioned before a white-manteld fireplace. Reverend Edmond moved a painted side chair from under the window to the center of the room for himself. The parlor was small, but nicely furnished and well-kept, with crocheted doilies and knick knacks scattered about on top of the mantle and the Queen Anne side tables. Pictures with religious themes hung from wires on the floral-papered walls; Jesus feeding the multitudes at the Sermon on the Mount, Jesus walking on the water, an angel ushering two small children across a precarious bridge. No Mrs. Edmond had yet appeared, but evidence of her hand was everywhere in this room.

When they were seated and introductions made, the Reverend answered Scott's question as though there had been no pause. "Yes, sir, I figured you'd be by sometime today. My neighbor, Glenna Bettmann, runs the telephone exchange here in Eufaula. She stopped by yesterday evening and told me that she had spoke with the telephone operator up there."

Scott nodded, unsurprised. "Yes, that's how I found out where you live. I expect she told you why we was coming."

"She said something about a young stranger who had got killed up that way, and because he had mentioned my name you figured I know who he is."

"That's about right, Reverend. I notice that you don't seem overcurious about this peculiar situation. Could it be you already have an idea who our unknown victim is?"

The Reverend smiled at this. Not a happy smile, either. "Truth is I don't know, Sheriff. But I have a fear that it may be my son…"

"Your son?" Alafair couldn't help her exclamation. She hadn't anticipated this possibility at all.

Reverend Edmond blinked at her as though he had forgotten she was there before he turned back to Scott and finished his sentence. "…who ran away from home more than two years ago, when he was thirteen. Though what he could have been doing up around Boynton, I don't know."

Scott picked the leather grip up off the floor next to his feet and placed it across his lap. "Well, Reverend, I don't know anything about your son or whether our murder victim is him. I only know that before he died this young fellow mentioned your name to my cousin. Said that you tried to make a Christian out of him."

A look of cautious relief passed over the Reverend's face. "That could be any one of a bunch of boys. I've been pastoring here in Eufaula for near to twenty years, first at the Indian school then at the Methodist church yonder. What's the boy's name?"

"That's the problem. We don't know for sure. He told my cousin that he was Crying Blood."

"A Creek boy?"

"He looked like a half-breed to me. He was dressed up like an old-time Creek, though. I was told that Crying Blood ain't a proper name."

Reverend Edmond's shoulders inched up and down. "Probably not. As I understand the Creek, it means he was trying to set right the untimely death of a relative."

"So I was told. I'd like to find out who he really was and get him back to his folks if I can. Need to find out something about him if we're going to discover who killed him, too."

"I'll help if I can, Sheriff. Can you describe him to me?"

Scott cast a glance at Alafair. "I can do better than that, Reverend. If you'll step over to the sideboard with me, I'll show you a photograph of the boy that I had took at the undertaker's."

The two men stood and moved to the side of the room where Scott put his leather case on the long bureau, opened it and withdrew a large brown envelope. Alafair sat where she was since she was plainly not invited to this viewing. Scott was being gentlemanly, she knew, protecting her feminine sensibilities. But she was irritated nonetheless. She had seen plenty of ugliness in her life, including the sight of a wooden spear protruding from a boy's heart, and she had yet to succumb to the vapors. She sat back in the chair, resigned to observing the proprieties.

At first, the only thing she could see was the men's serge-clad backs and inclined heads as Scott withdrew the photograph from the envelope. The reverend snatched it out of his hand and made a noise that caused Alafair's heart to sink.

Reverend Edmond could only manage a strangled whisper when he finally spoke. "That's my boy, Sheriff. That's Reed."

Chapter Forty-five

Shaw set up camp in the clearing in front of the house, just as he and James and the boys had on the night of the hunt. This time Shaw approached the derelict house and walked the perimeter. It was a sturdy enough house, built of tight split rails packed with mud and boar bristles. The south side was shaded by tall hawthorns. At one time, it must have been a pleasant home, a wonderful place to sit out of an evening with the family, tell stories and sing, have a piece of pie.

There wasn't much left of what had once been a wide, covered front porch. The roof of the porch had long fallen in and fallen apart, termite-eaten, rain- and sun-busted, blown about by the wind and storms. Weeds and brush grew up through the floorboards. The whole house listed dangerously to the right, athwart the prevalent wind. One more good thunderstorm and it would go.

He scanned the front of the house, and a spot of color above the lintel caught his eye. It appeared to be a painted stick. He moved up to get a better look, then took an involuntary step back when he realized what it was. A carving of a snake. It was about a foot long and less than the diameter of his thumb, smooth and straight but for a couple of undulations in the middle. One end had been whittled to a point. The other end had an oval head with two painted eyes that stared indifferently into the distance. The head had been painted red with ochre.

He knew why it was there. Indian families often put a clan totem over the door for luck. This family must have belonged to the Snake clan. He tamped down the dread that rose up in his throat, put his hand on the door post and gave it a good push before he entered the house. The structure could go down soon, but he wanted to assure himself that it wouldn't come down on his head for the few minutes he planned to be inside.

There were so many holes and breaches in the walls and ceiling that it was almost as light inside as out. Weeds were sprouting from the holes and cracks in the rotted floorboards wherever the sun reached. There was a musky, animal smell to the place. He could see some small animal bones scattered about and a shallow hollow in the dirt near the lee side corner. Some critter had denned here recently.

Shaw walked outside and unlooped his mare's reins from the fallen tree trunk he had secured her to. He touched his forehead to the horse's, rubbed between her ears with his fingers, breathed into her nostrils. She responded with a *whuff* and a nod of approval. "He's here, Hannah," he murmured. "Now let's see if I can get him to come out and face me."

Chapter Forty-six

The Reverend Edmond's eyes were dry, but he sagged in one of the armchairs and blew his nose into a large white handkerchief as Scott stood over him, arms crossed, waiting for the man to get hold of himself. Alafair had taken it upon herself to locate the tiny kitchen at the back of the house and put on the kettle. Fortunately, a canister of tea on the cabinet was nearly full and she was able to find a pretty, blue-flowered china tea pot without having to rummage around too much. She couldn't come up with any proper tea cups, so ceramic mugs would have to do. Considering the situation, she didn't care about presentation.

She was just setting a steaming mug on the side table beside the Reverend when he finally began to speak.

"Reed's mama brought him to the Boarding School at Eufaula in nineteen and six, when he was just a little feller, maybe four or five."

Scott lowered himself into the kitchen chair. "He wasn't your natural son?"

"No, but we felt that he was ours, nonetheless. I never met the mama myself. She told them at the school that the boy's father had died and she couldn't look after him any more. The superintendent said she was a full blood Muscogee. Even so, Reed spoke English of a fluent, if ignorant, variety. He was a smart youngster. Already knew his letters and numbers. Me and my wife took to him right off. We got permission to bring him home with us for Sunday dinner a few times. My wife liked to sew little things for him. Even when he was a tyke he enjoyed cultivating a sharp appearance. It wasn't but a little while later that the tribal government decided to turn Eufaula into a girl's school. The plan was to move all the boys to Nuyaka, over west of Okmulgee."

Scott nodded. "Yes, I remember when that happened, Reverend."

"Well, Alma and I had grown quite fond of Reed and weren't prepared to lose him. So we made shift to adopt him as our own. Unfortunately, it seems his mother dropped off the face of the earth, for we could find no trace of her nor any record of where she had gone after she left her allotment."

Scott and Alafair exchanged a glance before Scott urged the Reverend on. "She abandoned her allotment?"

"So I gather. This is not an unheard of occurrence, as I'm sure you know, Sheriff. Many of the Creeks were loath to abandon their communal way of life, and who can blame them? Who would want to leave his clan and his village, where each supports and comforts the other, and go live in solitude with none but his wife and children and try to eke a poor living out of a small farm? My guess is that Reed's mother joined one of the traditional bands. Maybe found herself a new man, started a new life. I'm sure she expected her half-breed boy would do better to be raised in this situation."

"So you adopted him?"

"No, though it wasn't for lack of trying. We did persuade the tribal court to declare us Reed's guardians until such time as we could locate his mother. After statehood, though, tribal law was superseded and we were able to get a legal declaration of abandonment and proceeded to file for adoption. But then Ira showed up."

Ira. The name linked Reverend Edmond's story with Crying Blood's. Scott stood up. Alafair sat down.

"Ira was his brother," Scott said.

"Yes. He told you about Ira? We knew he had a brother. But for some reason, Ira ended up at the Creek Orphan's Home in Okmulgee instead of here in Eufaula with Reed. Ira was some years older than Reed so he was a teenager when I first saw him. He had run away from the Orphan's Home and come looking for Reed. He intended to steal his brother away and go live Indian. My wife felt sorry for the scamp and tried to take him in for a bit, but he was incorrigible. He made no bones about his hatred of Whites, though it was obvious that he was part White himself. He stole and lied, and told Reed the most outrageous tales. I could see the bad influence he was having, so I contacted the law in Eufaula and had him picked up as a runaway and taken back to Okmulgee.

"We didn't hear anything of him for a couple of years after that, and I figured Reed had forgotten all about him. Though I realize now that I was fooling myself. Reed was a good boy, but he was intensely interested in his Creek heritage. I didn't see any harm in encouraging that, as long as he maintained his Christian values and learned the superior history and culture of his European ancestors."

The Reverend paused and took a long swallow from the mug at his elbow. He stared into its steamy depths for a moment, then heaved a sigh and continued. "I was dismayed when Ira showed up again early last year, looking for Reed. Fortunately we had sent Reed to school at Bacone just that term and he wasn't home. Nor did I have any intention of telling Ira where he was, for Ira had reverted, had gone native in the extreme. I told him nothing but it wasn't hard for him to discover where Reed was. Alma and I had determined to withdraw Reed from Bacone and send him back East for a while to remove him completely from his brother's sphere. Before we could put our plans into motion, Reed disappeared.

"We were told that he had climbed out the window of his dormitory in the middle of the night with nothing more than the clothes on his back. Some of Reed's friends said that more than once in previous days he had been seen near the perimeter of campus in clandestine conversation with a strange Indian. I'm sure Ira filled the boy's head with romantic notions of the aboriginal life."

Reverend Edmond stopped speaking abruptly and looked off into space. He teared up and took a moment to wipe his eyes with a corner of his enormous white handkerchief before he continued. "I don't understand how he could abandon us so easily. We loved him and we thought he loved us. He didn't even leave a note! His betrayal broke Alma's poor heart, for it gave out not three weeks later and she died."

Alafair leaned forward to grasp the Reverend's forearm. "Oh, Mr. Edmond, I'm so sorry."

He shook his head. "I've not heard a word of Reed since. If he had returned after Alma died, I fear I would not have taken him back."

He glanced down at her hand, covering his on the arm of his chair. When he looked back up, his expression had changed to one of extraordinary sadness and resignation. "What happened to him?"

"I'm afraid he was stabbed, sir," Scott told him. "Who did it, we do not yet know."

"Could it have been Ira?"

"No, sir. According to Reed, Ira was killed last year by a white-haired man. Reed had taken it upon himself to find this man and avenge his brother's death." Scott told the Reverend all he knew of the circumstances of his foster son's death. Reverend Edmond listened in silence, only an occasional look of puzzlement passing over his face. When Scott finished, the Reverend spent a long moment digesting the information.

"Do you have any idea who this white-haired man might be?" Scott asked, at length.

"I do not. I know little enough of Reed's past. Neither he nor Ira had a birth certificate that my lawyer could find, nor was either birth registered with the Creek Nation. All we knew of him was the name of his mother. Or at least the name she gave when she brought him here. Superintendent Walker told us that he was able to find a woman with the same name in the Creek tribal rolls, but she disappeared after leaving off her boy and no one knows where she went. She never told us anything about his father. We always figured the boys were just by-blows of some passing White wastrel."

"No father? Do you remember what the mother called herself?"

Edmond pondered for a moment. "I'm not entirely sure." He stood and went to a large roll top desk in the corner of the room, opened a bottom drawer and rummaged around a bit before retrieving a sheaf of papers and returning to his chair. He wet a thumb and riffled through the stack until he found the page he was looking for and pulled it out. He perused the document and nodded. "Yes, I do remember correctly. When Alma and I were attempting to locate the mother, Superintendent Walker gave us these records of his enrollment. The mother said her name was Jenny."

"Jenny?" Scott said. "The mother said her name was Jenny?"

"Jenny. Yes. Mr. Walker only saw her once, a pretty young Creek woman, he said, small, and well-spoken."

"And she said she was Reed's mother?"

A brief flash of annoyance at Scott's incredulity touched Edmond's eyes. "I don't think Mr. Walker would have lied about such a thing. He's a godly man."

Alafair could hardly wait for Scott to climb into the driver's side of the Ford after he cranked the engine. "Wasn't Lucretia Goingback's daughter named Jenny?"

Scott pulled the automobile's door closed with a firm click and let out the hand brake. "Jenny was the daughter's name, yes. I don't know that Reed's mother is the same woman, but it's quite the coincidence if she ain't. When the Reverend called the mother Jenny, that threw me for a loop. I had just about decided that Crying Blood and his brother Ira were those two younger sons of Lucretia and Hawkins."

"Well, I still think that may be so, Scott. It all fits. Could it be that Jenny claimed to be Reed's mother just so she could turn him over to the Boarding School?"

They began to move down the street. "Maybe. On the other hand, maybe Reed was Jenny's son. I did get the feeling that the reason Uncle Peter fell out with Roane Hawkins was because he was a wastrel and unkind to the ladies. Or maybe the boy's ma is somebody else altogether."

"I'll declare! How are we ever going to know which was the boy's mother?"

"Unless we can locate Jenny, or Lucretia, or Roane Hawkins, and they tell us, I don't think we are. Besides, what difference can it possibly make now which is the ma? The poor child is dead, and I want to find out who killed him."

Chapter Forty-seven

Shaw led his mare away from the copse that surrounded the ruined homestead and back into the sharp afternoon light. The air smelled fresh after the close mustiness of the cabin interior and he took a deep breath. He could smell the acrid crispness of dying leaves and the faint tang of a fire somewhere in the distance. *If I were blind and deaf,* he thought, *I could tell it's fall by the smell.*

He walked to the center of the clearing a few yards in front of the house to the fire pit they had used on their camping trip. The rock-lined, blackened, ashy, pit was there long before he and his kinfolks showed up to hunt birds a week ago. The Hawkins' and the Goingbacks before them had probably used this pit for years to make fire for washing, cooking, tempering wood, melting lead for bullets. And who knows, this may have been an old Creek hunting camp for years before that.

He relieved the mare of the blanket roll and saddle bags and began to make his own camp. He had cleaned out the fire pit and arranged kindling in the bottom and was in the brush, gathering dry sticks and pieces of wood, when he saw his mare Hannah, still hobbled in the clearing, lift her head and prick her ears toward the rough path that led through the woods.

He straightened, clutching his armload of firewood to his chest, and listened.

Hannah snorted, switched her tail. Shaw could finally hear the dry-leaf crunch and snap of someone moving toward the clearing on horseback. He took two steps back, fading into the shadow of the trees before putting down the wood and curling his fingers around the butt of his sidearm.

Hannah stretched her neck and curled her lip, tasting the air, then emitted a whinny of greeting. The approaching mount answered immediately and Shaw dropped his hand from the revolver, relieved and surprised at once. He recognized that neigh and the flash of a copper-colored flank through the trees as the animal approached.

He stamped out through the brush, no longer concerned with stealth. "Gee Dub, is that you? Damn it, boy, I like to shot you! What are you doing here?"

Gee Dub reined in, shocked in spite of himself to hear his father curse. "Well, Dad, I came to get you. And before you rip off my hide, I'll tell you that it was either me or Mama, and I figured you'd have better success dealing with me."

"This scrape don't concern you, son. It's between me and that haint out there in the woods."

One corner of Gee Dub's lip twitched. "I beg to differ, Daddy. If you get killed, I reckon I may as well not even bother going home to face Mama again but just mount up and ride myself off a cliff."

"I could say the same thing, Gee. How'd you know where to find me?"

"When Kurt told us you'd decided to go after the killer, I figured it had to be back here that you'd start looking. This is where everything started going south."

Several of Shaw's emotions were fighting for the upper hand as he watched the tall, rangy, young man step down out of his stirrup and loop his reins over the saddle horn. The truth was, he was glad to see him. He was glad for the company, glad to have another soul on his side. Shaw was confident in his own abilities as a marksman, but it did cross his mind that this boy of his was a natural born shootist, a prodigy with a rifle, perhaps the best shot he had ever seen.

But shooting game was one thing. Shooting a human being was a soul burden he wouldn't wish on an enemy, much less his beloved eldest son. "Capturing a child-murdering ghost is going to be hard enough for me without having to worry about you."

Gee Dub didn't respond. He slid his rifle from its holster on the horse's flank and turned to face Shaw, awaiting instructions.

Shaw nodded at the firearm, his mind suddenly made up. "You brought your Winchester? Good." He leaned in, lowering his voice in case an eavesdropper lurked nearby. "There's a stream back there behind the house. Take Penny and Hannah and water them. Then I want you to picket them back up there in that blind we used last time, as stealthy as you can. I wouldn't put it past our haint to go after the horses."

By the time Gee Dub returned, Shaw was feeding a new fire in the pit.

"You find anything in the house?" Gee Dub asked him.

"Nothing human has been in there for a spell."

Gee Dub sat down on the ground. The heat from the fire felt good. The shadows were long and the temperature was dropping rapidly. The air felt damp, too. He could see Shaw's breath in the air. There would likely be another fog tonight. "So how are you aiming to find this murderer, assuming that he actually came back here like Crying Blood thought? If even Mr. Skimmingmoon's bloodhounds couldn't get a handle on him, I don't hold out much hope for our chances."

Shaw didn't look up from feeding branches into the nascent fire. "I expect he'll find us."

"You think he's watching us right now?"

"I think he only comes out at night."

"How'd you decide that?"

"Something Crying Blood said to me before he got killed."

"So we have to run him down in the dark, on top of everything?"

Shaw smiled at the skeptical note in Gee Dub's voice, but he didn't feel the need to explain his thinking to his son. Besides, there was no way to explain the unexplainable. Gee Dub folded his arms around his knees and regarded Shaw quietly, waiting for him to elaborate.

"I aim to lure him," was all Shaw said.

Gee Dub adjusted his hat. He had worn the old black Stetson for so many years that it was losing its shape and the brim tended to flop down on one side. He could tell this line of questioning wasn't going to be very productive. He decided to try another approach. "So you think he's on to you being here already?"

Shaw finally sat back from the fire and dusted the wood ash off his hands. "Son, I think he's been on to me ever since that child walked into our camp during the night. Crying Blood thought he was after the white-haired man for killing his brother. But I believe that it was the other way around. I think the killer has been after those boys from the beginning. Crying Blood couldn't call to mind anything much about his family. Then his brother Ira brought him out here to show him where they sprang from and that's when the haint got a look at them. The law decided that Ira broke his neck by accident, but the kid told me he saw a white-haired man bending over the body. I reckon our killer haunts these woods and only leaves when he aims to track his victim and do murder. He accomplished his task when he killed the boy, and I think he high tailed it on back here."

"Do you think he'll come after you eventually?"

"Don't matter what he intends now. He killed a young'un, and I mean to see he pays for it."

"We are going to capture him and turn him over to the law, aren't we, Dad?" Gee Dub hesitated before he asked the question for fear of offending, but he had only seen that look in his father's eye once before. He didn't care to see it again.

Shaw noted Gee Dub's tone with a hint of irony. "If we can, son."

Chapter Forty-eight

It was almost dark by the time Scott and Alafair reached the front gate of the Tucker farm. Alafair could hardly get her legs to work when she moved to get out of the auto and open the gate for Scott to drive through. Neither of them had said a word since Council Hill. Alafair was so tired she could hardly see straight. She had reformulated her whole opinion about the comfort and convenience of long-distance automobile travel.

"What's going on?" Scott said, causing her to start to consciousness and look over at him. He gestured with his chin and she peered with bleary eyes in the direction he had pointed. They were close enough to the house now to see that several of the more grown-up offspring were in the front yard, standing together in a roiling, gesticulating group and engaged in an earnest debate about something. All heads turned toward them as the Model T bumped down the bare dirt drive.

Martha broke off from the group and came out through the front gate to meet them.

"Mama, Cousin Scott, thank goodness you're finally home! Daddy's gone and Gee Dub has gone after him!"

Alafair gaped at her from the open window, her tired brain refusing to function properly. "Gee Dub's home?"

It was Scott who asked the proper question. "Where'd your daddy take off to, hon? What's he taken it into his head to do?"

◇◇◇

John Lee and Phoebe had come over, bringing Grace and Zeltha, who were both clamoring for their mothers to pick them up as the group milled around on the front porch. That was as far from the Ford as they had managed to make it before the story of Shaw's quest had begun spilling out. Martha, Mary, and Phoebe looked worried. Kurt and John Lee were eager to take action. Charlie was so excited that his tongue wouldn't get around his words properly. Somehow, Scott and Alafair managed to get the tale in spite of many tellers all talking at once.

Scott held up a hand for silence before he attempted a summary of what he had heard. "So Shaw has an idea that the killer is gone back to Oktaha and has set out to find him. But when Gee Dub came home and heard about it, he decided to go after him and try to talk him into coming home before your mama found out."

"Well, that was the idea," Martha said. "But if Gee had found him and been able to persuade him to give up this crazy idea, they'd have been home by now."

Scott and Alafair eyed one another in silence for a long moment.

Long experience had taught Alafair to have faith in Shaw's instincts. She also knew that Shaw Tucker was not a man to act rashly. He knew exactly what he was doing, and he knew it was dangerous. Why else would he have gone to such particular lengths to conceal his plans from everyone? From her?

There was a thing that Shaw had to do and it didn't matter whether she understood or not.

She could tell by Scott's expression that he had the same thought. "Alafair, I reckon I'll go fetch James as soon as it gets light and have him lead me out there to Uncle Peter's place."

The older girls all began to protest at once, but Martha's voice overrode her sisters'. "You have to go after him now, Cousin Scott, before somebody gets shot!"

"I'll go with you, Sheriff," John Lee offered. Kurt was already half-way down the porch steps in his eagerness to be off.

"Stop!" Scott bellowed, arresting Kurt's forward motion and casting a pall of shocked silence over all. "I'll be the judge of what I have to do, children. I think your daddy's on a wild goose chase, so I have my doubts that he'll get into any trouble tonight. Even if the killer has gone back there, Shaw'll have to do some mighty fancy tracking to find him. And I didn't hear anything about him taking any dogs, either." He turned to face Alafair, who was standing next to him with a wide-eyed Grace on her hip. "Alafair, you've been close with your opinion. If you think it'd set your mind at ease, I'll go back into town right now and trade this bone-shaker of a Ford for my horse, roust out James, and set out tonight to try and find Shaw and Gee Dub."

Do it, she thought. *Go after him this minute and bring him back to me. If anything happens to my boy, I don't know what I'll do. But if I lose Shaw it'll be the end of the world.* "I think you'll have a better chance of finding them tomorrow," she said.

Scott was ready for this trip to be over. The two miles of country road between his cousin's farm and town seemed almost as long to him as the entire last leg of their trip back up from Eufaula. He was desperate to get home and let his wife Hattie fuss over him. He had told her that it was unlikely they would be back until after dark, and so she was probably expecting him about now. He wondered if she had a pot roast simmering on the stove. She knew that pot roast was his favorite.

But no matter how loudly that pot roast was calling him duty called even louder, and he stopped at the jailhouse to check up on his flame-haired deputy, Trenton Calder, and find out if anything of interest had happened while he was away.

Trent met him at the street door and ushered him inside. Scott sank into a wooden chair and allowed the youngster to pour him a mugful of potent, twelve-hour-old, jailhouse coffee.

It tasted like lye water, but it was hot and full of caffeine and Scott sipped at it gratefully.

Trent leaned back on one of the desks in the front office and gave his boss a moment to gather himself before he spoke. "How'd it go? Did you find out anything?"

Scott nodded. "A bunch. We found the boy's family. His name was Reed Edmond, and it seems he was born out on that property of Mr. McBride's. His mother left him at the Creek Boarding School in Eufaula when he was just a little tyke and he ended up getting adopted by a minister and his wife out there."

"Well, I'll be!"

"And when I took Miz Tucker home," Scott began, "we found out that..."

"Talking about Mr. McBride..." Trent interrupted him. Scott swallowed his sentence, more interested in what he was hearing than in relating the details of his exhausting day. Trent continued. "...he came by here this afternoon about four and asked that you come out and see him as soon as you got back."

Scott blinked. "I thought he was in Okmulgee."

"Well, he's back now. Said he had some real important information for you about the dead boy."

"What is it?"

Trent's expression didn't change, but his redhead's complexion betrayed him, and he flushed. "He wouldn't tell me, Sheriff. He said it was for your ears alone."

Scott sagged in his chair before pushing himself to his feet, resigned. No pot roast for him for a while longer. "I'll go by there right now. Go 'round to my house for me and tell Hattie where I am and that I'll be home as soon as I can."

Chapter Forty-nine

Gee Dub leaned back on his elbows and stretched his legs out toward the fire. Curly black tendrils of hair stuck out from under his cowboy hat at odd intervals. The sight made Shaw smile. The boy had inherited his mother's hair. Alafair's dark, wavy, tresses had never been ruled, as far as he knew. Much like Alafair herself.

Shaw poked at the coals with a stick. "I wish we had a spring-house at home, son. When I was a lad, back yonder around Mountain Home, we had a springhouse made of rock that straddled the creek. That spring water was cold as ice all year around. Ma kept her milk and butter in there. When it was summer, us children would go inside and dangle our bare feet in that cold water till they turned blue. I swear, you couldn't hardly feel your feet to walk, and we'd reel around like drunks, laughing to beat all."

Gee Dub listened without comment and Shaw wondered if the young man was thinking that his father had lost his mind.

He continued. "I've been reminiscing on my folks a lot lately. I always do, come butchering time. I don't know if you remember, but the woods are full of white tail deer back in them Arkansas hills. Every winter when I was a kid, Pa and us boys would go deer hunting. Pa'd bring back a young buck and him and Mama would dress it and hang it up to smoke in a hollow log. There ain't so many deer around here any more. Not like when we first moved to the Indian Territory. Them as hunt their own meat have to make do with small game now."

Gee Dub crossed one booted ankle over the other. "I've dressed a deer or two in my time. I don't miss it. I never was overfond of venison, anyway. It's too gamey for me." He sat up and brushed a speck off the leg of his trousers. "It's gotten chilly. Damp, too. I wouldn't be surprised if there's a fog tonight."

The thought caused Shaw to shudder. "I hope not." He poked at the fire again, causing a smoldering log to collapse and send up a shower of sparks. He looked up. Stars were beginning to pop out of the greying vault of sky overhead. "It's finally getting dark."

Gee Dub regarded him from across the fire pit, the expression in his dark eyes full of speculation. "What are you going to do now, Dad?"

Shaw didn't look at him. "I'm going to make a fuss with the fire and hope he's watching me. Crying Blood followed me home because he thought he heard the haint call my name, and I believe that he did."

"You think the man who killed Crying Blood is someone who knows you?"

"I do."

"And you know him?"

"I think so." Shaw reached into the saddle bag on the ground next to him and pulled out the muslin bag. He fished a fatty piece of pork out of the salt, impaled it on an applewood spit he had whittled down and soaked in water, and staked it over the fire. Gee Dub watched with interest as Shaw placed his three-legged spider in a hollowed out place in the coals, right under the meat. It was only a few moments before the pork began to cook and the fat to melt, dripping with slow, musical, *thwunks* into the skillet. A delectable smell wafted out over the clearing and Gee Dub drew in a deep lungful. "You sure do aim to lure him."

Shaw didn't answer. When the outside of the pork began to char, he sawed off a hunk of juicy pinkish-white meat and handed it to his son.

They ate in silence, their meal of roast pork supplemented by cornbread reheated in hot fat. As Gee Dub was licking the last of the grease off his fingers, Shaw began talking, his voice pitched low so only the two of them would be privy to the conversation. It was fully dark.

"Bank the fire, son, but stack on the wood so it'll burn long and high enough to cast some light. Leave that leftover hunk of meat on the spit. You and me are going to make a show of bedding down back there in the house. But I aim to watch that fire all night if I have to."

Gee Dub didn't question the plan. He helped Shaw gather up their equipment, and together they retired into the house.

The two men had to duck to enter through the lopsided door. "It's dark as a dog's gullet in here!" Gee Dub whispered. "Stinks, too. You didn't run across something dead when you were in here earlier, did you?"

A sudden beam of light gave Gee Dub a start. It illuminated a swath of the floor, then ran quickly over the walls and what was left of the rickety ceiling.

"Is that the electric flashlight I gave you a while back?" Gee Dub asked, delighted.

Shaw flicked the light off, plunging them back into blackness. "It is, son, and it's been right handy lately. The only trouble with it is that the battery don't last very long and I didn't bring a spare on this trip. So I only aim to use it when I have to. Let's spread our blankets here on this patch of floor by the door. I tested it earlier today, and I think the floor boards here are in fair shape."

They shuffled around in the dark as best they could, unrolling and arranging bedrolls, bumping into each other, fearful of moving around too much lest they fall through a hole or splinter a plank beneath them. It got easier as their eyes adjusted to the dark. The moon rose while they were working. It cast a dim light through the window and door openings and the myriad cracks in the walls.

Shaw positioned himself in front of the door, far enough back that he couldn't be seen from the outside yet near enough to the entry to give him a straight, clear view of the campfire. Gee Dub set himself up to his father's right. He had discovered a collapsed area of wall that afforded him not only a good line of sight, but provided a perfect place to rest the barrel of his rifle.

After they were arranged to their satisfaction, the clicks and thumps of two men checking their firearms and ammunition were the only sounds disturbing the silence.

Gee Dub crossed his legs Indian style and positioned his Winchester across his lap. The low-burning fire in the clearing some ten yards away cast an eerie bubble of light around itself, illuminating not much more than the piece of meat still suspended on a spit just to the side of the pit.

Shaw's disembodied voice spoke to him out of the blackness. "If you want to sleep a spell, son, I'll wake you when I get tired."

"I'll watch with you for a bit, Dad."

"All right, then. But we'd better keep the talk to a minimum. I want the villain to think we're asleep."

Gee Dub glanced to his left. He could barely see Shaw's shape next to him, a darker figure against the darkness. "Don't worry, Dad. I never miss an opportunity to shut up."

The two of them watched together in silence most of the night. The stars were very bright until past midnight, when a fog began to come up. At first it was only ghostly wisps floating up off the ground, becoming caught like drifting white spider webs in the top branches of the trees. Eventually it rose up from the forest floor to meet the tree-captured shreds, and the stars were obscured. A grey veil moved slowly out from the woods, flowing like smoke and water into the clearing. The trees became mere shadows through the mist. The fire was still visible, glowing embers and an occasional small lick of flame. Even so, Shaw was filled with dread that the fog would thicken even more before morning and even if his quarry did appear, he wouldn't be able to see him.

One chance, Jesus, he prayed. *I know that Scott, or Barger, or Lord forfend, Alafair, will show up in the morning, and if that happens the killer will go to ground. This is my one chance, slim as it is. If I've figured this right, Lord, give me the chance to do justice.* His mind stilled for a moment as he watched the campfire glow through the fog. An image of earnest young Crying Blood, dressed in his antique Creek garb, determined to set things right, rose up unbidden. Shaw added to his prayer. *Master of Breath, make things straight.*

Gee Dub had fallen asleep, but there was no danger of that for Shaw.

Chapter Fifty

Alafair sat in the kitchen in the dark, clad only in her nightgown, thick socks and a shawl, her long, dark hair in a braid down her back. It was cold and her breath fogged in the air. All the children were asleep, the only sound in the house the tick, tick, of the clock on the shelf in the parlor. The moon was beginning to wane, but it still cast enough light for her to see that a frost was forming on the windowpanes. It was close to midnight. She was wondering how one could be so filled with icy terror and still function as though everything were normal.

The sound of her own breathing coupled with the rhythmic tick of the clock caused her to fall into a reverie. She remembered those months, years before, when Shaw had gone to work for Roane Hawkins. That was a hard time. She and the children were living with Shaw's parents after the baby died. How kind Sally had been to open her home to a depressed twenty-five-year-old girl with five little children and a husband who was away for weeks at a time. It made her cheeks burn to think how much of an imposition they must have been. But her mother-in-law had acted as if it were the greatest delight to have them. Alafair still half-wondered if Shaw hadn't taken the job out by Oktaha partially to give himself a break from his wife's gloomy presence.

She had moved like a mechanical woman through her days, doing whatever she had to do to pull her weight around Sally's house. In her mind's eye, she could still see Martha's anxious little face watching her every move. She had tried to smile more, just to reassure the children, but hadn't been able to manage it.

She had sat for hours, every free moment she had, in her bedroom with a lap-sized quilt frame before her, piecing a quilt for Shaw to take to Oktaha with him after his next visit home. She had made it out of hers and the children's old clothes, so that he could have them all near him while he was away.

She could visualize that quilt. She had made it in shades of red and blue, a spectacular Morning Star, the colors shading from a deep blood red center through the entire spectrum of reds, ending in a starburst of the palest of pinks. The star was on a midnight blue background, and the perimeter of the quilt was bordered with a band of alternating blue and white patterned triangles. The border was pierced by the four cardinal points of the star.

Alafair could see her own hand plying a needle over one of the blue and white triangles. She drew a breath. Indigo birds, flying across a field of white. She recognized the triangle pattern of the border. It was called Wild Goose Chase.

Shaw had taken that quilt out to the Hawkins place with him after a sojourn at home. He had never brought it back.

How is it I didn't remember that before now? she wondered. *He said Miz Hawkins admired it and he gave it to her, along with most everything else he had with him. I was put out at the time, but that's like Shaw, to be so generous. Whoever owned the bones that Shaw had found, he had taken a piece of Lucretia Hawkins' quilt into the grave with him.*

"Mama?"

Alafair started. "Oh! Martha. I didn't see you. What are you doing out of bed?"

"I could ask you the same question. Are you worrying about Daddy and Gee Dub?"

"I reckon I am, honey. You, too?"

Martha padded into the kitchen and took a seat at the table across from her mother. "Why did you tell Scott that it was all right to wait for morning to hunt them? There's no telling what could happen between now and tomorrow."

Alafair's gaze returned to the frost-covered window. "Scott will have a better chance of finding them in the daytime. Besides, Daddy can take care of himself."

"What about Gee?"

"He's with your daddy. Otherwise he would have come back home."

"Well, if he couldn't persuade Daddy to give up his chase, he should have come back anyway and got some help."

In the pale moonlight that illuminated the kitchen, Alafair's smile was barely visible. "I expect that Gee Dub is the one who got persuaded, honey. It'll be all right. It's good that they're together. They'll watch out for each other."

Martha was surprised that Alafair had so much faith in Gee Dub's abilities. In her mind, her mother still thought of them all as drooling infants. "You really think it'll be all right?"

"I do." Alafair reached across the table and squeezed Martha's hand. "I know your father."

Against all reason, the certainty with which Alafair uttered this statement made Martha feel better. She rose and circled the table to give her mother a hug, then went back to bed.

Alafair sat where she was, in the dark, making contingency plans for life as a widow.

Chapter Fifty-one

Shaw sat with his back up against his saddle, slumped forward, his knees raised and one hand placed on the rifle next to him on the floor. He was staring at the clearing, hypnotized by the eddying fog and the flicker of the fire. He heard an indistinct noise. He didn't move, but his eyes widened as he listened. The fog diffused and misdirected sound, so there was no way to tell where it came from.

He saw a movement at the far edge of the clearing and leaned forward, hardly daring to breathe. Was he imagining it?

No, there it was. A hulking shape, hunkered close to the ground. It scuttled toward the fire, stopped, crept forward again.

Shaw felt a stab of disappointment. An animal. Then the figure raised up on two feet and lifted its head. The fog was too thick to allow him to make out detail, but even through the gray veil he could see the figure's tangled crown of white hair.

Shaw reached out a hand and touched Gee Dub's arm. The young man sat up, instantly awake.

Shaw pointed toward the clearing and heard Gee Dub draw a breath. "When I speak," Shaw whispered, "you shine this light on him." He held out the flashlight, and when Gee Dub reached for it Shaw seized his wrist. "No matter what happens I don't want you shooting anybody. So if it comes to the worst, you high tail it out of here and bring the law."

"Dad…" Gee Dub's voice was barely audible.

"Do as I say, son. Promise me."

"All right."

Gee Dub got to his knees and watched anxiously as his father slipped out the door, rifle in hand, and made a stealthy circle around the front of the cabin. The young man tried to swallow, but his mouth was too dry. If he hadn't known exactly where to look, he would have lost Shaw in the fog as he moved away. He couldn't help but feel impressed at how quietly Shaw was moving.

Gee Dub held his Winchester under one arm and gripped the flashlight with his left hand, watching as Shaw crept out just to the edge of the clearing. Did he step on a twig or catch the firelight with the rifle barrel? Gee Dub didn't think so, but the dark shape in the clearing suddenly lunged forward to grab the piece of meat from its spit and bolted for the woods. Shaw stepped forward into the open and shouldered his firearm.

"Stop!" he called, and Gee Dub clicked on the flashlight.

Was it an animal after all? It lumbered forward, stopped, looked back over its shoulder. The meat was in its mouth. It's head was covered with a mat of white fur, its body with a brown pelt. It had one eye, milky pale in the beam of light. Gee Dub almost dropped the Eveready. A monster!

Except now he could see that the fur was a mess of white hair and the brown pelt was a garment made of rags and skins. And the creature was holding a rifle of its own. It ran.

"Stop!" Shaw called again, but the cyclops didn't pause. Shaw fired and the running creature made a shrill noise before it disappeared into the woods. The flashlight started to fade and Gee Dub frantically banged it against his thigh until the beam strengthened. When he looked up he saw that Shaw was standing beside the fire pit, his outline clearly visible in front of the banked fire.

"Roane Hawkins!" Shaw bellowed into the darkness. "Come out. I know you. Why'd you do it?"

A moaning noise came from all around, scattered by the fog. It was a human sound that rose up at the end. Like a question. A shot rang out and a flash appeared from between the trees near where the creature disappeared. A ricochet pinged off a tree behind Shaw.

Gee Dub stood up, alarmed.

Shaw didn't move. "You killed your own boys, you varmint. It's time for you to go back to hell."

Another shot split the night, another flash. Shaw raised his rifle and fired back. Gee Dub suddenly realized what his father was doing. He was trying to goad the cyclops into firing, then guiding his own aim by the muzzle flash. Gee Dub scrambled out of house and began to work his way around the edge of the clearing, hoping to catch a sight of the creature before it shot again. He wondered if Shaw remembered he was there.

A third shot came from the trees. Shaw jerked and stumbled, but straightened quickly and raised his rifle.

Oh, Jesus. Gee Dub dropped to one knee and sighted along the barrel of the Winchester. At nothing. It was pitch black. If he shot now and hit anything it'd be a miracle. He could feel the flop sweat start under his arms. He needed a reference.

"Roane Hawkins!" Shaw called again. "You remember who you are. You used to be Roane Hawkins. You kilt your boys. You kilt Reed and Ira, too. You know who I am, Roane Hawkins. I come to get you."

Silence. Had the white-haired haint slipped away?

A single, icy, sigh of wind passed, causing Gee Dub to shiver and ruffling the remaining dry leaves on the trees.

The creature made a sound, almost like a voice. *Shaw,* it said.

Two shots exploded at the same time, one from the woods and one from Shaw, so close upon one another that it was impossible to tell which came first. The two muzzle flashes momentarily blinded Gee Dub and he blinked desperately to regain his night vision.

A yowl like a wounded dog arose from somewhere. Then nothing. Shaw took a step back and fell flat, spread eagle on the ground.

Gee Dub sprinted across the clearing and dropped to his knees at his father's side. Shaw was staring straight up, a look of surprise on his face.

"Daddy!" Gee Dub grasped Shaw's face with both hands.

Shaw's eyes shifted to Gee Dub's face. "Did I get him?"

Gee Dub sat down heavily. "Great day in the morning, Dad! I thought you were killed for sure! Are you hit?"

Shaw put a tentative hand on his own chest. "I don't think so. I just tripped over that hunk of firewood. Get out of this light, son, in case he's still alive and looking to shoot something."

"You hit him for sure, Dad. I see him lying over yonder like a pile of rocks."

Shaw didn't try to look. He kept his gaze on Gee Dub's face. "Is he moving?"

"No."

"Help me up. I'll see what's what."

Gee Dub grabbed his father's shoulder and shoved him back down. "You lie still."

Shaw opened his mouth to protest, but the nineteen-year-old was too fast for him. By the time he had rolled up onto his elbow, Gee Dub was leaning over the dark figure. "He's not moving, Dad, and I don't hear breathing. Looks like you got him in the chest. I think he's dead."

Shaw managed to drag himself to his feet. A sharp pain in his ribs caused him to clutch his side and double over, one hand on a knee. He struggled to catch his breath.

"Are you all right?" Gee Dub said.

"I got the wind knocked out of me is all." He straightened as best he could and got himself over to his son's side. Gee Dub turned on the flashlight for Shaw's benefit and shone it into the creature's face. For a long moment, the two of them stared at the monstrous figure with the gaping wound in its chest. It was a man, all right. After a fashion.

"This is Roane Hawkins?" Gee Dub asked at length. "Grandpapa's friend?"

"Well, now that I get a look at him I can't be sure. Might be. I haven't set eyes on Roane Hawkins for fifteen, twenty years. But he is the only one who I could figure would be old enough to be white-haired, have lived on this place, and known me to see me, all at once."

Gee Dub cocked his head, the better to study his subject. "Half his head is sheared off. It almost comes to a point. There isn't even a socket for that missing eye. What do you suppose happened to him?"

"Who knows, son? It was bad enough to take the human soul out of him, looks like."

"If this is him, why would he track and kill his own sons?"

Shaw grimaced at the pain in his side. "If this is him, I expect he didn't have mind left enough to figure a reason." He sighed. "Get the horses, son. It'll be dawn soon. We'll pack up and haul this carcass into Oktaha."

While Gee Dub was gone, Shaw stood over the body and tried to connect this half-human thing with the tall, wise-cracking Irishman with the sly blue eyes and greying blond curls he remembered from his youth. Roane Hawkins had been charming as all get out, but slippery, too. If you intended to keep company with Hawkins you kept your eye on your wallet.

Was this really him? The wide open eye could have been blue and the curly white hair perhaps had been blond years earlier. More importantly, was it at all possible that he had murdered Crying Blood? Did this creature have the capacity to plan a hunt and kill two healthy young men? His gaze shifted to the discarded rifle lying next to the body. Even in the dark, he could see three stripes painted on the stock. Hawkins had known enough to pick up Crying Blood's rifle. And he still knew how to shoot it. Thank God his injuries hadn't improved his aim.

Shaw was mulling the possibilities when the rag pile moved.

He straightened, surprised. The cyclops eye blinked at him. Shaw kicked the rifle out of the way and drew his revolver.

"Shaw Tucker. You tell her…" The voice was not much more than a rasp, but Shaw understood it, all right. His heart began to thud uncomfortably.

"Who? Tell her what?"

"…that's what she gets." The white-haired man emitted a noise that was part bark, part laugh, part cackle that turned into a snarl. He flung himself over on his side and grabbed the ankle of Shaw's boot with a clawlike hand.

Shaw shook him off and took a step back, his hair standing on end. The thing—Roane Hawkins, he was sure of it now—was writhing on the ground, hissing and trying to move toward him, leaving a smear of blood on the ground as he slithered on his belly. Shaw moved back out of his reach, watching the horrifying display with a cold detachment that surprised even him. His lips thinned with distaste.

"You should have stayed dead."

He leveled the revolver in his hand and shot the creature in the head.

The echo of the gunshot dissipated into the mist, leaving total silence. Shaw looked up at the sky. The fog was thinning. He could see the diffuse light from two or three stars directly above his head.

He turned around to see Gee Dub standing behind him, holding their horses' reins. Both mares snorted and sidled unhappily at the blood-covered heap on the ground. It was too dark to judge his son's expression.

When he spoke, Gee Dub's tone was matter-of-fact. "Are we going to take him into town now?"

Shaw stretched a little to ease his sore ribs. "I guess we ought. It'll go better if I turn myself in."

Gee Dub didn't move. "Looked like self-defense to me."

"It was, until I shot him in the head."

"Because he was trying to take your leg off."

Shaw smiled. "Maybe that'd fly, son, if one thing followed close upon another. But I don't think the law will see it that way."

Gee Dub shifted his weight to one leg, prepared to stand there and reason with his father all night if he had to. "What do you mean? I saw what happened. He came at you like a wounded mad dog and you shot him."

"Gee Dub, you're splitting hairs. I don't aim to lie."

"I don't see as you have to. Besides, what good would come out of you spending a year in jail for manslaughter and leaving Mama and the children all alone, just for the matter of ten seconds? Daddy, there's the legal thing and then there's the right thing."

Shaw looked down at the bloody pile at his feet. He had no regret over his action. In fact, he felt better than he had felt in months. He had done what needed to be done and his heart was straight. He raised his head. "Now you do sound like your mama. But I guess you have a point."

He barely heard Gee Dub's relieved exhale. "Well, thank you. I think."

"Let's roll this critter up in that old horse blanket and see if Hannah will deign to carry him back of the saddle. If she shies, I reckon we'll have to rig a travois."

Shaw's step was noticeably lighter as he moved to pull the blanket roll from behind his horse's saddle. "We'll wire Scott from Oktaha, get him to ride out to the farm and tell your mother what's going on."

Chapter Fifty-two

Shaw removed his black woolen jacket and steeled himself for Alafair's reaction. It wasn't as bad as he feared. She drew in a breath between her teeth but didn't gasp or exclaim.

"It's just a scratch," he said.

This was the first time he'd actually gotten a look at the long gash in his side, but he had known from the first that the wound was minor. It had bled enough to ruin his tan shirt but not so much that he had been weakened from the loss of blood.

No, it wasn't the wound that threatened to do him in. It was sheer exhaustion.

When Shaw and Gee Dub had finally ridden up to their farm's main gate, it was already late enough in the day that the shadows were growing long. Shaw had not slept for a couple of days, and for much of the trip Gee Dub had kept an anxious eye on his father lest he fall out of the saddle.

Deputy Morgan released them earlier in the day, after taking charge of Hawkins' body and questioning them five ways from Sunday. It was Gee Dub, then, who had navigated the return journey from Oktaha. He had ridden as straight a path as he could manage, across farmers' fields, through patches of woods, fording shallow creeks, until they got close enough that the horses could smell home and he could give them their head.

When Gee Dub dismounted to open the gate, a black and tan blur rushed up the drive to meet him.

"Howdy, Buttercup!" The dog jumped up on him and he paused to scratch her ear before he pushed her down and returned to business.

Shaw, still on his horse, laughed at the sight. "I see you've been let out of solitary, girl."

The dog happily trotted along beside the horses as the men neared the farmhouse. Normally they would have called out to alert those inside of their approach, but Alafair was already standing in the drive, the older girls behind her, the younger ones in front, a bulwark around her.

Gee Dub had wired the Sheriff's Office in Boynton early that morning, so Alafair knew the broad details already. She had meant to alert Shaw to the fact that visitors were waiting and then usher him immediately into the parlor. But the moment she saw his face she had insisted he take the time to wash and change before he had to deal with anything else.

He was standing in their bedroom now, as Alafair inspected his wound from her seat on the bed. She wiped the blood from his side with a wet cloth. "This must hurt like fire." Her tone was perfunctory. "I don't think you'll need sewing, though."

"The bullet just barely nicked me. He was a bad shot."

She dabbed ointment on the gash and bandaged it with white cotton strips, practical and competent, her silence telling her thoughts better than words.

He regarded the top of her head for a long moment, weighing whether it was wiser to speak or keep his counsel. He decided to chance it. "Are you vexed with me?"

She made a noise that could have been a laugh or a sob. She seized his jacket off the bed and stuck her fingers through the bullet holes on the left side, one in the front, one in the back, and waggled them at him. "This coat is ruined." When she looked up at him he could see the tears welling on her lower lids.

He bit his lip to keep from smiling at the way she had chosen to voice her displeasure. "I needed a new one anyway." He put his hand on her hair. "Me and Gee will have to go into Muskogee next week and talk to a judge. Barger doesn't think it'll take very long. Good thing, because I've got to get to…"

"Shaw, I'm proud of you," Alafair interrupted. "I know you did what you thought was right. But I wish you hadn't of run off like that without so much as a how-do-you-do. I was scared stiff. And what if you had been killed? These children need you. The girls need an example of what a good husband and father looks like so they won't settle for nothing less. And as for the boys…well, a girl can just naturally become a woman but a boy needs to be taught what it is to be a man."

Shaw was taken aback, touched and regretful all at once. "I understand you, Alafair, and I apologize for causing you grief and worry. I didn't undertake to go after that creature lightly nor did I do it for fury or revenge. My aim was not to punish him for what he done, but I couldn't let that evil remain abroad in the same world as you and the children. Not if I could help it."

She heaved a sigh. "Well, I just had to say it."

"I know, honey." He nodded toward the closed door that led into the parlor where their company, bolstered by cake and hot tea, awaited them. "How long have they been here?"

Alafair stood and helped him into a clean shirt. "A couple of hours. Scott asked Deputy Morgan to wire him when y'all left Oktaha this morning. He wanted everybody to be here already when you finally made it home."

"I nearly dropped my teeth when I saw Doolan and Papa together in the same room."

"I expect you did."

Shaw drew a sharp breath through his nose. The iodine had made the wound tender. "What about the woman?" he asked.

"What about her?"

"Are you going to tell me who she is?"

Alafair didn't answer. The question was meaningless. Shaw knew very well who the visitor was.

Chapter Fifty-three

"I figured from the first that it was him who done in Goingback. That was when the world got throwed out of whack, and if I had put things straight right then, all this wouldn't have happened. But Goingback was a bad husband and I was glad to get shet of him. Hawkins wasn't no prize, but he was a good provider. My children liked him, and he never did beat me."

Shaw studied the little brown woman with the face like a dried apple, trying to connect her in his mind with Roane Hawkins' pretty wife who had brought him fried squirrel and cornmeal dumplings every day for dinner twenty years earlier, when he was clearing trees for her husband. Last he had heard she had dropped off the face of the earth, abandoning her children—or were they her grandchildren?—and selling her property to Peter McBride after her husband disappeared.

Yet here she was, Lucretia herself, sitting on the horsehair-stuffed settee in his parlor next to Peter's nemesis, Doolan. The long, black hair he remembered had turned slate grey and was now parted in the middle and cut in a severe, shoulder-length style. When he had known her she didn't speak much English. She was fluent enough now, speaking easily with a tonal, sing-song, Creek accent. Her black eyes gazed at him out of a mass of wrinkles. "I remember when you come to work for us out to the farm, Shaw. Hawkins always was partial to you. Said you was a good worker, gave an honest day's labor."

I could have done without that kind of 'partial,' Shaw thought. He turned to his stepfather. "You knew all along that she was living in Okmulgee with Doolan and not in Nebraska?"

Peter was aware of the flash of irritation in Shaw's voice. "There was a reason she didn't want to be found, son. Hear her out before you judge."

Shaw looked back at Lucretia and settled himself in the armchair to listen. Scott and Peter were seated in cane-bottomed kitchen chairs to his left. The young people had been sent about their various afternoon tasks. Except Gee Dub, who was listening discreetly from his place on Charlie's cot in the far corner of the parlor. Sally and Alafair were perched on the piano bench at Shaw's right side. Alafair reached out and placed a supportive hand on his thigh.

Lucretia nodded and began her tale. "Hawkins, he had the white man's sickness. A worm got in his head and made him want to own land. That worm give him a idea that if he was my man he could control that plot the tribe passeled out to me. So he fixed it that a tree fell on Goingback, then offered to marry up with me. I suspicioned all along what he done, but I wanted him. So I believed it was a accident like he told everybody.

"But that worm had took up housekeeping in his head, and even after he got what he wanted and we had children of our own, that worm whispered to him that Goingback's boy, my oldest son Chitto, he had him a parcel of land, too. And Chitto's piece connected our land to the main road that led to the railhead. And if that boy died the Creek courts would say his land belonged to me."

Shaw leaned forward with his elbows perched on the arms of the chair. "Chitto! Was that your son's name?"

Lucretia blinked, momentarily disoriented from being taken out of her story. "Yes. Chitto. That is my family name. My clan. My son was Chitto Goingback."

Shaw flopped back in his seat, the hair on his arms prickling. He didn't speak much Creek, but he knew that word, *Chitto*. Snake.

"So he took my son out hunting," Lucretia continued, "like he done a hundred times before. But this time he aimed to rub him out. He'd of buried Chitto, I reckon, and told me that he run off. But my second boy, Ira, my oldest son with Hawkins, he seen what happened. Now, Hawkins tried to kill Chitto, but they went to fighting and ended up killing each other. Ira come back to the house and told me what happened. I went out there to the creek bed and brought my boy back home. Ira covered up Hawkins' body with dirt and rocks and stuff. We just left him there.

"For four days me and my family, we sat with Chitto. Then we buried him up there in the woods. We put tobacco in his grave and wrapped him in his favorite quilt. You give me that quilt, Shaw. He slept under it 'til he died. I put a piece of it in his medicine bag to keep him comfortable in the place up there. Then we lit a fire and kept it burning 'til his spirit found the passage to the sky."

Shaw rubbed his mustache with two fingers. "What about Reed? Where was he while this was going on?"

"Reed was just a little fella. My daughter Jenny took care of him while me and Ira buried her brother.

"After Hawkins and Chitto killed each other, I figured everything was straight again, and it was all over. Then near to a year later the ghost started haunting us. It stole all our meat. It busted things and took our tools. It killed our goats and chickens, hamstrung the mule. Spoiled the well. I thought at first it was Chitto, mad at me 'cause I didn't cry blood for his father. But then I seen it late one night when the fog came up. It spoke to me. That's how I knew it was Hawkins. He aimed to send us all to the dark place where he lived. We never showed him how to get to the world above, so he was still wandering around in this world with that worm still eating his brains. It had almost eat his head clean off. I knew he'd get us all if he could. So I give away my young ones. I split them up so he'd never find them."

"Was Jenny Reed's mother?" Scott asked.

"Jenny?" Lucretia repeated. "Naw. Who said so?"

It was Alafair who explained. "When Sheriff Tucker and I were visiting the Reverend Edmond in Eufaula, he told us that Jenny was the one who brought Reed to the Boarding School. She told them that she was his mother."

Lucretia's eyebrows peaked. "I told her to say that. They wouldn't have took him without his mother signed him over. I'd have done it myself, but I was taking Ira to the Orphan's Home west of Okmulgee." She continued with her tale before her audience could sidetrack her with more questions.

"I went to McBride." She looked at Peter. "McBride is a good man. He give Hawkins money when y'all first came to the Territory. Him and Sally give us food and furniture and clothes for the children. Then Hawkins and McBride fell out. Over money, a woman, I don't know. I never saw McBride for ten years until I went to him for help. I didn't know nobody else with money. I told him that Hawkins had left me and Chitto had run away. I told him about the haint, too. I said I was scared it'd get me or my children. But I never said I knew that it was Hawkins.

"McBride bought that land so Jenny could go to school in Kansas. She's still there, wife of a fine man. It was her told me that the preacher took in Reed. I didn't have nowhere to go. But McBride told me he knew a good fella in Okmulgee, another old friend of Hawkins', who would help me find a place and settle in. Doolan was real kind to me and we hit it off. That was all right with me." She added this without looking at the man sitting next to her. "I was thinking maybe if I lived in Okmulgee I'd see Ira now and then. But he run off from the Orphan Home directly and I never did. I never knew where he went."

Her gaze wandered off into space, and she fell silent for a moment, remembering. No one intruded on her thoughts.

Would I be willing to never see my children again if I thought it would keep them safe, Alafair wondered?

"Sheriff Tucker took me to the death house where Reed's body is. I recognized him right off. He favored Ira a bunch." Lucretia sighed and looked down at her hands. "If Ira hadn't found Reed and took him back to that dark place, the ghost wouldn't have got a look at them and they'd be alive." She lifted her head. "Shaw, you done laid him down at last. All my menfolk's blood, after all these years, it cried to you."

Her tale was done. The room was so quiet that Alafair could hear Charlie on the back porch murmuring comforting words to Crook as he changed the bandages on the dog's leg. She was aware of Martha and Mary standing discreetly back from the kitchen door, listening.

"What now, Scott?" Peter asked.

"Nothing, I guess. Barger already knows what happened out by Oktaha. The murderer is finally dead…" He turned to address Lucretia. "…which he plainly wasn't before, ma'am. But now he is, killed in self-defense. Reed's body can be returned to his mother. Miz Doolan, I'll help you make whatever arrangements you want. You're free to go back to Okmulgee any time you like."

Lucretia and Doolan made a move to stand, but Scott put out a hand and the couple hesitated. "Hang on, Mr. Doolan." Scott looked to his left. "Uncle Peter, do you still want to press charges on Mr. Doolan for stealing Red Allen's stud services?"

Lucretia settled back into the settee. Doolan still had nothing to say, but the look in his steel-blue eyes sharpened as he gazed at Peter.

The two old pony soldiers leveled narrow stares at one another as Peter answered the sheriff. "In view of all that's happened, let's leave that for another day."

Chapter Fifty-four

Scott and Peter had gone to take the Doolans into town, leaving Shaw in the parlor with his wife and his mother. Shaw Tucker now knew the facts of how Crying Blood's death had come about, but his most important questions had not been answered. He knew it was unfair, but the only people with whom he felt safe enough to ask the unanswerable were these two. "If I hadn't thought to go hunting out there just when I did would that child still be alive?"

Alafair resisted the urge to get up and throw her arms around him. "Shaw, I know that's been on your mind since he died. But if y'all hadn't gone out there when you did and the poor boy hadn't followed you home, Hawkins would have killed him there in the woods and nobody would have ever known. Reed, and Ira, and Chitto, and even old Goingback, they'd of never got justice in this world."

Shaw Tucker had a lot of Indian blood. The Tuckers were woven through with Choctaw and Cherokee ancestry from as early as anyone could remember. And the woman sitting in front of him with a speculative expression, his mother, was the daughter of a full-blood Cherokee woman. Shaw had grown up around his Cherokee relatives. He had attended the Green Corn Festival every year of his life, played in day-long stickball games, knew his clan and his kinship obligations. He even spoke passible Cherokee.

But he was raised to be White. In fact, even though he was an enrolled tribal member, he was White enough in blood and looks and way of life that the U.S. Government never bothered him. No one had ever come to take his children away and put them in boarding school. No one had ever proscribed his movements or told him where he had to live, or how. Shaw Tucker was White and he viewed the world in the way of a White man. Mostly. He was well aware of his mother's knowledge of an existence he could barely comprehend.

"But why me, Ma?" he asked Sally.

His plaintive question caused Sally to turn away and gaze into space for a long moment. Finally she faced him. "Tell me about the snakes."

His breath caught. "Who told you?"

Alafair's brow crinkled. "What snakes?"

Sally shrugged before she seized Alafair's hand and lifted it into her lap. "I have seen that you have a troubled mind, Shaw. And Alafair told me how Grace found that snake in the barn. And I noticed just now that you were mighty interested to hear that Lucretia's son was named Chitto."

How she had made that leap of logic he didn't know, but this was not the first time she had seemingly plucked his secrets out of thin air. "Yes, I've been seeing snakes out of season," he admitted. "I don't know why, but I took a notion that they had something to do with all this business."

Sally nodded. "Shaw, there are some things we'll never know. Sounds to me like Chitto Goingback died trying to set things right for his murdered father. But he failed. And because he failed his brothers died too. Could be his spirit has been watching and waiting for years, praying for Master of Breath to help him choose the right man to finally do justice."

Alafair was nodding unconsciously, her brown eyes glued on Sally's face.

Shaw was a bit more skeptical about his mother's logic. *Sometimes you'll be walking along, trip on a rock and fall on your face. Did Master of Breath choose you for that as well?* Even so, her explanation made him feel better whether he entirely believed it or not. He smiled. "Mama, can I ask you a question? Right after Pa died sometimes you'd disappear. Seemed like you'd be gone for days on end. I've always wondered why you'd go off like that?"

Shaw was relieved to note that the question didn't appear to cause his mother any discomfort. In fact Alafair looked more surprised than Sally. Shaw wondered if he'd ever mentioned this to her in the twenty-five years they had been together.

"Your pa died young," Sally said, "and didn't leave us with much. Both your pa's family and mine did good to keep us supplied with meat and canned goods and such. But every once in a while I didn't have a choice but to go off into Mountain Home and do a job of work to get some cash money for you children's clothes, or salt, or nails and the like. Mostly your Tucker uncles would roust up something for me to do at the sawmill. But during the season I'd pick cotton or vegetables, or candle eggs, or anything else I could come up with."

Shaw was dumbstruck. Why on earth had that never occurred to him? It was so logical.

"You've been pondering on this since your pa died?" Sally wondered. "Why didn't you ever ask?"

"I don't know. I guess when you're a little kid you just know how things are and never think to wonder why. I always felt sorry for Josie having to wrangle us savages like she did."

Sally nodded. "Your sister Josie had to grow up in a hurry."

"Now, how old was Josie when this happened?" Alafair asked. "Eleven, twelve?"

"She was almost twelve," Sally told her. "Not much older than Blanche."

All these years. I thought Ma was so wrapped up in her grief that she left her children to struggle on her own. Instead, I was so wrapped up in mine that I didn't see the sacrifices she was making for us. His cheeks felt hot. *The things we get in our heads that affect the rest of our lives!*

Alafair brought him out of his reverie. "You'd best start being nicer to Josie from now on." She wasn't entirely teasing.

Chapter Fifty-five

The whole family turned out to see Grandma Sally off when she finally left for home, everyone standing in the front yard and waving at her buggy until it disappeared into the distance.

When the dust had settled and Martha had ushered most of the children back into the house, Alafair took Shaw's arm and glanced at Gee Dub. He had leaned his long frame against the picket fence and crossed his arms, making no move to go inside with his siblings. "Come on then, both of you," she said, "and get cleaned up for dinner. Gee, you look like the bottom of a rat hole and you're not too fragrant, either."

"We're both mighty hollow, too," Shaw admitted, "after a couple of days of my camp cooking."

Gee Dub peeled himself away from the fence. "We'll be along, Mama. I want to talk to Dad for a minute."

Alafair's first reflex was to shoo him inside like a goose, but she caught herself in time. "Hurry it up, then," she said, and left them alone on the walk.

Gee Dub had watched in silence the entire time that Lucretia was telling her tale and had yet to offer an observation. Shaw was curious. "What is it, son?"

"Dad, did you believe that woman's story about Hawkins and Chitto killing each other?"

Shaw's mustache twitched, a sign that he was surprised by the question. "I believe that she believes it. I think Hawkins probably killed Chitto, but it's plain that Chitto didn't quite finish off his stepdaddy. I'm guessing that Hawkins eventually crawled out from under the grave of rocks and dirt Ira buried him in with his brains all scrambled and set about making mischief for the next ten years. Whatever sort of critter I shot, it wasn't a ghost. You have a different idea?"

"Well, something's been eating at me. You remember the last thing Hawkins said?"

Shaw grimaced. "I don't care to reminisce about the occasion."

Gee Dub nodded absently, barely letting his father finish in his eagerness to say what was on his mind. "I expect not. But I heard him. He said, '…tell her that's what she gets.' What do you think he meant by…?

Shaw cut him off. "I don't know what he meant, Gee. You saw what he had become. I doubt he knew what he was saying." He put his hand on Gee Dub's shoulder. "Remember what your grandma said, son. There are some things we'll never know."

Chapter Fifty-six

Shaw made his way alone across the cemetery to stand beside the newly filled graves. The rest of the members of the funeral party were still in the basement of the little Creek Methodist Church helping themselves to the barbeque feast that the ladies of the congregation had provided.

Since she had become Lucy Doolan, Lucretia had acquired quite a circle of friends, Shaw thought. He was sorry that life hadn't worked out as well for her sons.

When he had finally managed to slip away from the crowd, Shaw had been aware of Alafair's eyes on him. But she hadn't tried to follow or to ask him what was on his mind.

He stared down at the two mounds of raw earth. During the funeral, Crying Blood—Reed, he supposed he should call him—had rested in his open coffin. A very young Creek man at perfect peace, dressed in a new tunic with his medicine bundle under his folded hands and his snake vertebrae necklace peeping out from under his collar, sleeping the sleep of the innocent. Shaw imagined that their mother had provided similarly for Chitto, but his coffin had been nailed shut over his bones.

Where the third brother, Ira, reposed, no one knew. Reed had never had the chance to tell where Ira had met his end at his own father's hands. Shaw expected he lay with his people in some Indian burial ground deep in the Kiamichi or Winding Stair Mountains.

He squatted down beside the near grave. "Go on now, Chitto," he said. "Take your brother and go on home. We did the best we could do."

Shaw scooped a shallow hole in the soft earth and returned Chitto's snake bone necklace to him, to protect him on the journey.

Chapter Fifty-seven

January 1916

The new year was off to a wet start. It had been raining in earnest for days, but today the heavy clouds only spit a light, intermittent drizzle. It was cold as sin, and muddy, but Shaw seized whatever slim window he could to do some fence mending. Oklahoma was hard on wooden structures, soaking them with rain, freezing them in thick coats of ice, steam-heating them in the summer humidity and always, always, blowing at them from one direction or another. Sometimes all directions at once. Riding fence around his paddocks and fields was an unending chore. The truth was, though, that fence mending was one job that Shaw didn't mind.

Occasionally he rode the perimeter with a son or a hired hand, especially around the larger fields. But today he was working on one of the paddocks next to the stables, maybe a quarter acre square. A job perfectly suited to doing alone.

He loved the sheer physicality of lifting rails and nailing them back in place, or pulling off and replacing rotten boards. Even digging post holes or wrenching out broken posts gave him an opportunity to use his muscles, to enjoy the feeling of strength and warmth in his back and biceps. And when he was done he would know that he had accomplished a real and useful task.

He could see his breath in the frosty air as he hammered a top rail, his hands encased in leather gauntlets that covered his forearms half-way to his elbows. There had been a front come in last evening with a big wind and lots of rails were down. His chaps and boots were covered with mud, wet grass, and wood splinters. He had draped his coat over his saddle horn since the exercise made him warm in spite of the weather. Ironically his mustache was stiff with ice and his nose felt like it was going to freeze into a solid ice cube and shatter right off his face. His black mare, Hannah, was standing behind him, alternately trying to graze what soggy, trampled, winter-yellowed grass she could find and nibbling at the wooden handle of the pliers Shaw had stuck in the back pocket of his Levis. Shaw waved his hand behind himself in an attempt to swat her away.

"Dang it, gal, either quit nipping at my rear end or haul them pliers out and twist some wire around this rail."

Hannah snorted and moved away long enough for Shaw to lift the rail to the top of the post and hammer a couple of ten-penny nails into the top. He was just standing back to inspect his work when he heard a high-pitched call in the distance. Alafair calling the family for dinner. Over the years she had developed her own peculiar method of long-distance calling that served as well as any dinner bell, a sort of *yoo-hoo* which had eventually transformed into in an upper register *ooo-eee* that could be heard from anywhere on the farm. It reminded Shaw of a hog call, which he thought was probably appropriate. In his mind the sound was so associated with food that his mouth watered when he heard it.

He had seen Alafair scrubbing sweet potatoes earlier. He hoped that she had baked them whole in their jackets. There was nothing he loved better than to peel a warm sweet potato and slather it with butter.

He packed up his tools into his saddle bag before he mounted up and rode back to the house. Kurt Lukenbach was walking up the path toward the kitchen and they met in the yard. Shaw had barely swung down out of the saddle before Grace came crashing out of the back door. He lifted her into his arms and she ran her hand over his stubbly face.

"Daddy! Buttercup had her puppies!"

"Did she now?"

Dark-haired, emerald-eyed Blanche and dimpled Sophronia with her auburn pigtails followed their little sister down the steps. Sophronia threw her arms around Shaw's waist and Blanche tugged at his hand. "There's five of them, Daddy. Come and see!"

Shaw laughed and looked up at Alafair, standing at the back screen wiping her hands on her apron tail. This was not an unexpected event. It had become clear last fall, not long after Buttercup's parole, that her incarceration had come too late.

"There's a few minutes before I get dinner on the table," Alafair said. "I'll get Charlie to put the nose bag on your horse if you want to go have a look."

Shaw walked out to the barn, his three skipping little girls in front of him and Kurt and Charlie Dog trotting behind. Buttercup had been ensconced in the empty stall where Crying Blood had died. The stall had been scrubbed with lye water and Alafair had well removed any lingering aura of death with raw eggs and plenty of sage and cedar smoke. Buttercup seemed happy there and so did Crook, who rose from his place near the stall gate and greeted them with a wagging tail. His broken leg had healed well and he seemed to have suffered no permanent damage from the wound. Shaw knelt down at Buttercup's straw-filled nursery crate and rubbed her head. Grace squatted down next to her father's elbow and leaned in so close that Buttercup snuffled at the child's ear and made her laugh.

Shaw laughed too when he got his first look at Buttercup's babies. Four beautifully marked, pure-bred little coon hounds, and one yellow, flop-eared little mongrel. "Charlie Dog, you scamp!"

The old yellow shepherd cocked his head when Shaw said his name. His fluffy tail waved in the air a couple of times.

"John Lee wants one of the hunters, Daddy," Blanche informed him.

"He can have his pick. As for the rest, I can always sell a good hunting hound. But what am I going to do with a little half-breed mutt?"

"I'll take him."

Shaw looked back over his shoulder. He had forgotten Kurt was there. Kurt grinned. "After we wed, me and Mary will need a good-hearted dog at our new place."

"All right, then!" Shaw stood up and brushed his hands together. "Now, girls, did Mama bake sweet potatoes for dinner?"

"Ham and red-eye gravy, Daddy," Sophronia told him. "And creamed corn and biscuits."

Grace jumped up and down. "And sweet potatoes, too!"

"Well, then, sounds like everything is just like it ought to be. Let's go eat."

Indian Territory

1905

The hunter's bullet slammed into the man's leg and the gun in his hand went flying. He howled with pain and crumpled over. He scrambled around in the dirt, trying to dig himself into the ground like a badger to escape his terror, pain, and the sight of his own blood pouring down the front of his shirt from his missing ear.

It suddenly dawned on him that he was alive. His ear was bleeding like Moses and the leg hurt like hell, but he was alive. And for the past couple of minutes his pursuer hadn't been trying to alter that fact.

The man didn't move, listening to the silence for a good while before finally lifting his head to assess the situation.

Through the bushes, he could see the toes of his pursuer's boots protruding over the dry yellow grass three feet from his face. The man dared take a breath and raised up on his elbows.

The hunter lay on his back, spread-eagle, his hair radiating like a corona around his head. He was staring at the sky with a look of profound surprise on his face and a neat hole in the middle of his forehead.

The man emitted a sob of relief mixed with amazement. That was the goddamned, son-of-a-gun, Jesus, Mary, and Joseph, luckiest shot ever shot by a living human being on the face of this earth.

He was motionless for a minute or two, trying to calm his heart. It was hard to wrestle his mind around to where it needed to be. Instead of planning his next move he couldn't stop himself from reliving the stupid things he had done to get himself into this situation.

But it had been so easy to kill Goingback. Just clomp him in the head when they were out in the woods together alone, then chop down a tree so it would fall on the body. A horrible accident. Nobody questioned his story or even looked at him sidelong.

He told the widow that he was beside himself with remorse. By that time he had lived in the Indian Territory long enough to know that the Creek believed even an accidental death had to be made right. The tribal council had thought it only logical that he should marry the widow and support her and her children for the rest of her life. The widow was amenable. Goingback wasn't much of a husband in the first place.

And everything had gone so well for so long! They built a sturdy house, cleared land for a sawmill, built a road to the high-way so that when the time came he could haul wagon-loads of finished lumber to the railroad. Ten damn years he had worked like a coolie. He was satisfied with Lucretia and got along with her children. They even had the two boys of their own, bright little lads.

Then the government had decided to give each and every member of the tribe a piece of land for his or her very own. Many chose plots on or near where they already lived. Some refused to choose and had plots assigned to them. Lucretia got hers, which was really his since she didn't care one way or the other. The children all got theirs, adjoining their mother's. Things couldn't have been any better. He was the patriarch of an empire! Him, who had left Ireland with nothing but the clothes he stood up in.

And then the KATY had decided to put their railroad spur somewhere else. That was bad enough. But after the shock wore off he realized he may be able to salvage the situation by building another road. His stepson's allotment abutted the Ozark Trail.

Now, the widow's son had worked along side of him for years, happy as a lark. But all this allotment business had put the youth out of joint. That land belonged to all the people together, he said. He wasn't going to take it up, he said. And even if the government forced the boy to take title it wouldn't do the man any good. After the new law went into effect in a few months, White folks wouldn't be able to buy land off of full-bloods for twenty-five years.

It was all so complicated. Killing Goingback had been so easy. And if any of her children died without issue the widow would inherit his allotment to add to her own.

But everything had gone awry. The man was getting old and the widow's son was young and quick. They had gone out together that night, just the two of them, like they had many times before, intending to hunt in the morning. The lad arranged his blanket beside the fire and went to sleep, or so it seemed. One blow of the axe ought to have done it. But the damn kid had ears like a bat. The axe came down on bare dirt where the young man's head had been a split second before.

They were both on their feet then, and looked each other in the eye. The lad didn't even look shocked. You could tell by his expression that he knew everything. He had figured it all out in the time it took for that axe to plunge into the earth.

That's also how long it took the man to see that he had been mistaken about who was likely to die this night. He took to his heels.

Damn, if he just hadn't tried to take the easy way out. He and the lad could have figured something out, come to an agreement.

The man leaned back and stared at the sky for quite a while, trying to think. But his mind was unable to function properly. A handful of dirt and small stones cascaded down the sheer bank behind him, loosed by a gust of wind. He blinked and scrubbed his face with his sleeve to remove some of the blood and sweat fouling his vision, then cast a quick look around the brushy clearing. No boy to be seen. Perhaps in his panic he had just imagined that he'd seen the young face at the edge of the woods.

He felt the side of his head where his ear used to be. It stung like the devil but was clotting up already. What a mess. He attempted to stand but his shot-up leg wouldn't support him. He regarded the wound in his thigh. Not bleeding much, certainly not pumping blood. No artery hit, so he wasn't in immediate danger of death. He'd have to have the slug out, though, before it poisoned his blood.

He was just beginning to form a plan of action when he heard movement and sank back down.

His wife was standing on the brushy edge of the dry creek bank with the boy behind her. He caught his breath and said nothing. He didn't think she could see him, still half hidden behind a bush under the overhang.

The woman crossed the wash and bent over the hunter's body, her face impassive. The man puffed out a breath. She never failed to surprise him with her stoicism. He liked to think that if his own mother had found him dead she'd shed a tear or two.

The boy tugged at the woman's sleeve and whispered in her ear. Her gaze lifted, eyes black and hot as coals, staring right at him. She straightened and walked to his hiding place with the boy on her heels. She parted the brush and stepped into the space under the ridge. Her eyes went to the hand axe that had taken off his ear, still embedded in the bank.

The man gasped and scrabbled as far back into the little cave as he could manage. It was a desperate move, but futile. She was standing over him now with the axe in her hand.

"You killed my son," she said. Her tone was matter-of-fact.

"Lucretia, he tried to kill me! I had no choice!"

"That ain't what Ira says."

He gaped at the small figure with the intense expression who was standing behind his mother. "Ira, you saw, laddie! You saw!" He despised the wheedling tone of his own voice but couldn't do anything about it. "It was self-defense!"

The blank expression on the kid's face was impossible to read. For a moment the man was hopeful. "You wouldn't want for him to kill your dear dad, would you, boy?"

Ira didn't have an opportunity to answer. Lucretia took a two-handed grip on the axe handle and brought the blunt edge down on the man's head with all the force she could muster. The man sprawled unmoving in the dirt, one of his eyes nearly popped out from the force of the blow. He hadn't tried to defend himself. He hadn't had time to realize what was happening.

She knelt, leaned close to check for signs of life, and started when he snatched a handful of her long black hair and drew her down to breathe his curse into her ear.

I'll claw my way out of hell and make you pay.

Lucretia wrenched herself free. With a blow from the sharp edge of the axe, then another, she sent him to the hell he expected and deserved. She stood and stepped back to inspect her handiwork, then placed the axe down on the ground.

Ira and his mother regarded one another for a long time before she said, "We got to bury him."

Ira nodded and gave Lucretia a sign to move away from the mutilated body. Small and light, he grabbed one of the dead tree roots protruding from the cliff face and hoisted himself hand over hand to the top. It was hard to negotiate the precarious overhang, but he was strong and lithe and managed to swing himself out enough to grab the grassy lip of dirt and haul himself up. Even his slight weight caused a crack to open in the overhang, but he had to jump up and down on it for a bit before it gave way. He sledded down on top of the mini-avalanche and arrived at his mother's feet with only a skinned knee and a bruise on the heel of his hand. He got to his feet and dusted off the seat of his trousers.

The man with the busted head was good and buried. Only the fingers of one hand protruded from the pile of scree and red dirt that had once loomed over the creek bed.

Ira and Lucretia turned back to the hunter Chitto, who was staring upward relentlessly, as though surprised at the sight of heaven, and made their plans to take him home.

Producing, Preserving, and Cooking Meat

Butchering Time

Shaw Tucker was a breeder of mules and work horses, so pork wasn't a primary part of the Tuckers' income. However, he kept one or two breeding sows to provide the family with meat and made a little money on the side by selling the surplus piglets to his neighbors. But like everything else Shaw did on the farm, he approached the raising of pigs as an art, and the animals he sold were much in demand because of their high quality meat.

Shaw kept a special penning area for hogs being readied for slaughter. It was a good-sized sty, big enough for four large hogs to have individual shelters, troughs, and room to roam. Shaw always chose animals that were big and healthy but not huge or too fat. Not because of any extra effort that may be entailed in the slaughter or the processing. It was a hard, miserable job no matter how big the carcasses were. But smaller, leaner pigs with just the right amount of firm, white fat made for higher quality meat and lard. Had Shaw been raising pigs for a large-scale business, he more than likely would have fattened them on more economical feed corn. Since he never had very many hogs to feed at once, he decided he'd rather be a little persnickety about their eats and get the best meat out of them he could.

So he chose two or three likely shoats in the spring and moved them into the equivalent of a hog luxury hotel, where they were fed apples and hay, milk and molasses, as well as table scraps. They were regularly put out to pasture and sometimes turned out in the woods to root for acorns and grubs and any other delectable morsel they could find, and to get some exercise and fresh air. Alafair swore that pigs who ate meadow flowers had the tastiest meat of all. Shaw had never heard Alafair's peculiar pork belief before she came into his life, but since she was the one who was responsible for turning much of the pig into a year's worth of meat products, he respected her opinion and saw to it that his pigs spent most of their one and only summer of life in a flowery pasture.

In the fall, after the first freeze of the season, two well-grown hogs were moved from the feeding pens into the much smaller retaining pens next to the processing area behind the barn, coaxed along the path with a bag of apples and prodded in the right direction with a cane.

The hogs spent their last two days in small pens close to the slaughter area, fasting but drinking plenty of clear well water. A few hours before they were to meet their doom, Shaw fed each of them a small pan full of sugar. Just as Alafair was convinced that a diet of wildflowers flavored the meat, Shaw's Irish stepfather had taught him that a final meal of sugar made the pork sweet. Besides, the hogs loved it.

Some years Shaw raised a calf for slaughter, or a goat or two, and when he did, he made very sure to kill the beast in isolation so as not to upset its companions. But when it came to pigs he never bothered. Swine are smart but totally unconcerned about each other's fate. In fact, if a pig died at night in the presence of its fellows, Shaw seldom saw the carcass. There wouldn't be a bone or hair left by morning, thanks to its cannibal litter mates.

Shaw sent Charlie out to scrub the pigs down the day before slaughter. They didn't stay all that clean in their little pens, but it helped and they enjoyed it.

A block and tackle was rigged over a stout tree limb and a second huge iron cauldron sitting close to the trunk was filled with water the day before. First thing in the morning, Shaw lit the fire under the cauldron, and by the time the hogs were moved into the chute the water was already steaming in the cold air.

Once the hog was confined, Shaw killed the animal with a single shot in the forehead. His father and grandfather had killed pigs by sticking them in the carotid artery with a sharp knife. If a pig wasn't properly bled the meat could spoil. Besides, no self-sufficient homesteader ever wasted any part of an animal, including its blood. The first hog slaughter Shaw ever witnessed when he was a boy was a bloody affair. The butcher had stuck the pig and then hauled it up by its hind legs to hang head down and bleed out while it was still conscious. The squealing of the dying pig gave the young Shaw nightmares for a month.

His father had usually stunned the hog with a hammer before slitting its throat, but that wasn't much more pleasant for a boy to witness. Shaw had never seen a hog shot until the first time his stepfather slaughtered. He figured he and his brothers must have looked startled, because Peter McBride had winked a lively blue eye and assured them that if they looked sharp and got that hog up the tree in good order, its heart would keep beating long enough to insure a good bleed.

Shaw didn't know which method a professional butcher would prefer. But as for him, he'd never lost a carcass to contamination, and besides, if he never heard another dying pig that would suit him just fine.

As soon as the hog dropped down dead, Shaw opened the gate and threw a sturdy rope around one hind leg. He and his helpers hauled the animal out and hoisted him up off the ground with the block and tackle. Shaw quickly slit the pig's throat, careful to sever the large veins and arteries. The blood flowed in a pulsing stream into a large tub on the ground beneath.

Proper bleeding took several minutes, so the boys washed the pig yet again and Shaw cleaned his knife before leaning against the tree with a great sigh. Eventually the pulsing stopped and the stream became gouts, then drops, and finally ceased altogether.

They removed the tub full of blood and rotated the block and tackle enough to suspend the carcass over the cauldron, then lowered it head first into the scalding water. Three or four minutes of scalding was long enough to loosen the hair on the hog's skin.

Then they hoisted the hog out and put it on an enormous sled for transport to the covered butchering house just a couple of yards away. It took two or three men to maneuver the animal onto the table, where they scraped off the remaining hair and removed the hooves. Farmers who butchered meat for a living often used a gambrel, a tool especially made for hoisting a carcass for cutting up. But Shaw's main business was horses and mules, so whenever he butchered an animal he used the utensils he had at hand, which meant a piece of harness equipment called a singletree. He inserted ropes through the Achilles tendons, attached them to the singletree and once again hoisted the carcass to hang head down from a rafter in the center of the shelter.

The young men proceeded to sluice down the table and the sledge while Shaw removed the animal's head. Just about the time he was severing the gullet Alafair and her daughters joined them, all dressed as scruffily as the men and boys. The killing was done. The hard work of butchering and preparing the meat was about the begin.

Alafair and the girls filled washtubs with water as Shaw carefully split the hog open from stem to stern, careful not to pierce any organs. The intestines slopped out, but were still attached inside so never hit the ground before Shaw could cut them loose. He didn't check first to see if Alafair was at his side, ready to take the internal organs away in a tub. She always was.

Alafair and one of the boys hauled the tub of innards to the table where she and the girls separated out and washed the individual organs. Her aides cleaned the intestines while she trimmed up the heart and chopped it up for chilling. She trimmed off as much fat as she could to save for making lard.

For years Charlie was in charge of cleaning the hog's head, at least while he was still young enough to get a perverse thrill out of cutting out brains and eyeballs.

As the women began the work of preserving the innards, the men thoroughly washed the now-organless body cavity. Then they left the carcass suspended from the ceiling while they repeated the whole bloody process with the second hog.

Alafair's Recipes

Quail Pie

Quail are delicious little birds that can be used in any recipe that calls for chicken. Keep in mind, though, that the bobwhite quail that Shaw and the boys shot on their hunting trip in 1915 are smaller than chickens, so it'll take more of them. Since they have lived their lives in the wild, quail are also tougher than home-grown poultry, so often game birds are 'hung' for a few days to help tenderize the meat. But if the birds are young they can certainly be cooked fresh.

There are innumerable ways to make quail pie, both simple and complex. The easiest is to cut the quail into pieces and fry it in butter. Take the birds out of the skillet and mix the pan juices with a little flour to thicken. Remove the meat from the bones, arrange the quail in a baking dish and pour the pan gravy over all. If the quail are dry, add some bacon on top of the quail meat. Top with pie crust and bake for 20 minutes or so in a hot oven (400 degrees) until golden brown.

The quail pie that Alafair took to her in-laws' house for Sunday dinner was more like a traditional pot pie. The quail were boiled in salted water until tender, then removed from the bones and returned to the broth while she sauteed an onion in butter in a skillet. When the onion began to brown, she added two or three tablespoons of flour and stirred until smooth, then added in the quail meat with its broth and cooked it over a low flame until the mixture thickened. She then added a couple of cups of cooked vegetables—peas, potatoes, carrots, winter squash, sweet potatoes—whatever was on hand, and poured the whole thing into a deep baking dish. She then covered it with a pie crust or biscuit dough and baked as above.

Bear Soup

When butchering time comes, it behooves the family cook to have a repertoire of quick and easy recipes for feeding an exhausted crew in a hurry and with a minimum of effort. Bear soup certainly falls into that category. It is the easiest dish imaginable to make and surprisingly satisfying and delicious.

How it came to be called "bear soup" is a mystery lost in time, for it has nothing whatsoever to do with bears. Maybe this is what Goldilocks found sitting on the table when she perpetrated her B&E at the home of the three bears.

For each individual serving, finely chop a slice of onion and add it to a cup and a half of milk. Cook the milk and onion together in a saucepan over low heat until the milk is simmering and the onion becomes transparent.

Crumble a large piece of leftover cornbread into a bowl and pour the hot milk and onion mixture over it. Salt and pepper to taste, and enjoy.

Pork

Hog butchering is hard, messy, unpleasant work, so Shaw and Alafair wanted to make sure that the animal's sacrifice was appreciated and its meat properly utilized. When you raise and slaughter an animal in order to feed your family, the order of the day is "waste not, want not." Every scrap of the carcass was used. Even the ears were smoked and given to the dogs.

Alafair and Shaw would have used the entire hog carcass in ways that would never occur to someone who could simply go to the supermarket and buy whatever she needed.

Shaw was in charge of preserving most of the muscle meat by smoking and salting. This would include the back, loins, shoulders, hams, ribs, and bacon. Alafair's purview was mostly the innards and extremities, which she would transform from something disgusting into delicious edibles that would keep for a long time.

Lard

One of the most useful products to come from a hog carcass was lard, which is nothing more than the purified fat of the hog. The pure white fat was used for more than just cooking. It was used as a lubricant, to make lotions and medicines, and to make soap. Though the very word lard conjures up visions of fat-clogged arteries and multiple-bypass heart surgeries, lard in and of itself is not unhealthy. It becomes dangerous when it is hydrogenated, which is what food companies do in order to keep lard from spoiling on the shelf. Home-rendered lard actually has its benefits and is in fact healthier than hydrogenated vegetable shortening. It has less saturated fat than butter, a high smoking point, foods fried in it tend to absorb less fat, and it has and a neutral effect on blood cholesterol. And a pie crust made with homemade lard cannot be beaten, tastewise.

The best fat to use is the "leaf lard", which is found over the kidneys and in the hog's back. The intestinal fat is yellower and of a lower quality and makes a lard that is of a lower grade, but still useful, especially for noncooking purposes. Rendering lard is not a complicated task, but it isn't fragrant. Alafair rendered lard in a large iron cauldron over an open wood fire in the back yard.

Cube the fat and add it to a small amount of water in a large pot. Heat on fairly low heat, stirring occasionally, until the fat melts. This will take a while, about an hour for a pound or so of fat. Stir often with a wooden utensil. The fat will pop and crackle as it melts and the air pockets burst.

Eventually, little pieces of crispy pork will begin floating to the surface. These are the **cracklins.** Their proper name is 'cracklings,' but Alafair would never have called them that. When the cracklins begin to sink, the lard is done. After it cools, pour the liquid fat through cheesecloth into sterile jars. The cracklins will be caught in the cheesecloth. Save them and eat them as a snack, salted, if you wish. Alafair would then chill the jars of lard outside on the porch in the crisp fall air, or in the cool root cellar. It will solidify like butter and turn snowy white.

Sausage

One of the great staples of American farm cooking, sausage is the perfect dish for utilizing every edible piece of meat in such a way that it keeps for weeks and months. If the cook knows what she's doing, she can get twenty pounds of sausage out of 250 pounds of live hog. Sausages can be preserved as patties or links.

Leftover trimmings from the hams, loins, and shoulders were used to make sausage. At the discretion of the maker, the "sweetbreads" (heart, brains, liver) were also used. The different meats were minced together finely with fat and mixed with salt, herbs, and spices. Southern American sausages are always highly spiced. Sage and onion are commonly used, as well as garlic, clove, thyme, and both red and black pepper. The sausage meat was usually mixed in a large bowl, and at intervals a pinch would be fried and tasted to check the seasoning. When the mixture suited all the tasters present, the meat was either stuffed into sausage casings or preserved as patties. The patties were fried up, a stack of them placed into a sterile jar, and hot fat poured over them to cover. This keeps out the air and preserves the meat. The jars were then sealed and stored upside down on their lids.

Traditional link sausage casings are made from the hog's small intestine, a long, continuous tube which has been washed and scraped, then turned inside out and soaked, washed, and scraped with a dull knife again and again, until it is practically transparent. The casing is left soaking in a tub of brine until it is ready to use, in order to keep it clean and supple enough to stuff. When the time comes, the casing is removed from the water and one end placed over the spout of the cast-iron stuffer. The prepared sausage meat is fed into the top of the stuffer and depressed with a plunger, which forces the meat out the spout and into the casing. Sausage stuffing is a two-woman enterprise; one to feed the meat into the stuffer and one to guide the casings with her hands as they fill so that they will fill evenly and not tear. The 'guider' determines the size of the links by twisting or pinching the casing at regular intervals. Sometimes the ends of the links are tied with string. Link sausages could be canned. A sterile jar was simply filled with links and hot lard poured over them to remove the air. Then, like the canned sausage patties, the jars were sealed and stored on their tops in the pantry or root cellar.

The best thing about link sausage is that it could be smoked. Great loops of sausage links would be hung from a pole in the smokehouse and slowly cured by the smoke from the hickory or applewood fire in the middle of the floor.

Head Cheese

Bear soup has nothing to do with bears and head cheese has nothing to do with cheese. Head cheese is more like a kind of pan sausage and is quite tasty. However, it is one of the ickier hog products to contemplate.

Take one hog's head and remove the eyes, brain, ears, and jaw. Saw the head in half, place it in a large pot and cover it with water. Add an onion and spices as desired, such as sage, bay leaf, clove, garlic, and pepper, and boil until the meat falls off the bone. Remove the bones, grind the meat and onion together, then put the ground meat back into the water and boil again until it thickens. It will thicken on its own because of its natural fats and gelatin, but one can add cornmeal to the water to help the process along and also because it's tasty. Pour the mixture into a shallow pan and cool until it sets. Slice into pieces for frying or for making sandwiches. A pan of head cheese will last several days if chilled.

Blood Pudding

Like head cheese, blood pudding is a sausage-like mixture made with hog's blood. The blood is caught in a pan during slaughter and must be stirred constantly until it cools to prevent clotting. Once it has cooled, mix one quart of blood with about one cup of lard or other fat, salt and pepper to taste, two cups of dry oatmeal, cornmeal, fine bread crumbs, or cooked rice or barley. Mix all the ingredients together and boil until thick. Put in a cool place to set, then slice and fry.

Pickled Pigs Feet

The author spent many happy hours of her childhood sitting on her father's lap eating pickled pig's feet out of a jar and thus retains fond feelings for the dish, howsoever much she may be put off by it now.

Wash the pig's trotters carefully, trim, and scald them in hot water. Split the feet in half lengthwise. Bring them to a boil in fresh water and simmer for an hour and a half or until tender. Stir often. Remove the feet from the water and rinse again.

In a large pot, simmer together enough vinegar to cover the feet, a chopped onion, a bay leaf, mustard seeds, peppercorns, and cloves for about thirty minutes. Then add the pig's feet, bring the mixture back to the boil and remove from heat.

Remove as many bones as you can, then place the feet in sterile jars and pour the vinegar mixture over and seal. Let the mixture pickle for a month or so before eating.

Historical Notes

The Indian Territory

In the 1830s and 1840s, the federal government confiscated the lands of many of the great Native American nations in the South. The tribal members were removed from their traditional lands in a series of forced marches along a route that later became known as the Trail of Tears and settled into the Indian Territory, which was outside the then-borders of the United States in what is now the State of Oklahoma.

The Indian Territory (I.T.) was divided among the so-called Five Civilized Tribes, which included the Cherokee, Choctaw, Creek (Muscogee), Chickasaw, and Seminole Nations. For many years, the nations were left to govern themselves. And govern themselves they did, with their own tribal courts, laws, and legislatures, businesses, trade, newspapers, towns and farms, schools and colleges. In the traditional way, tribal land was held in common, with families and clans living in townships or on farms, the wealth of which was communally shared. Many of the native peoples were even slave holders.

Unfortunately, many, though not all, Indians in the I.T. supported the losing side during the American Civil War. This was excuse enough for the U.S. government to extend federal jurisdiction over the territory, and the nations were forced to sell off or cede their lands west of the 98th Meridian to the United States. This effectively divided the territory into two relatively equal parts, the I.T. in the east for the Five Nations, and the Oklahoma Territory in the west. The U.S. then exiled several Plains Indian tribes, including Comanche, Apache, and Arapaho, from their homelands onto reservations in the newly formed Oklahoma Territory.

In the early part of the twentieth century, there was some discussion in Congress of admitting the territories into the Union as two separate states, Oklahoma in the west and Sequoia in the east. But at the last minute the two territories were combined and became the State of Oklahoma.

Allotment

In the 1880s, a U.S. senator by the name of Henry Dawes decided that it would be best for the Indian peoples if they were "Americanized" in order to make it easier for them to assimilate into White society. He proposed that the best way to do this was to do away with communal lands and allot a parcel of land to each tribal member, thus introducing them to the joys of capitalism and individual ownership.

The Dawes Act was passed in 1887, following which Congress set out to conclude a treaty with each of the Five Tribes. Since the tribal governments weren't in the least interested in participating, it took several years of pressure before they gave in to the inevitable and sat down with the U.S. Government to negotiate the details and particulars of the allotment program, including who was to be considered a tribal member and thus entitled to receive a piece of land. The treaty with the Creek Nation was signed in September of 1887, but not passed into law until 1901.

Each enrolled member of the Creek Nation, male and female, adult and child, was given 160 acres of his own choosing. Every member who accepted allotment was automatically given U.S. citizenship, but many restrictions were placed on the individual's ability to dispose of the land as she or he saw fit. The government deemed the Indians, especially full-bloods, not quite competent to handle their own affairs. So, to keep greedy speculators from taking advantage of the new landowners, the law stipulated that from his 160 acres each citizen had to designate 40 acres as his "homestead." This homestead could not be sold at all, to anyone, for twenty-five years. A minor's allotment was chosen for him by his parents or guardian and could not be sold during his minority. After the owner's death, title to the homestead passed to her children or to her heirs, according to the laws of descent of the Creek Nation.

Therefore, in 1906 Roane Hawkins would have been able to control his wife's land, but he could not have owned it. Oklahoma became the 46th state in September, 1907, so had Hawkins been patient for one more year, the laws of the United States of America would have superseded the treaty when the sovereignty of the Creek Nation and all the Native nations of Oklahoma, was dissolved.

"I would not mind so much playing the White man's game if only the White man would not make all the rules."—Chitto Harjo (Crazy Snake), leader of the Creek traditionalist band known as the Snakes.

Oklahoma Creek Place Name Pronunciations

Bacone (*bay-CONE*)—established in 1888. Named for Almon C. Bacone, Baptist missionary. Bacone Indian University, now Bacone College, is located in Muskogee, Oklahoma.

Checotah (*shuh-KO-tuh*)—established in 1886. Named for Great Chief Samuel Checote, Muscogee Creek minister and politician.

Eufaula (*you-FALL-uh*)—Near the banks of the North Canadian River, Eufaula came into its own in 1872 when it became a stop for the Missouri Kansas and Texas (KATY) Railway. The James-Younger gang had a hideout just north of the town. Belle Starr is buried in Eufaula.

Hitchita (*HIT-chuh-tah*, rhymes with *Wichita*)—A market town from about 1900, located in northern McIntosh County some 18 miles SSW of Boynton. It was named for a band of the Muscogee tribe.

Muskogee (*mus-KO-ghee*)—Founded in 1872 when the KATY railroad first crossed the Indian Territory. Named for the Creek tribe.

Nuyaka (*noo-YAHK-uh*)—A mission site for the Creek tribe, established in the 1880s. Located near Okmulgee.

Okmulgee (*ok-MUL-ghee*)—Became the headquarters of the Muskogee Nation in 1866, and is the location of the Creek Council House. *Okmulgee* means "bubbling water".

Oktaha (*ok-TAH-ha*)—named for Muscogee chief Oktarharsars Harjo. Originated in 1872 as a stop on the KATY railroad.

Note: *Muscogee is the peoples' own name for their confederation. Creek is the name given by the English to a band of the people living along a creek by the Ocmulgee River in Georgia, and the term later expanded to include all the Muscogee-speaking bands which were originally located all across Georgia, Alabama, and Mississippi.*

To receive a free catalog of Poisoned Pen Press titles, please contact us in one of the following ways:

Phone: 1-800-421-3976
Facsimile: 1-480-949-1707
Email: info@poisonedpenpress.com
Website: www.poisonedpenpress.com

Poisoned Pen Press
6962 E. First Ave. Ste. 103
Scottsdale, AZ 85251